## Outstanding praise for *Bobby Blanchard, Lesbian Gym Teacher*!

"Shamelessly campy!"
—*Instinct Magazine*

"Nolan's pell-mell pastiche of varied genres is great fun."
—*Pittsburgh's Out*

"If you're looking for silly, satiric fun, Bobby
will show you a good time."
—*Edge Magazine*

"A fun, fresh, and feminist satire on pulp fiction
of the fifties and sixties."
—*Orange County Blade*

## Outstanding praise for *Lois Lenz, Lesbian Secretary*!

"Unabashedly campy and titillating, Nolan's debut novel is a
tale of 1950s lesbian career girls loose in the big city. . . ."
—*Publishers Weekly*

"Nolan squeezes her kicky premise for plenty of juice, leaving
the pulp in *Lois Lenz, Lesbian Secretary* deliciously intact."
—*Entertainment Weekly*

"Monica Nolan's first novel, *Lois Lenz, Lesbian Secretary*, is a
delicious contemporary homage to queer pulp novels. . . ."
—*Bay Times*

"In her second book, Monica Nolan gives us what we really
want—a campy pulp filled with gratuitous lesbian sex,
communism, reefer madness, and ruthless dictation. . . ."
—*Curve Magazine*

"The 1950s. Virginal young women. Small-town values.
Repressed deviant desires. Big-city temptations. No, it's not
lurid new fiction from lesbian pulp pioneers like Ann Bannon
or Paula Christian—though Nolan's campy novel is an
exhilarating homage to their lusty novels of yore. . . ."
—*Bookmarks*

**Books by Monica Nolan**

THE BIG BOOK OF LESBIAN HORSE STORIES
(with Alisa Surkis)

LOIS LENZ, LESBIAN SECRETARY

BOBBY BLANCHARD, LESBIAN GYM TEACHER

MAXIE MAINWARING, LESBIAN DILETTANTE

Published by Kensington Publishing Corporation

# Maxie Mainwaring, Lesbian Dilettante

## MONICA NOLAN

KENSINGTON BOOKS
www.kensingtonbooks.com

*For Julie Ann
and librarians everywhere*

# Chapter 1

## In the Powder Room

"Damn," exclaimed the brunette with the bee-stung lips. "I have a run!"

Maxie Mainwaring glanced over from her side of the mirror, where she was busy freshening her lipstick.

"What a shame," she began politely, then stopped, transfixed, as the girl hiked up her narrow skirt to mid-thigh to examine the state of her stockings. "A real shame," Maxie breathed, her eyes riveted on the girl's legs.

She'd always been a sucker for a shapely pair of legs, ever since she'd fallen for the swim instructor at Camp Pottawatomi when she was twelve.

"They're ruined," fretted the brunette. "What am I going to do now?"

"Why don't you just take them off?" Maxie suggested boldly. "No one will notice."

But the brunette shook her head. "Maybe if I'd gotten a tan this weekend at Loon Lake, but it rained, and I'm still as white as a fish belly—simply gruesome! Besides, those old biddies at the DAP tea would be scandalized!"

"Oh, are you attending the DAP tea too?" Suddenly Maxie's dishwater-dull afternoon was looking decidedly brighter.

Madcap Maxie had only agreed to attend the 1964 Daughters of the American Pioneers Spring Tea under duress. Her mother had threatened to withhold her monthly allowance unless Maxie accompanied Mrs. Mainwaring to this annual inauguration of Bay City society's summer whirl, the round of parties, fetes, and galas, whose sole purpose was to determine the social pecking order.

And her attendance alone would not suffice, Maxie's mother told her sternly. She was to behave in a manner befitting a girl of her position: no cocktails instead of darjeeling, no smoking in front of Mrs. Lund, Mrs. Thorwald, Mrs. Houck, or any of the other DAP officers, no wearing those outré styles she affected with her disreputable chums at that horrible boardinghouse in Bay City where she insisted on living for some ungodly reason, and no provocative comments on politics or shocking stories about her bohemian habits.

"Am I allowed to breathe?" Maxie had inquired sarcastically.

"And whatever you do, don't talk about your—your *job*," Mrs. Mainwaring had concluded, ignoring the interruption. Her tone of voice suggested that Maxie worked in the sewers instead of at a newspaper. "I've let everyone think you're busy with volunteer work for the Junior League. Is there *any* young man in your life, not too embarrassing to mention?"

Maxie had twisted the cord of the front desk phone impatiently. "No, Mother—you know I spend most of my evenings with my girlfriends."

"Well." Her mother's disapproval had vibrated over the line. "I'll put it out that you're choosy. But, Maxie, I warn you, I'm not going to tolerate this situation much longer—"

It was a pity Pamela Prendergast wasn't a fellow, Maxie had thought to herself as she hung up the phone, because

Pamela was just the kind of rising young executive Mrs. Mainwaring was always introducing to Maxie, or seating next to her daughter at society functions. But on the other hand, if Pamela had been a fellow, Maxie would never have given the fetching redhead a second glance. There was simply no way she could please both herself and her mother when it came to dating!

She'd resigned herself long ago to having as gay a time as a girl could, while making the occasional concession that kept Mabel Mainwaring signing the checks.

For the hundredth time Maxie wondered if she should follow Pamela's advice and try to make a real career in journalism. Her salary as a part-time assistant for columnist Mamie McArdle scarcely covered her bar bills. But who was she kidding? She was no Pamela. She could never have started at the hosiery counter in Grunemans department store and worked her way up to Junior Sportswear Buyer in such a short time, the way her dynamic girlfriend had.

It was only on afternoons like this one, at the Bay City Women's Club, listening to the droning of the DAP minutes and evading questions from her mother's blue-haired cronies about her work with the Junior League, that Maxie felt like she'd do anything—dig ditches, drive a cab, even be a dental nurse—to get out from under her mother's thumb!

When she saw Mrs. Houck heading her way, undoubtedly in another attempt to fix Maxie up with her son Harvey, she'd escaped to the powder room. And there the girl with the bee-stung lips had driven her dilemma right out of her mind.

"Oops!" The girl clapped a hand over her mouth in mock dismay. "I hope I haven't spoken out of turn. I count my mother as one of the old biddies I mentioned. I'm Elaine Ellman."

Elaine Ellman, daughter of Eddie Ellman, granddaughter of Erwin Ellman, the bicycle heiress. Maxie placed her instantly. "Maxie Mainwaring." She held out her hand. "And my mother's another old biddy." The two girls shared a laugh as they shook hands.

Elaine must have been placing Maxie as well. "Didn't you go to Miss Gratton's?" she asked. "I think you know my cousin—Sookie Carmichael."

Maxie blushed faintly. Of course she knew Sookie Carmichael. Sookie had been at Miss Gratton's the year Maxie was caught with Mingy Patterson, after lights-out, in the nurse's office. She couldn't help wondering if Sookie had told Elaine of the school scandal and Maxie's own starring role in it.

"She sounds familiar," Maxie said cautiously, wondering whether Elaine was the type to be put off by such high jinks, or the kind who was intrigued. The second possibility made her pulse quicken. "But let's solve your stocking situation before we start reminiscing. Maybe the maid has an extra pair."

But the powder-room maid, after looking through a basket of lotions, sewing notions, and sanitary napkin belts, came up with only one pair, sized large, dark tan.

"Gruesome," Elaine said again, wrinkling her pert, freckled nose. "I guess I'll just have to hide in here for the rest of the afternoon."

Maxie was eager to help her new friend. "I'll tell you what," she suggested impulsively. "Why don't you wear mine? I've got enough of a tan to get away with it. No, really," she interrupted Elaine's protests. "I often skip stockings—I guess I'm the bohemian type. And I've been shocking the old biddies since I was born."

Maxie's friendly generosity won Elaine over. Retreating to the inner lounge, away from the curious eyes of the maid, the two girls made the switch. While Elaine was smoothing down her pastel printed skirt, Maxie wadded up Elaine's ruined hose and threw them into the wastebasket. Her own legs felt agreeably bare under her brown linen two-piece with the white piping. She began to revive from the hour and a half she'd just spent repressing every natural instinct under her mother's icy glare. Here, with Elaine, in the pink-and-green powder room, she felt sort of—free, like she was her own woman again.

Maxie took a cigarette from her purse and lit it. "Don't let's go back yet," she proposed, sitting on the pale green pouf at the powder-room dressing table.

Elaine was turning this way and that in the mirror. "Much better," she said, dropping to the pouf beside Maxie. "You've saved my life!" She took the cigarette Maxie offered her. "You *must* be the girl Sookie told me about. She said you were awfully generous."

Maxie leaned forward to light Elaine's cigarette. As the two girls' dark heads came together, she noticed the enormous diamond on Elaine's left hand. "What else did Sookie tell you?" she asked huskily.

"She said you were always getting into trouble with your crazy pranks." Elaine's voice was just a whisper and her big brown eyes made Maxie think of Bambi. The movie had made a strong impression on the tender-hearted girl as a child, and the thought of the orphaned deer could still bring tears to her eyes.

"Nothing ventured, nothing gained, I always said." Maxie was mesmerized as she stared into those big Bambi-like eyes, feeling an overwhelming impulse to cuddle this fawn-like creature to her bosom.

Elaine's eyes never left Maxie's as she put her cigarette in the ashtray. "I like your philosophy," she said as she leaned forward.

Maxie knew she shouldn't, but Elaine's bee-stung lips were simply begging to be kissed, and her engagement ring glittered like a kind of challenge in the periphery of Maxie's vision. As their lips met, she slid her arms around the warm, silk-covered torso, and it seemed to Maxie that she felt the girl tremble, like a frightened fawn hiding from a hunter. But who was hunting who, or rather whom? she asked herself, as Elaine's eager, experienced lips started a small forest fire in her loins. Then she didn't care anymore, as the fire grew, burning up all thought of hunters, woods, and small, furry mammals with it. She tightened her arms around Elaine as the other girl's head fell back, exposing the tender white throat. Not like a fish belly at all, Maxie thought hazily, as she nibbled the delicate flesh, while Elaine's pink-polished fingernails dug almost painfully into her shoulders.

She was about to suggest they go upstairs to one of the club's guest rooms, when Elaine suddenly pushed her away. In the mirror behind Elaine Maxie noticed her mussed hair and smeared lipstick before spotting the shocked reflections of two doughty dowagers, Mrs. Ingeborg Lund, President of the Bay City Chapter of the DAP, and Mabel Mainwaring, Maxie's own mother.

Elaine cried, "What on earth are you doing?" in simulated horror. It took a confused second for Maxie to realize that the bicycle heiress had hurled the accusation not at the interrupting society matrons but at Maxie, the girl who had given her the very stockings off her legs.

"Me!" said Maxie indignantly. She whirled to face the intruders. "She started it! She said she had a run in her stocking, and—"

Mrs. Lund was patting Elaine soothingly, as the attractive brunette wept convincingly on her flowered shoulder. "I should have believed the shocking things Sookie told me!" she sobbed as Mrs. Lund led her from the powder room.

Scarcely had the duplicitous debutante made her exit

than Mrs. Mainwaring turned on Maxie with a tight-lipped fury that made her daughter quail.

"This is the limit, Maxie! I've had it up to here shushing one scandal after another and putting up with your boorish behavior to boot! I was never so mortified in my life as when Inga and I came in and saw your shameless attack on the poor Ellman girl!"

"I tell you, Mumsy, she started it!" Maxie protested. "She isn't even my type!" It was that fawn-like quality, she thought to herself with fierce resentment. If Elaine hadn't reminded her of Bambi, none of this would have happened.

Her mother snorted. "Everyone knows Elaine Ellman is engaged to Ted Driscoll, of the dry-cleaning Driscolls," she snapped. "The Lord knows your father and I have done our best for you—the best schools, the best society—we even paid for a psychiatrist after the embarrassing incident at Miss Gratton's—"

"He was loonier than I was," Maxie muttered.

"And how have you shown your gratitude? Broken engagements—disreputable friends—a preference for the gutter rather than the fine, decent people you were raised with. And then taking a job working for that unsavory columnist!"

"Mamie McArdle is a well-respected newspaper woman," Maxie protested. "And the girls at the Magdalena Arms are nice, hardworking kids, all of them!"

"Well, you have a choice, Maxie." Mrs. Mainwaring grew frighteningly calm. "You can come home with me now, or you can go back to the gutter and find someone else to support you—because you're not getting another dime from your father or me until you're back at the Manse under our supervision!" And with that parting bombshell she wheeled around on her well-shod heel and stalked from the powder room.

Maxie's mind was in a turmoil, like a washing machine that had been fed too many nickels. How could a simple visit to the powder room have gone so horribly wrong? How could a girl who kissed so well behave so badly? Did she have enough money in her purse for a cab back to the Arms? If only she'd collected her allowance before her mother had issued her ultimatum! She was behind on the rent and she'd already overdrawn her account!

And how on earth was she going to explain this to Pamela?

# Chapter 2

# A Date with Pamela

Maxie let herself into Pamela's place with her key. She bustled about the airless apartment, heels clicking on the parquet floor as she opened drapes and windows. Then she sat down on Pam's new couch to wait for her girlfriend. She plucked the latest issue of *The Step Stool,* the homophile newsletter Pamela subscribed to, from the kidney-shaped coffee table.

Maxie flipped through it, barely seeing the words on the page. Her mind was too full of the solution that had come to her on the way to Pamela's: She would finally move in with her faithful girlfriend!

Not only was it the ideal answer to her dilemma, but Pamela would be overjoyed—she'd been pestering Maxie to move in with her for years. *Maybe Mumsy's ultimatum was actually a blessing in disguise,* Maxie mused.

Tossing *The Step Stool* back on the coffee table, Maxie got to her feet and prowled around the picture-perfect apartment, looking at the familiar surroundings with a newly possessive eye. The little galley kitchen seemed even more charming than ever, chock-full of cunning conveniences, including a nickel-bright, built-in can opener. And penny-pinching Pamela had done herself proud, purchasing not only the new couch and the coffee table, but a French fondue set—all at Grunemans, naturally, using her employee discount.

Maxie paused in the kitchen doorway, picturing herself in a frilly apron, dipping a chunk of crusty bread into a pot of melted cheese with one of those clever forks. Didn't the *Sentinel* always print those articles on their Women's Page, proving two could live as cheaply as one?

The ex-deb wandered back to the living room and leaned on the windowsill, contemplating the city skyline and enjoying the faint breeze that wafted from Lake Washington—so much more pleasant than the stifling rooms at the Magdalena Arms. Surely Pamela wouldn't mind supporting her until she came into the trust her grandmother had left her? She'd pay Pamela back, eventually—every penny!

Maxie sat on the couch again and emptied the contents of her pocketbook onto the coffee table. Lipstick, compact, an old stained handkerchief—was that coffee or blood?—a comb, her reporter's notebook, three matchbooks, her cigarette case, some loose change and two singles. She counted the change. Two dimes, a nickel, and two pennies. $2.27. Goodness, that was barely enough for the veal plate at Luigi's! Maxie turned her pocketbook upside down and shook it. Another penny fell out. Maybe she shouldn't have taken that taxi from the Women's Club to Pamela's.

There were other ways she could contribute—cooking, for example. Maxie jumped up again and went to the kitchen to dig out the fondue pot. But after she read the recipe book and looked through Pamela's cupboards and the contents of her refrigerator, Maxie realized that Pamela was missing several key ingredients, including the necessary quantity of cheese.

Undiscouraged, Maxie decided she'd mix some drinks

and have them ready for Pamela when she came home from a hard day at work. Maybe she could rustle up a tray of tasty cocktail tidbits as well.

Shaking the silver cocktail shaker with a practiced hand, Maxie imagined herself comparing prices at the A&P, or making Pam bacon and eggs in the morning and then sending her off to work with a good-bye kiss. Of course, Pam got up awfully early and Maxie was used to sleeping in. But she was sure they'd adjust.

Maxie sampled the contents of the shaker. Just right! She tied a gay, red-flowered apron around her waist, and admired the picture she made in the mirror. Now for some delicious hors d'oeuvres; she could set out some olives, or maybe Ritz crackers with that bit of cheese she'd seen. Rummaging in Pamela's pantry she found a painted tin tray. Perfect!

When Pam came in at five-thirty, Maxie was on her second shaker, her feet were up on the coffee table, and Chubby Checker was on the stereo. She was poring over a fashion spread in the latest issue of *Vogue*, trying to decide between the raw silk shift and the cotton playsuit in the mad flower print.

"Pam!" Maxie jumped up and aimed a kiss at Pamela's mouth. "I made you a drink!"

Pam looked hot and tired. She dropped her big handbag to the floor and kicked off her shoes. "I see you made yourself one too," she observed, surveying the coffee table. "Did you finish the crackers?"

Maxie looked at the tray and was surprised to see the plate of crackers was only a plate of crumbs. Had she eaten them all? And they'd looked so nice with the blue cheese spread and pimento on top!

"I'll go get some more." She hurried to the kitchen while Pamela headed for her bedroom to change. "Why are you wearing that apron?" her voice floated back.

Oh dear. She *had* finished the crackers. Maxie opened the refrigerator and peered hopefully inside. Deviled eggs would be nice, but didn't you have to hardboil the eggs first?

Pamela appeared behind her in a sleeveless blouse and bermudas. "What's the fondue set doing out?" she asked a little crossly as she made herself a ham sandwich. Maxie hastened to put the copper pots away, and followed Pamela back to the living room. The record had come to an end, and the needle was making a knocking noise. Maxie switched it off, while Pamela poured herself a drink and sipped. "Needs ice," she grunted.

Maxie hurried back to the kitchen again, and returned carrying the silver ice bucket.

"No need to make a big production," Pamela said sourly.

"You're welcome!" Maxie untied her apron and threw it on a chair, thinking the job of happy homemaker was underpaid. She definitely would *not* be getting up early to make Pam her bacon and eggs!

"I'm sorry, honey," Pam sighed. "Evelyn had all us junior buyers checking inventory in our departments all afternoon, and this hot weather makes me cross as a bear! Who expected a heat wave in May?"

"You ought to get some air-conditioning." Maxie plopped down on the couch and fanned herself with the fashion magazine. "Then this place would be perfect!"

"And pay for it how?" Pamela's question was tart. "Unlike you, I have a budget I need to stick to." She took a gulp of her drink and rattled the ice in the glass impatiently.

Maxie was silent. She wondered if they would quarrel about money when they lived together, as so many young couples seemed to do. The two girls had drastically different approaches to money management. Maxie never kept track of her spending, while Pamela quoted her budget as if it were a federal law and not some notations in a notebook. Her stock response, whenever Maxie suggested a weekend away or a spontaneous purchase, was always an impatient "Money doesn't grow on trees" followed by, "You just don't understand."

But Maxie *did* understand. She knew Pamela's sad story by heart: how her dreams of going to college had crashed around her ears after her mother discovered her necking with Carol Claver in the family Ford one night. How she'd left her hometown of Walnut Grove and boarded a bus to the big city with only a high school diploma in her suitcase and a weeping girlfriend on the seat next to her. How she and Carol had gotten a room at the Y, surviving on cold soup and sleeping on a narrow cot while they looked for work. How Carol had fallen for a uniform and joined the WACs to be with her new crush, leaving Pamela an apology pinned to the pillowcase of the bed they'd shared. How Pam had struggled on, burdened now with a broken heart and the full rent for the little room.

Maxie suspected Pamela was secretly proud of her suffering. Surely she could have heated that soup somehow? Anyway, the story had a happy ending: Pamela was no longer a scared teenager renting a room at the YMCA, but a self-confident merchandiser with her own apartment. Couldn't she begin to relax and live a little?

"I guess you had a hard day too." Pamela's voice broke in on Maxie's ruminations. "How was the tea? Did you manage to keep your mother happy?"

"Well, I wanted to talk to you about that." Maxie felt a little anxious. "Mumsy got so upset with me she cut off my allowance! She said she'd only support me if I moved back to the Manse. So you see"—she spread her hands helplessly—"I haven't a *sou,* and I'm not sure how I'll survive!"

Pamela put down her drink. "What? She was serious?" At Maxie's nod, she rose and paced the room, thinking hard for the space of a few seconds. "Why, that's blackmail!" She sat next to Maxie and took her girlfriend's hand. "Maxie," she said solemnly, "you simply have to move in with me!"

Relief flooded Maxie. This was the Pamela she depended on—decisive, determined, and ready to defy the world. How could she have criticized, even in her head, her wonderful girlfriend? "If you say so," she said adoringly.

Pamela picked up her purse and pulled out her memorandum book, all business now. "How much money do you have in your account?" she asked Maxie.

"I'm not sure," Maxie told her, not wanting to admit that she was overdrawn. Pam frowned, obviously disapproving of Maxie's feckless ways, but said nothing. "All I know for certain is that I have two dollars and twenty-eight cents in my pocketbook." Maxie added blithely, "Enough for a couple rounds at Francine's!"

"You'd better stay away from Francine's until your financial position is a little more solid," Pamela advised, making some notes. Maxie listened meekly. Of course she'd been kidding about Francine's. She'd spend the $2.28 on something more practical, like groceries.

"I figure I can save us lots of money, cooking dinner and doing the shopping and things," she told Pam eagerly.

Pamela looked dubious. "Better concentrate on getting a job," she advised.

Her homemaking effort had been a dud, Maxie gathered, feeling disappointed. Pam thought aloud, "I wonder if there's anything in Grunemans packing department? That's one place that takes unskilled girls."

The packing department! Maxie had seen the window-less room in Grunemans basement where young, uneducated girls sat at a table wrapping packages for mail and C.O.D. orders. She was shocked that Pamela would think of such a place for her. "I'm not completely unskilled," she said with some heat. "I've gone to secretarial school."

"You never finished it," Pamela reminded her.

"I've taught!"

"One spring quarter at that crazy progressive kinder-garten."

"What about my stage-managing experience?"

"Summer stock at Loon Lake," discounted Pamela. "Do you know how competitive theater is?" Her face dark-ened. "And you only did it because you had a thing for the girl doing lights."

Maxie had forgotten that her stint doing summer stock was a sensitive topic. Now Pam snapped, "Next you'll bring up your job helping Ramona roll reefer cigarettes! Don't leave that off your resume!" The young merchan-diser stopped, took a deep breath, and spoke more calmly. "Face it, Maxie, you're a dabbler, a dilettante. You have lots of enthusiasm, but no real experience."

Offended, Maxie improvised, "I was planning to ask Mamie about a job at the newspaper. Maybe they have an opening for a reporter!"

"Ask by all means." A patronizing smile played around Pamela's lips. "But don't expect your own byline right off the bat. Everyone has to start at the bottom—including you."

"You needn't sound so pleased," Maxie told the self-made girl tartly, and was rewarded by the expression of embarrassment on Pamela's face.

"I'm not, honey, really, I'm not." Pamela put an arm

around Maxie. "I think the whole situation's a rotten shame. I'm just glad you're finally going to move in, and that I'm going to be able to help *you* a little bit, instead of the other way around."

"You never let me help you half as much as I wanted to." Maxie leaned her face into Pamela's soft bosom. "When I get the money Grandma Nyberg left me, I'm going to buy us an air conditioner!"

"Okay," Pam laughed. "I guess I can wait the ten years until you're thirty-five and come into your inheritance." They sat there for a minute, arms around each other. Maxie nuzzled into Pamela's neck, running her lips along Pam's firm jaw. Pam's arms tightened. "You never said what it was that ticked off your mother. Did you light a cigarette in front of Mrs. Lund?"

Maxie froze in Pam's arms, and Pam felt it. The temperature, which had been heating up, suddenly cooled. Pam drew back so she could look at Maxie. "Or was it something else?"

The ex-deb had practically forgotten about Elaine and the kiss that caused the mother-daughter quarrel—how could she explain the situation to her loyal girlfriend, without Pamela leaping to the wrong conclusions?

She essayed an airy little laugh. "No, not smoking—well, I was smoking, but I was in the powder room, and it was the craziest thing. Mumsy and Mrs. Lund happened to walk in just as I happened to be getting acquainted with Elaine Ellman—you know, the bicycle heiress? Her cousin Sookie was at Miss Gratton's with me. Anyway, Mumsy completely misinterpreted our friendliness—"

Maxie knew her breezy approach had failed when Pamela disentangled herself from her girlfriend's arms. A tide of red was rising from the neckline of her blouse, staining her cheeks scarlet. Maxie quailed inwardly. Pamela didn't exhibit it very often, but she had a redhead's temper.

"Friendliness?" Pam spat at her. *"Friendliness?"* It was amazing how she made the innocent word sound like a slur.

"Now don't you go misinterpreting too—" Maxie's attempt to stem the storm sunk like a stove-in ship.

"You and your wandering eye!" blasted Pamela. "Last month it was the cigarette girl at Club Lucky, the month before, that co-ed who wandered into Francine's by accident—"

"All right, I kissed Elaine," Maxie admitted. "One little peck! But only because she kept flashing that diamond engagement ring in my face and then making remarks about my reputation—"

"So you had to add another notch to your belt! You're like that duchess, Maxie; you like whatever you look at, and your looks go everywhere!"

Maxie regretted, now, those romantic evenings they'd spent reading poetry to each other in the early days of their affair. But Pamela was ranting on.

"I'm tired of playing second fiddle to some sorority girl just so you can prove she's as queer as you are! I'm through waiting around for you to come out of the powder rooms of Bay City, always wondering if your lipstick will be smeared! If we're going to live together, I expect to see some real changes in your behavior, no more empty promises . . ."

Looking at Pamela as the angry words tumbled out of her mouth, the disinherited heiress had a sudden sense of déjà vu. Why, it was her mother's ultimatum all over again! A sudden anger seized Maxie. Why was everyone trying to mold her into some model girl they had in their heads? Was she really so awful as she was?

She jumped up from the couch, unable to play the penitent any longer. "Maybe it's not such a good idea for me to move in with you after all," she told Pamela hotly. "I might as well move in with Mumsy! Both of you treat me like a juvenile delinquent who needs constant supervision. I'm twenty-five years old, and I've been managing on my own for quite a few years, thank you very much!"

"Managing!" Pamela practically frothed with fury. "On an allowance from your parents! You have *no* idea what it takes to survive on your own in this world. You think you can waltz into the *Sentinel* tomorrow and become a columnist or a reporter—"

"I don't think any such thing!"

"—when you have no skills, no particular aptitude for writing, no experience doing anything but drinking, shopping, and chasing girls!"

Maxie flinched as if she'd been slapped. "So that's what you really think of me!" Jerkily she collected her pocketbook, her hat, and her gloves. "A dipsomaniac dimwit! A social parasite! Well, thank you very much for your honest opinon!"

"Maxie, stop." Pamela laid a placating hand on her arm, and Maxie shook it off. "Maxie, please, stop. You know you're as bright as anything, I'm sure there's loads of things you can do. I'm just saying you have to be realistic—" The older girl broke off abruptly. "Why am I apologizing? You're the one who's been cruising the powder room!"

"No one's asking you to apologize." Maxie tried to brush past her hot-tempered girlfriend, who stood between her and the door, but Pamela grabbed her arm.

"Fine, leave," she said, as she held on to Maxie. "Maybe tomorrow you'll have cooled down enough to listen to reason. But here—" She dropped Maxie's arm and extracted a five-dollar bill from her bag. "I still want to help out."

Maxie just glared at Pamela as the redheaded career girl held out the money.

"Don't be a fool, Maxie! You know you need it!"

Maxie was more enraged than she'd ever been in her life. Snatching the bill, she struck back at Pamela where she knew it would hurt the old penny-pincher the most. She ripped the bill in half and let the pieces float to the ground. Stepping over them, she walked to the door through Pamela's stunned silence.

"Fine!" Pamela came to life as Maxie exited. "You're on your own!" And the door slammed shut behind her.

# Chapter 3

## Maxie Drowns Her Sorrows

Ten blocks from Pamela's, Maxie's boiling rage had settled to an angry simmer. She was glad she wouldn't be keeping house for that cranky, critical career girl, glad! Her feet hurt, and she longed to flag down a passing cab, but she was determined to prove she could economize as well as tightwad Pam. With the money she saved, she'd buy a couple beers at Francine's.

Leaning on a stoop, she slipped off one coffee-colored pump and wiggled her cramped toes, then set off again, footsore, but full of resolve. Hadn't her great-grandfather Mainwaring trekked into the wilderness of Loon Lake with only his rifle and his wits? And he'd made a fortune in timber, then wheat, and finally dairy. Surely his descendant could conquer her own little slice of Bay City!

But by the time Maxie limped down the block toward the Magdalena Arms, the only territory she wanted to conquer was a cool bath and a colder drink. Her hairdo, the Fairweather Flounce she'd gotten at the House of Henri, was flat and matted, her linen two-piece was sweat-stained, and she had a blister on her left heel. Not only had her bouffant lost its bounce, but her spirits had fallen lower then the Magadalena Arms basement. She didn't want to make her fortune in the wilderness of Bay City. She just wanted to wake up and find that this whole day had been a bad dream.

But as she approached the Arms, her steps slowed. Mrs. DeWitt might be hanging around the entrance hall, and she was sure to ask Maxie about the rest of her rent for May. Her elderly landlady never seemed to mind that Maxie seldom paid on time and sometimes not in full— but she had a sixth sense that told her when Maxie was due to receive her allowance, and she magically materialized the minute Maxie had money in her pocket.

While Maxie tried to decide the best way of slipping past her landlady, a petite, tanned brunette in an orange-flowered cotton dress came out of the building. She didn't even notice Maxie standing there, so intent was she on the letter she read as she slowly descended the steps.

"Hey, Lois," Maxie called. "Psst, Lois!"

Lois Lenz, Maxie's neighbor on the fifth floor, looked up with a lost air. Maxie saw that her friend's eyes were red and puffy, as if she'd been crying.

"Why, Lois!" Maxie hurried toward the forlorn girl, forgetting her aching feet. "What's the trouble?"

"It's Netta," Lois choked out. "She left today!"

"Oh, Lois." Maxie put a consoling arm around the now sobbing former secretary. "She'll be back. It's just for the summer."

The two girls were almost exactly the same size and had the same coloring, although the bouffant framing Maxie's heart-shaped face was a shade darker than Lois's hair, and Lois's complexion was a trifle more olive. But they were similar enough that even their friends sometimes confused them from a distance, especially as Maxie was in the habit of sharing her extensive wardrobe with Lois.

"But it's so dangerous!" Lois cried. Maxie had never seen the upbeat office manager in such low spirits. "You know how reckless Netta can be when it comes to matters of principle!"

Netta Bean, Lois's teacher girlfriend, had decided to spend her summer vacation in Mississippi registering voters. This meant that there would be an empty room on the fifth floor and an empty place in Lois's heart.

"She'll be fine." Maxie tried to reassure the bereft girl. "She's going with that Progressive School Alliance, isn't she? And don't forget, she's been practicing jujitsu for almost five years now!"

"Jujitsu won't be much use against the Klan!" retorted Lois. Tears filled her eyes anew. "It's not just her safety. Look at this—" She waved the letter she was holding beneath Maxie's nose. "She didn't even stop by the office to say good-bye before catching her bus—just left this note on my bureau. Sometimes I think she wants to get away from *me* as much as she wants to work for the advancement of the Negro!" The revelation brought a fresh burst of tears. Maxie patted Lois's heaving shoulders and came to a decision.

"We're going to Francine's and drown our sorrows with a couple of beers," she said, taking Lois's arm and guiding her down the street. "I'm in the same boat as you are—Pamela and I had a terrific blow-up, and I'm temporarily single too. Maybe for good!"

"Oh, Maxie, not again!" Lois was temporarily distracted from her heartache by Maxie's news. She'd always been the biggest cheerleader for Maxie and Pamela's on-again, off-again romance. "You two are meant for each other," she'd told Maxie more than once.

Lois had looked up to Pamela ever since high school days, when Pamela had been the captain of the Walnut Grove High School Pep Squad, and Lois had been a freshman cheerleader. When Lois arrived in Bay City to work as a secretary, she'd discovered her high school idol was with Maxie, who dazzled the naïve teenager with her city sophistication. Perhaps it was natural that Lois idealized Maxie and Pam's romance, even now that she was no longer naïve or a teenager. The talented business girl had just been made office manager at Sather and Stirling, a prestigious advertising agency.

"What was it this time?" Lois asked, wiping her eyes and blowing her nose.

"Well, there was this brunette in the powder room," began Maxie as they turned the corner. She described the tempting Elaine in lascivious detail, while Lois wavered between titillation and loyalty to Pam. Loyalty won, of course.

"How can you play around on Pamela, just because some strange girl gives you the glad eye?" she scolded as they settled at a quiet table in Francine's with their beers.

"She isn't a stranger," corrected Maxie. "She's Sookie Carmichael's cousin. Besides, I won't have anyone telling me what I can or can't do—not my mother, not Pamela! Even if I am down to my last two dollars and twenty-seven cents, I mean two dollars and twenty-eight cents." Maxie looked down at the coins left after buying her and Lois's beers, and amended, "One dollar and eighteen cents."

Lois puzzled expression turned to perturbation as Maxie explained her financial embarrassment. "And I don't know what I'll tell Mrs. DeWitt," she concluded.

"But, Maxie, this is worse than any brunette," Lois cried. "And you just paid for our beers!"

"I'm economizing," said Maxie proudly. "A beer is a lot cheaper than a cocktail!"

"I should be buying *your* drink." Lois opened her pocketbook.

Maxie waved her hand dismissively. The chat with Lois and the beer in front of her had lifted her sagging spirits.

"You can get the next round," she said, looking at her half-empty glass.

Lois pushed a folded bill across the table. "Of course I'll get the next round, but put this in your purse."

"I couldn't," Maxie began, but Lois interrupted firmly, "Of course you can. Think of the millions of ways you've helped me over the past few years!"

"It's swell of you, Lo." Maxie gave in, tucking the bill into her pocketbook. "But I'll need more than this to stay in Bay City." Her buoyant spirits began to sink again. "I guess I'd better resign myself to moving back in with Mumsy." She shuddered, and signaled the waitress: *another round.*

"You *can't* move back to Mainwaring Manse!" Lois was adamant. "The Magdalena Arms wouldn't be the same without you!" She chewed her lower lip thoughtfully. "Have you considered looking for a full-time job?"

Maxie gave a bitter, "Ha!" continuing, "What would be the use? According to Pamela, I'm an empty-headed society girl with no qualifications or experience!"

"Who are we gossiping about?" queried a jovial voice, and Dolly Dingle pulled out a chair and sat down at their table.

Dorian "Dolly" Dingle, ex-child actress, currently eked out a living with radio commercials and modeling jobs for "art" photographers, while hoping for another shot at stardom. Now she waved at the waitress. "You girls have a head start on me. Where's Pam, Maxie? Did you two have another fight?"

"And how! But what's really worrying me—"

"Wait for Phyllis," Dolly told Maxie. "Or you'll have to tell your story twice."

Earnest Phyllis Densher, her frizzy dishwater-blond hair caught back in a simple barrette, balanced a glass of beer as she squeezed herself in at their table.

"The waitress will come to take your order, you know," Dolly told her.

"She's so busy, I didn't want to bother her," Phyllis explained.

Do-gooding, self-effacing Phyllis worked in the statistical department of the Bay City Harbor Commission. She devoted herself in equal parts to public policy and pining after her former supervisor, Miss Ware, who'd transferred to another branch of city service. Maxie was fond of the well-meaning young bureaucrat, but could never resist teasing her.

"But, Phyllis," she said now, "don't you realize that when you get your own drink, you're depriving Jill of her tips?"

Phyllis looked stricken. "I never thought of that." She eyed her full glass of beer remorsefully. "The next one," she resolved, lifting the glass and taking a long gulp.

"I'm sure Phyllis tipped Tobey at the bar," said a new voice. "And Dolly will tip Jill at the table. Either way, someone gets tipped."

The cool logic could belong to none other than—

"Janet!" chorused the girls. "We thought you were permanently buried in your books!"

Their old friend stood above them smiling down. Her smooth brown pageboy and tortoiseshell glasses were part of the brainy elegance that had always been Janet Kahn's hallmark. Working in a law office by day and studying jurisprudence at Bay City College by night, Janet was the one all the girls looked up to. Only Pamela rivaled her work ethic, and Maxie knew that Pamela envied Janet her education, however much the merchandiser argued that experience was the best teacher.

"I just stopped by for a moment," said Janet, slipping between Dolly and Lois. "I was hoping to see Netta before she left, but she's—" Janet hesitated.

"Gone," said Lois mournfully.

"Buck up, Lois," said Dolly with a hearty pat.

"Think of all the good she's doing," urged Phyllis.

With an effort, Lois smiled. "I'm all right, really. I'm going to keep myself busy taking a course in the automated office at Bay City College and apartment hunting. Netta and I have decided to take the plunge and get a place of our own, when she comes back."

There was a buzz of chatter and congratulations. But Dolly voiced Maxie's own feeling: "Gosh, there'll just be three of us left on the fifth floor—Maxie, me, and Phyllis. The last three musketeers!"

"I'm not sure how long I'll be there myself," Maxie said gloomily, reminded of her predicament. "Mrs. De-Witt is pretty tolerant, but she'll toss me out if I can't pay the rent."

The table of girls looked at Maxie in astonishment. This was monied Maxie talking, the open-handed heiress, who dabbled in journalism for fun, not profit.

"What's the gag?" demanded Dolly.

"Maxie's mother cut off her allowance," explained Lois.

"It's true." Maxie confirmed the story, as the girls turned startled faces toward her. "I'll have to crawl home to the Mainwaring Manse and live under Mumsy's thumb unless I can find some way to pay the rent."

Her friends broke into a babble of questions and exclamations and the whole story came out. "Good God," Dolly exclaimed, when Elaine Ellman's role was revealed, "that was one expensive kiss!"

"A slip of the lip sank this allowance ship, you might say," quipped Maxie to cover her depression. She rose to her feet and lifted her glass. "Farewell, old gang! I guess I'd better go home and pack. Is this the end of Maxie?"

Half a dozen hands pushed her back into her seat. "Why, this isn't the end, it's the beginning!" Dolly declared. She signaled the waitress with a snap of her fingers. "A martini for the little lady here." She jerked a thumb at Maxie. "It's her independence day!"

"You're not really going to give up your principles and move back in with your parents, are you?" Phyllis asked earnestly.

"I don't want to," admitted Maxie, "but what else can I do?" She looked around the circle, half hoping her friends could come up with another solution.

"What about an old-fashioned rent party?" suggested Dolly. "Ask everyone we know to contribute a few dollars."

"You could sell some of your jewelry, or even clothes," Lois added.

"I can give you tips on reducing expenses—the department has a budget book we hand out to destitute Docksiders." Phyllis began digging through the woven straw bag she carried.

"Isn't the allowance from your grandmother's trust?" Janet mused. "Perhaps there's a way to force your mother to give you the allowance—or even to break the trust."

Maxie sat up straight, as a brimming martini was set down in front of her. "You mean I'd get all of Grandmother's money at once, instead of waiting until I'm thirty-five?" This appealed to the heiress much more than Phyllis's budget book.

"Don't get your hopes up," warned Janet. "Even if it's possible, it might take quite a bit of time and money."

"Of course." But the idea was more intoxicating to Maxie than her martini—why, she'd be free of her parents, permanently!

"Meanwhile, you need to either pay your rent at the Magdalena Arms or go back home to Mumsy." Janet ticked off the options on her fingers in an orderly fashion. "There's no way around it, Maxie—you need a job!"

"But what can I do?" demanded Maxie earnestly. "Pamela seemed to think that with my lack of experience and history of dabbling no one would hire me."

"Pamela's just mad you were smooching that Ellman girl." Dolly dismissed the clothes-buyer's career wisdom. "There's no reason you can't make a living like the rest of us ordinary folks! Let's see . . ."

The gang eyed Maxie judiciously, as if fitting her for a suit of clothes. "The problem," murmured Lois, "is that you have such varied interests."

"And talents," added Phyllis thoughtfully.

It was true. Maxie had never been able to make up her mind what she wanted to do. She'd played with painting, trifled with cooking, and even toyed with the trumpet. She followed fashion, loved jazz, easily identified most Bay City bugs, and could recite the rules of polo and list the game's principal players. To top it off, she spoke a smattering of French, and could fool native Finns when she exclaimed, *"Kaipasin sinua paljon!"*

Her job as assistant for columnist Mamie McArdle had seemed ideal. She loved roving around Bay City, investigating all sorts of abstruse topics. But at her current pay rate, the part-time position was a lark, not a career.

"If I could just figure out what I'm *best* at." Maxie spoke her thoughts aloud. Suddenly Lois grabbed her arm. "There's someone who can tell you!" She pointed a finger at the bar.

Talking to the bartender, her chestnut hair coifed in a smooth bouffant, her lime-green skimmer making her look as fresh as a Popsicle, the woman looked vaguely familiar to Maxie. "Who—?"

"That's Doris Watkins!" Lois said proudly. "The career counselor!"

# Chapter 4

## Miss Watkins Is Perplexed

"**M**iss Watkins!" The tipsy gang of friends surrounded the startled career counselor like bobby-soxers besieging the latest teen idol. "You have to help Maxie!"

Doris Watkins had risen in the working world since her days advising high school girls stymied by the choice between nursing and teaching. From Walnut Grove High School Guidance Counselor, to Girls Reformatory Vocational Liaison, to Hospital Vocational Counselor, Miss Watkins had climbed to the top of her profession, rung by rung. But even now, in her prestigious position as Head of Personnel at the Business Machines Corporation, she was always ready to offer advice and aide to any girl suffering career confusion.

In fact, it appeared that Maxie and her friends had interrupted an impromptu counseling session with Francine's bartender. "This business has me so bothered I can't concentrate," Tobey was telling the sympathetic counselor.

"I'm sure I can find a solution," Miss Watkins said, before turning to the eager group of girls. She smiled at them, radiating her reassuring air of warmth and competence. "What's all this about?"

"It's Maxie." Lois acted as spokeswoman for the group. "She simply has to find a job!"

"But I have too little experience and too many interests," Maxie explained.

"Sounds like you're a candidate for the Spindle-Janska Personality Penchant Assessment," Miss Watkins told her. "If you're free tomorrow, I can—"

"Oh, Miss Watkins, wouldn't it be possible to take this Personality Assessment thing tonight?" Maxie interrupted eagerly.

Miss Watkins was taken aback, as the rest of the group echoed Maxie's plea for immediate testing. "But maybe Miss Watkins doesn't have the test with her," good-natured Phyllis suggested, offering the dubious career counselor a way out.

"N-n-o-o-o, I always carry extra copies of the PPA," said Miss Watkins, putting a protective arm over the leather satchel balanced on the barstool next to her. "It's simply that I've never administered the test in such unusual circumstances, to someone who's perhaps under the influence of alcohol—"

"Just two beers and a martini," put in Maxie.

Miss Watkins continued, as if thinking aloud, "Of course that would be an interesting data set . . . if I could compare to . . . especially given the current predilection for the liquid lunch . . ."

Tobey, who had lingered nearby wiping the bar, suggested, "She could take the test in the storeroom, away from the noise, if you want." She winked at Maxie. "It's a crazy test, but it does the trick!"

"All right, we'll try it," decided Miss Watkins. "But you must promise, Maxie, that you'll come to my office next week and retake the test under standard conditions, so I can compare the data."

Excited by the sudden turn of events, Maxie would have agreed to much more. While the gang returned to their drinks, Tobey ushered her into the little storeroom behind the bar and provided her with a rickety stool. Miss Watkins handed Maxie a copy of the test, along with a clipboard, which had a ballpoint pen attached to it by a silver chain.

"Don't dwell too long on any one question," she instructed Maxie with a smile. "Your instinctive reaction is what we're after. This test is about you and your personality—there are no right or wrong answers."

The door latched behind her, and Maxie was alone in the dimly lit storeroom. The ex-deb felt a wave of trepidation, as she wondered what the test would reveal about her personality. She'd never worried about her character before—that kind of introspection was for squares and dullards! But what if her penchant proved to be for partying? What if the test showed she had an aptitude for exactly nothing? What if Pamela was right, and Maxie *didn't* have what it took to make it as a career girl?

"There's only one way to find out," Maxie told herself firmly as she picked up the pen and bent over the test.

The Personality Penchant Assessment started with easy questions: did she prefer to work outdoors or indoors; with a group or alone; how many windows did she think were ideal in an office? *Either,* wrote Maxie. *Both, but I like to be in charge. Two, at least.*

*You prefer to be . . . You're attracted by . . . When doing x, y, or z you a) rapidly become bored, b) work for an alloted time and then stop, c) lose track of time and only stop when recalled to your surroundings by some outside force . . .* The questions and choices marched on.

Next Maxie was confronted by a succession of hypothetical scenarios that had her furrowing her forehead. If she found a $10 bill . . . if she missed her train . . . if she was suddenly orphaned; "Which I have been, in a way," she muttered to herself.

*You are walking through a dense forest and you come to a log that lies across your path. Do you leap over it or walk carefully around it?* Maxie lifted her head and stared unseeingly at the case of Old Taylor 86, The World's Most Popular Bourbon, trying to imagine the situation. It would all depend on how thick the underbrush was, and whether she was wearing an old pair of dungarees or a new pair of capris. She envisioned the forest at Loon Lake, majestic pines casting tranquil green shade on the velvety forest floor, the hum of mosquitos, the cool damp; she saw chipmunks scurrying, and down the path, a big-eyed fawn, still as a statue. Then the fawn was Elaine, her diamond engagement ring glittering in a shaft of light that penetrated the thick canopy, as she parted her scarlet lips in surprise.

*Leap,* wrote Maxie decisively.

After that there was a series of word associations, with printed instructions which told Maxie to write rapidly, without thinking. That was fun! Next to *Knife* she wrote "fork." *Table* prompted "chair." *Girl*—"girl-friend," *Mirror*—"lake," *Home*—"prison," *Mother*—"death," and so on.

At the end there was a page of inkblots, and Maxie was to choose the description that corresponded most closely to what she saw. She couldn't help amending some of the choices she circled. To "a butterfly" she added "with two heads," and "Man with a mustache" became "Man (?) with a mustache."

Finally she had circled her last answer, filled in her last blank. Fatigued, her head aching with the unusual mental activity, Maxie stumbled out of the storeroom and handed the test to the waiting Miss Watkins.

Miss Watkins shuffled the scrawled pages on the bar, aligning the edges neatly. "I'll call you as soon as I've made my analysis," she said briskly.

"Can't you give me a little hint?" Maxie pleaded. "Just a teensy one?"

"You are in a hurry," Miss Watkins observed, her pleasant smile becoming a trifle fixed. "But you see, interpreting the Personality Penchant Assessment is never the work of a moment."

"It's just"—Maxie let her shoulders droop and looked as woebegone as possible—"I've lost my allowance, and my girlfriend told me I was too impossibly empty-headed to find employment. I know I won't sleep a wink tonight without some sort of hope for the future!"

Miss Watkins laughed gaily. "No one with your persistence and persuasive powers need worry about that! And I'm sure this test will bear out my personal observation . . ." But as she glanced at the assessment, the career counselor's voice trailed away and she knit her eyebrows together. Sitting down on an empty barstool, she spread the test before her, studying it intently.

"This is odd," Miss Watkins murmured to herself. Maxie felt a shiver of anxiety.

"Have you ever been involved in planning illegal activities?" the personnel head asked the nervous girl abruptly.

"Not the planning part." Maxie tried to be honest.

"How about show business or religion? Perhaps you've produced some sort of extravaganza or organized a revival?"

"I was just an assistant stage manager for summer stock. What is it?" Maxie couldn't take the suspense. "Am I abnormal or something?"

"Of course not!" Miss Watkins almost snapped. "But these results are highly unusual—in fact, almost unique in my experience."

"Is that bad?" asked Maxie, half suspecting the test showed signs of mental deficiency and Miss Watkins was trying to sugarcoat the truth. Maxie's great-aunt Alta had recently declared that she was Queen Christina of Sweden, and was quickly committed to a sanatorium outside the city. "Don't I have a penchant for anything?" Maxie demanded plaintively.

"The peculiar thing is that you have so many penchants!" Miss Watkins told her, clearly perplexed. "Ordinarily the PPA eliminates all but a few. But according to this, I might equally well encourage you to become a private investigator, a professional gambler, or to open a motel franchise!"

Maxie thought all these possibilities were intriguing, but Miss Watkins was still talking. "There are bewildering contradictions at an even deeper level." She flipped to the inkblots. "Cold logic coexists with intuitive insights. You show every sign of high-functioning within the group, while at the same time you have a better-than-average chance of surviving a prolonged period of solitary confinement with your sanity intact!" Miss Watkins's voice rose as she spoke.

Maxie's head was spinning. The personnel head recovered her professional poise. "I certainly need more data and the time for a really in-depth analysis before I can make any firm conclusions." She put the test in her satchel. "I want you to take the test again, sober. And please provide me with all your educational records, including any Girl Scout badges." Miss Watkins smiled reassuringly at Maxie. "One thing you *don't* have to worry about is being 'empty-headed.' You're an exceptional girl, and I feel sure you have a unique and rewarding career path before you . . . What's that flashing light?"

Maxie had been so intent on Miss Watkins's words that she hadn't noticed the red and blue light flashing on the wall. Girls were clustered below the two high windows of the cellar bar, standing on their tiptoes and trying to see what was going on outside. Maxie went over to Dolly, who'd climbed on a chair and was peering out.

"It's a police car," reported Dolly. "It's parked right outside. I wonder what's going on—do you think there's been another mob hit? Mamie wrote in her column there's going to be a gang war!"

"Don't believe everything you read," cautioned Maxie, speaking as a seasoned newspaperwoman. She knew better than anyone how shaky some of Mamie's sources could be.

Just then, the door to Francine's swung open, and footsteps descended the short flight of stairs. All eyes turned to the man in blue, standing on the bottom step, surveying the crowd with a slow, cold stare.

# Chapter 5

## A Visit from the Police

"Get down from there," ordered the police officer when his gimlet gaze reached Dolly, still standing on the chair. Hastily Dolly descended, her mouth agape in astonishment.

"Shut it," muttered Maxie, elbowing the shocked actress.

She couldn't blame Dolly. Francine's had never had a visit from the boys in blue before, not in Maxie's memory. The girls at Francine's felt safe, secure. Francine's was okay, they told each other, not like the Knock Knock Lounge with its catfights and raids, the rendezvous of lowlifes and petty criminals. At Francine's, the twilight world they all lived in took on a rosy, cozy hue. Now Francine's customers exchanged uneasy glances as the man in blue stalked to the bar.

"We've had a report that two females in this establishment were dancing together and otherwise engaging in a lewd and lascivious manner," he told Tobey in a voice that was heard throughout the hushed room.

"That's all wrong," Tobey said as she nervously wiped down the spotless bar. Maxie reflected that, strictly speaking, Tobey was telling the truth. Not just two, but dozens of women had been dancing together in the course of the evening.

The policeman turned away from the bar, a sneer on his face. He strolled slowly around the room, shooting suspicious looks from side to side. He was searching for some violation, Maxie realized. He intended to shut Francine's down!

"That's a man's tie!" He stopped suddenly at a table, addressing a woman Maxie recognized as a teacher friend of Netta's.

"This? Why this is my favorite foulard," the woman faltered, fingering the paisley-figured neckpiece nervously.

"Are you making fun of me?" The policeman's heavy brows lowered.

"No, no, not at all," her friend quickly broke in. "You can see this very item advertised in the Grunemans catalog as 'Foulards for Femmes de Mode'—that means for women of style," she translated helpfully.

"He certainly doesn't know his fashions," Maxie whispered to Dolly.

The policeman seemed stymied. "I'm keeping my eye on this place," he told Tobey, retreating up the stairs.

As soon as he was gone, a low murmur of talk broke out, which grew and swelled like a tidal wave until it drowned out the jukebox. Almost simultaneously an exodus began. "I'm afraid *my* fun is over for the night," declared the woman in the paisley foulard as she and her friends hurried past Maxie, leaving their half-drunk beers behind. Other patrons finished their beers first, but exited just the same.

"This is poor policy on the part of the police!" expostulated Phyllis. "We ought to protest, not play along with the game!" Phyllis seldom got angry and then only on matters of principle. But now she radiated indignation to the ends of her crinkly blond-brown hair.

"Who can afford to?" Janet was pragmatic. "I know I can't." With a sigh she picked up her purse. "At least I'll get more studying done!"

After Janet's departure, Lois asked in a troubled voice, "Do you think he'll be back?"

"You can bet on it!" declared Dolly. "It's what I was saying earlier, a gang war! That mob that runs the Knock Knock is trying to get more territory—turf, I mean to say—and they've set their sights on Francine's!"

Maxie heard similar rumors racing around the bar like frightened bunnies. Someone said that the mob hit last week was connected. Another girl knew someone in the anti-racketeering task force, and her source said a new boss was in charge of the Larsen gang. "You mean the Swenson gang," objected a third. "And I heard it's an out-of-town organization muscling in." Several girls agreed that all these gangs should be deported back to Sweden, Norway, and the other faraway Northern European countries they'd come from. Immediately an opposing group argued that it was unfair to punish *all* Scandinavian Americans, just because there were a few bad apples.

The high-pitched arguments, fueled by unspoken fears, swirled around the room as Francine's patrons grasped at any straw to explain the sudden shattering of their safe haven.

Maxie looked around the familiar surroundings, the warm patina of the worn oak bar, the framed photos of Amelia Earhart, Eleanor Roosevelt, and a smiling woman in a feather hat said to be the bar's namesake. The floorboards were worn with the tread of oxfords, saddle shoes, ballet flats, boots, and pumps. The square of linoleum in the back had been polished by everything from the foxtrot to the frug. The old jukebox, the new cigarette machine—at the beginning of the evening they'd seemed as certain as death and taxes. Now the whole shebang was threatened.

It was certainly a day for upheavals! Maxie decided.

Dolly and Phyllis had fallen into conversation with a motley group of Francine faithfuls. "They've already knocked over the Knock Knock, I heard," reported an earnest young co-ed, pushing up the glasses that were almost sliding off her nose. "My soc prof's awfully excited about it. He says it's a chance to study the criminal underworld in action!"

"Sure, but while you're studying the underworld, where are we going to get a quiet drink?" queried her friend mournfully.

"I always knew Francine's was too good to be true," put in an older woman in a voice of triumphant doom. "I remember when we just had house parties. We had a darned good time then, and we can again!"

No one else seemed enthused by this prospect. "There's always the Blue Danube." The earnest student named a restaurant popular with all members of the third sex.

"It's not the same," Dolly objected. "You can't dance and they're always after you to order food."

"What do all these gangs want with Francine's anyway?" demanded one of the students.

"Protection money," the earnest one explained patronizingly. "Weren't you paying any attention in class last week?" She turned to Tobey, who was glumly washing glasses. "Isn't that right?"

"The less you know the better," Tobey said to the student. It had been her stock answer all evening long.

"I don't think Francine Flicka will be a pushover, as they say in mob parlance," remarked Miss Watkins as she picked up her leather satchel.

"You mean, Francine is still around?" Maxie was amazed. "I've never seen her."

"She hardly ever comes into the bar anymore," explained Miss Watkins. "And it was never more than a sideline to her true calling." As Maxie wondered what Francine's true calling was, Miss Watkins took a card from her purse and gave it to Maxie. "Are you free to meet me at my office on Monday, for our follow-up?"

"I have a part-time job as an assistant for Mamie McArdle, the crusading columnist," Maxie told her. "But I pretty much make my own hours."

"Ah!" Miss Watkins was impressed. "That's very fine. Your PPA did show signs of a penchant for the written word."

"Really?" Maxie lapped up this crumb of encouragement like a hungry bloodhound. Pamela had never approved of Maxie's job with Mamie—another thing she had in common with Maxie's mother. "I thought I'd ask Mamie about a full-time job at the *Sentinel*."

"An excellent idea," approved Miss Watkins.

Suddenly red and blue lights began flashing their garish warning on the walls of Francine's once more. A universal groan rose from the remaining patrons.

"Good-bye, Maxie, I'll see you Monday." Miss Watkins gathered her gloves and set her hat at a jaunty angle. "Keep your chin up, Tobey. Apparently you've chosen the right time for a career move." She led a second exodus up Francine's stairs and out the door.

"Time to go, Phyllis," Dolly told their frizzy-haired friend, who was studying the photo of Francine. Lois was long gone.

"I'm staying right here," Phyllis declared. "I'll show those goons they can't push the little people around!"

Dolly took her elbow firmly. "Don't be a dope, Phyll," she said, not unkindly. "It's late and it'll be even later by the time you get done with night court." She escorted the recalcitrant policy maker up the stairs, and Maxie trailed behind.

The unemployed heiress had been struck by an idea. If that sociology prof found career opportunity in gang warfare, why couldn't Maxie? She could sell the *Sentinel* a series of stories! PART I: INSIDE A RAID, she planned mentally.

When she reached the street, the flashing lights had just winked off. Maxie guessed that they'd served the policeman's purpose—they'd emptied the bar as fast as a fox empties a dovecote.

Maxie stopped in the shadow of the brick building and watched curiously as the policeman got out of his car. Was he going to pull in poor Tobey and Jill, or drunken Mattie Bye, who'd fallen asleep at the back table? But the cop walked past Francine's entrance and turned into the alley, casting a glance behind him.

Now Maxie's investigative instincts were aroused. She followed him, peering cautiously around the corner. No one was in sight. Feeling her way along the brick wall, she went down the dark alley to where it joined another alley, the one that ran behind Francine's.

There was the policeman, deep in conversation with a second figure. Heart pounding, Maxie hid behind a clump of metal trash cans. Her brown two-piece melted into the shadows, except for the white piping, which made Maxie feel as conspicuous as a glowing firefly. She made a mental note to eliminate white from her wardrobe.

Maxie peered over the top of the trash can, ignoring the sour smell of stale beer. A light went on in the rear window of one of the apartment buildings, giving her a look at the mystery man, as he talked with the cop.

*Why, he's just a kid!* she thought. *And a good-looking*

*one at that.* He stood in the dark alley with the easy grace of an athlete, nonchalantly slapping something against his left hand. The policeman talked on in a monotonous murmur.

"Good enough," the youth finally interrupted. He handed the policeman the thing in his hand. It was a thick envelope.

*A payoff!* Maxie realized, and the light went out. She couldn't restrain an ecstatic sigh. Maybe this was the new crime boss they'd been talking about in the bar! No— Maxie dismissed the idea. No crime boss worth his weight in Cuban cigars would stand around in a dark alley making payoffs himself!

She heard footsteps coming and crouched back down. The policeman didn't glance her way, as he counted the money in the envelope. *He pocketed the tainted money, shaming the very uniform he put it in,* Maxie mentally composed her lead.

Then she turned her attention to the man who had made the payoff, the—what was the term Mamie used? The bagman. PART II: INTERVIEW WITH A BAGMAN; that would be a stunner. If she could just get it across to this fellow that her only interest was as a journalist—

"Excuse me," she began boldly, but the mob flunky was closer than she'd thought, and the two collided as she emerged from behind the trash can. "Hey!" he exclaimed, and grabbed Maxie, whether to maintain his balance or hold her captive, she wasn't sure.

"Sorry—I just wanted to ask you a few questions— anonymously, of course—could you please let me go!" With a final twist Maxie partially freed herself. "Why— you're a girl!" she gasped.

"That makes two of us." The husky voice vibrated in Maxie's ear and raised a crop of goose bumps on her bare arms. He—no, she—released Maxie and retreated a step. Maxie felt a queer twinge of regret.

"You paid off that policeman to make trouble at Francine's!" she accused the stranger. "How could someone like *you* be party to such a thing?" The discovery that the bagman was a girl, and a distinctly boyish one, had turned Maxie's journalistic objectivity into indignation.

The girl seemed amused at Maxie's anger. "Did I interrupt your sorority do?" she drawled. "The Knock Knock is still swinging—why don't you go there? Too hoity-toity?"

"So you're from the Knock Knock," Maxie sniffed. "I should have guessed!"

"Why?" demanded the stranger. "Because of the way I look? I'm not *respectable,* not the kind you want at Francine's, is that it?" There was resentment in her voice as she flung out, "You college girls make me sick!"

"I never went to college," retorted Maxie. "What have you got against college girls anyway?"

She felt oddly excited as she peered at the stranger's face, trying to make out her features. She sensed the mannish girl was doing the same. They were standing quite close to each other now, and Maxie felt that funny tingly sensation all over, even as she told herself that the girl's part in the raid was reprehensible.

"Maybe one of them broke my heart." Now the stranger's velvety voice held a teasing note.

"Are you sure it wasn't the other way around?" *Why, I'm flirting with her!* Maxie realized, half horrified. *What's the matter with me?*

"You'd know something about heartbreakers, wouldn't you?" The stranger's voice dropped a notch and became infinitely more suggestive. She moved a fraction of an inch toward Maxie and lifted her hand to fluff Maxie's tousled tresses. "You're all mussed," she murmured.

*I'm going to kiss her,* Maxie realized in a daze. This unexpected alley meeting was a far cry from her playful powder room encounter with Elaine. This girl was no Bambi, and what Maxie felt now was as different from her attraction to Elaine as the call of the wild was from a petting zoo.

"Who are you?" she whispered, lifting her face to the stranger, lips dry with desire, her pulse pounding in her throat.

"My name is Lon," said the girl, bending toward her. "I'm—"

"Maxie Mainwaring, heiress to the Mainwaring fortune," the girl murmured as her lips brushed Maxie's.

Maxie pulled back. "How do you know so much about me?"

They both stared into the impenetrable darkness. A car honked in the distance. Lon lifted her head, as if at a signal only she could hear. "Good night, Maxie," she said. "Time all good little girls were in bed." Then she was sauntering swiftly toward the street, leaving Maxie, swamped in frustrated sensation, behind. After a dazed split second, Maxie hurried after her. She reached the street just as Lon slid into the passenger seat of a black Buick. The slanting streetlight illuminated a pair of shapely legs next to her before Lon shut the door and the car slid away from the curb and disappeared into the night.

## Chapter 6

## Advice from Mamie

The brunette in the red twill overblouse and white crepe shirt-shift stood on the corner of 47th Street and Dock, smoking a cigarette in short, impatient puffs. Just as she dropped her stub and ground it out with an impatient twist of her red patent-leather toe, another brunette, this one wearing a pleated dress in jonquil yellow with a white piqué collar, came out of the Magdalena Arms and hurried to join her.

"I see it worked," said the girl in yellow. "But I can't help thinking it was a mean trick to play on Mrs. DeWitt."

"No it wasn't, Lo," Maxie said earnestly. "You saved my life!"

It hadn't been easy, convincing the honest office manager to loan Maxie her favorite spring ensemble so the penniless heiress could sneak by Mrs. DeWitt. She'd only persuaded Lois by offering her imported Italian dress in exchange. But it had worked like a charm. Mrs. DeWitt had given Maxie a bleary-eyed glance as the faux-Lois crossed the hall, her heart pounding under the borrowed red twill, and resumed her watch for her errant tenant.

"I hope Miss Watkins finds you a job soon," Lois said now. "Or *I'll* be organizing that rent party."

"You've done enough for me," Maxie assured her worried doppelgänger, patting the borrowed red-and-white purse, where Lois's loan from last night was safely stashed. "I'm going to wangle an advance out of Mamie, as well as a full-time job, and then all my problems will be solved."

The two girls were walking to the bus stop together. Maxie felt virtuous and energetic. In assuming Lois's identity, she'd had to adopt her schedule as well. It was now seven forty-five A.M.—the earliest she'd been up in years.

"That dress really does something for you." Maxie laid on the flattery to distract her friend from further pangs of conscience.

"Really? You don't think it makes my complexion too yellow?" Lois took out her compact and held it at arm's length, in an effort to evaluate her outfit.

"Not a bit," Maxie assured her as the bus arrived and they climbed aboard. They found two seats together. "I should at least give you back your pearls." Lois sank her voice to a whisper.

"Keep 'em," Maxie ordered.

The loan of her pearls was the only way Maxie could show Lois her appreciation right now. The unemployed heiress chafed at the thought that she could no longer treat a girl to a drink or dinner; she'd always been the open-handed benefactress of the fifth floor. But how could she maintain that position now? Who was she, without her family's money? She gazed at her reflection in the window of the bus as it plunged into a tunnel. Then her questioning face disappeared as they emerged into sunlight, and Maxie's moment of introspection passed as well. Her only thought was for breakfast.

"See you later, Lois." She pulled the cord for her stop as they reached the outskirts of Bay City's business district. There was a coffee shop across the street from the offices of the *Bay City Sentinel* that served the most delectable buns. Maxie swung off the bus and headed for it.

"Cuppa joe and a honey bun," she told the waitress as she slid onto a stool at the counter. She surveyed the shop, crowded with typists, stenographers, proofreaders, and receptionists, all grabbing a hasty bite before their workday began. This would be *her* schedule, Maxie realized, if she obtained the full-time employment she sought. The thought was a little daunting.

Her wandering gaze was arrested by a plump woman with graying blond hair, sitting by herself in a booth. Mamie McArdle, too, was up early. Maxie took her coffee and half-eaten bun and carried them across the crowded restaurant to join her employer. The columnist looked up from her study of the *Bay City Tribune*, the *Sentinel*'s rival.

"Maxie Mainwaring, what are you doing up before dawn? Or have you been up all night? Where, why, and who else was there? Don't hold out on me now!" She shook her finger reprovingly at Maxie.

"Do I ever hold out on you, Mamie?" Maxie held out her cup for the waitress to refill, and added a generous dollop of cream. Mamie was having waffles and bacon along with the diet fruit cup. Maxie wondered if she should order a side of sausage, and then reminded herself sternly that she was economizing.

"Well"—Mamie mopped a forkful of waffles in a puddle of syrup—"I had to hear about the powder-room fracas at the Bay City Women's Club from *another* source."

Of course, Mamie McArdle would already have the whole story of the powder-room scandal. Her "Confidentially" column was scorned by girls like Pamela for its scurrilous stories and salacious gossip, but read by all of Bay City, from the society matrons down to their maids and masseuses. Maxie always defended the newspaper-woman, who was only meeting public demand when she wrote of the sins society tried to keep secret. No one knew more about Bay City than Mamie. If she put in print a quarter of the shocking things she'd uncovered, she'd blow the lid off the town!

Now Mamie looked at Maxie with knowing eyes and asked, "Tell me, Maxie, confidentially, is it true your mother said you were only helping Elaine Ellman get a fish bone out of her throat?"

"Ha!" said Maxie bitterly. So that was the story her mother was spreading. "If that was the case, I wouldn't have been kicked off the Mainwaring payroll." She leaned forward, all earnestness. "That's why I'm up so early, Mamie. I need some extra income, pronto! How about a full-time job?"

Mamie shook her head. "No can do, Maxie. There's no room in the budget. The editors are already kicking about my expense account, and the price of payoffs to cigarette girls and bellhops is rising faster than inflation."

"What about another position at the *Sentinel*?" Maxie persisted. "Maybe on the crime beat? I talked to a career counselor who said I had a penchant for writing—"

Mamie laughed kindly. "The paper wants reporters with experience—samples and published pieces, not penchants." She signaled for her check.

Maxie followed Mamie to the cash register, a little cast down. The only thing she could show the city editor was the piece she'd written about horned beetles for the Camp Pottawatomi paper, *Rise and Shine*.

"And another thing," Mamie added as they exited. "When you're on the job you deliver, but half the time you're vacationing at Loon Lake, or flying off to Europe, or sunning yourself in Acapulco. News never stops, you know!"

Maxie bit her lip. It was her mother's fault. Always insisting Maxie come up to Loon Lodge for one of her everlasting parties for "nice people." That European trip had been Mumsy's attempt to separate Maxie from Pamela. Unbeknownst to Mrs. Mainwaring, Pamela was following the fall fashions for Grunemans and the two girls had connected in every city from Paris to Milan. As for Acapulco—Maxie shuddered, remembering. It had been Christmastime, and she'd hated every minute of false festivity!

She crossed the street with Mamie to the *Sentinel* offices, wishing she could explain this to the columnist. Instead, she pulled out her ace. "What if I told you I witnessed a mobster paying off a policeman last night?"

Mamie's eyes gleamed. "When, where, how?"

Maxie told her the story, leaving out her conversation with Lon. "You always could get the good stuff!" Mamie said admiringly. Then she sighed. "But I can't use it. The editor got so many complaints about my piece on mob murders he put the kibosh on any more crime stories for a while. The DAP says I'm giving Bay City a bad name."

"But if they're true . . ." Maxie began.

"And then the accidental death of a fellow named Swen*sen* somehow got mixed into the list of hits on the Swen*son* mob," Mamie admitted. "I don't know why I didn't catch it. But the upshot is, nothing but society gossip in 'Confidentially' for a while." She patted Maxie consolingly as they climbed the broad marble stairs to the *Sentinel* newsroom. "Maybe your cop will keep."

Mamie picked up a sheaf of messages from the receptionist and went into her office, reading all the way. Maxie wandered after her, not knowing what to do next. Her schemes so far had all fallen flat!

"I think I'll do an item on the Driscoll-Ellman engage-ment," Mamie announced, as if she'd forgotten all about crime. "Scuttlebut is, the Driscolls are selling off a string of dry cleaners to raise some cash. 'Decimated dry-cleaning empire delays wedding bells.' How does that sound? I don't suppose," she suggested in her most persuasive voice, "you'll be seeing your little friend Elaine again?"

"Certainly not," said Maxie. She felt a wave of wrath when she thought of the underhanded Elaine and the trouble she'd caused. And how tame Elaine seemed, com-pared with handsome Lon. *Who's just a gang girl,* Maxie reminded herself.

"What about Ted Driscoll?" Mamie was asking. "Do you see the Driscolls socially?"

"I suppose I could call up Elaine's cousin, Sookie," Maxie said halfheartedly. "Isn't there any way to cash in on my corrupt cop? I need money *now,* Mamie!"

Mamie only laughed. "Oh, pshaw! A Mainwaring needing money! Your mother will be handing out your allowance again in a week. Unless"—an inquisitive gleam came into Mamie's eye—"the Mainwaring fortune isn't as solid as it seems?"

"Of course it is!" Maxie retorted indignantly. "Don't you dare print anything to the contrary!"

Evidently full-time employment at the *Sentinel* wasn't going to be as easy as she'd thought. But she still had a paycheck to collect, thank heavens. Her weekly pittance suddenly seemed a significant sum. However, when she picked up her pay envelope and tore it open with unac-customed eagerness, her check was for only fifteen dol-lars.

"There's been a mistake," she said, returning to the payroll window. The clerk pursed her lips and opened a heavy ledger. "No mistake," she said, her spectacles flashing triumphantly. "Salary of thirty-five dollars, less twenty advanced last Wednesday."

Maxie remembered then—she'd needed money to pay for the hairdo at Henri's, the Fairweather Flounce she'd gotten to make her mother happy.

"Can I get another advance?" asked the ex-deb desperately, but the clerk was already shaking her head. "I'm sorry, Miss Mainwaring. Payroll policy limits salary advances to three per month, and you've reached your limit."

Maxie turned away, clutching her meager check. She couldn't help overhearing the clerk, who commented to her colleague in an undertone, "All that Mainwaring money and always asking for advances! Those rich girls give me a headache!"

# Chapter 7

## Raid on the
## Mainwaring Manse

Standing in Bay City's Central Station, which had recently been renamed the John F. Kennedy Memorial Station, Maxie counted her money. Had her breakfast really cost sixty-five cents? It was disconcerting, the way she always had less money in her pocketbook than she thought she did. After she bought her ticket to Waukesset, her loan from Lois would be half gone!

Maxie had decided that a visit to the Mainwaring Manse was in order. She needed to retrieve the educational records Miss Watkins had requested, and the sooner she got them to Miss Watkins, the sooner the career counselor would come up with a real job, paying a real salary.

And Maxie was determined to collect one last allowance. Mumsy always kept a quantity of cash in a lacquered box on her dressing table for household emergencies. Sure, some might call it stealing, but to Maxie's mind, her mother owed her that money!

Mabel Mainwaring was unlikely to see it that way, but fortunately Fridays were Mumsy's days to get a facial and massage at Countess Elfi's. The coast would be clear.

Money, money, money—it was monotonous to be preoccupied with filthy lucre to the exclusion of all else. Somehow, knowing that she shouldn't buy even a magazine made Maxie long for one more desperately than on previous train trips. How did poor girls stand this constant obsession with cost? Maxie's membership in this sad sorority was only a day old and already she felt she'd go mad from this—this fenced-in feeling.

Getting off the interurban at Waukesset, Maxie looked longingly at the taxi stand. It was three miles to the Mainwaring Manse, and Maxie felt utterly conspicuous trudging her way down tranquil streets past the lavish lawns and well-tended gardens, under the curious glances of gardeners trimming the shrubbery.

At least she'd had the sense to wear flats today. She turned up the Mainwarings' curving driveway toward the big redbrick mansion, built by her great-grandfather in 1882 in the style of an English manor house. Patrick, the groundsman, was clipping the box hedge, but he stopped what he was doing when he saw Maxie.

"Good morning, Miss Maxie," he said, taking a few steps toward her. "Your ma said you weren't to come to the Manse no more."

Maxie essayed a little laugh. "Oh, Mumsy! I guess she was mad for a couple minutes—we had a small tiff yesterday, but she's over it now. It's all right, Patrick, really it is." She took a step up the drive, but Patrick blocked her passage.

"Your ma said 'under no circumstances,' " he said stolidly. "You better come back later, when she's home."

Maxie bit her lip in vexation. Patrick was obviously determined and bigger than her to boot. "Well, of course I don't want to get you in trouble," she said with a wide, false smile. "And it isn't important anyway." Damn Patrick and his loyal retainer act! Well, there was more than one way to skin a cat. No one was going to stop her from getting inside the Mainwaring Manse today!

She retreated down the driveway and turned toward the Thorwalds' turreted, gingerbreaded mansion known as Viking Hall. Along the far side of the house was a narrow path, little more than a beaten track in the grass, which led to the ravine where she and Ginger Thorwald had played as children. Maxie turned into it. "Quiet, Odin," she muttered, as the Thorwalds' aging Newfoundland barked at her inquiringly. Odin followed her, panting in a friendly fashion, but left off when Maxie began inching down the steep hillside. Losing her footing, she slipped and slithered down the side of the ravine, landing feetfirst in the muddy creek at the bottom. *Wonderful,* she thought in disgust. Now Lois's shoes were soiled and would have to be cleaned. Another expense.

"In for a penny, in for a pound," she muttered, making her way along the creek until she saw the fence that marked the Mainwaring property. On hands and knees, she inched her way back up the side of the ravine. Now, if no one had noticed the broken boards by the oak tree . . . No one had. Maxie wriggled through the narrow opening, realizing she'd grown some since her teenaged years, when she'd used this route for many an illicit excursion. Brushing herself off on the Mainwaring side of the fence, she saw that she'd acquired a vivid green grass stain down the front of Lois's borrowed ensemble. That tied it. Her mother was paying all the expenses of this little outing!

Darting from tree to tree, then to the arbor, the sauna, the poolhouse, and finally the bushes that fringed the terrace, Maxie reached the house without being seen. She slipped inside the little door that led to the service corridor. On her right she could hear a clatter from the kitchen. She pushed open the swinging padded door in front of her and tiptoed into the great hall, empty but for the familiar suits of armor her grandfather had brought back from some European shopping spree. Crossing hurriedly to the library, Maxie opened the paneled door cautiously, on the off chance Dad was dozing on the overstuffed leather sofa instead of at the polo club.

The sofa was empty, the needlepoint pillows symmetrically arranged, which meant that the maids had already done this room. Maxie dropped to her knees by the walnut filing cabinet and pulled out the lower drawer. *Waukesset Day School, Miss Gratton's, Dr. Ridgeway, Circle School, Woodbury Secretarial School.* Maxie pulled out the files, deciding Miss Watkins would probably want the records of her analysis by loony Dr. Ridgeway as well as her grades from Miss Gratton's. She looked around for something to put them in, and spotted her father's briefcase standing next to the desk. That would be perfect, and Dad hardly ever used it.

Setting the briefcase on the desk, Maxie's eye fell upon the papers spread out there. The words *Hedda Nyberg Trust* leaped out at her. Who was looking at Grandma Nyberg's trust papers—and why? After a moment of hesitation, Maxie gathered up the legal documents and put them in the briefcase with her educational records. She'd show them to Janet.

Now for the upstairs. But first—Maxie went to the bookshelf and took down the gilt-bound copy of *Hard Times*. This was where her father kept his secret supply of betting money. As an eight-year-old, she'd displayed to an awed Ginger Thorwald a hundred-dollar bill she'd come upon while reading. She flipped through its pages, then shook the book vigorously. A bill fluttered out and Maxie pounced, but it was only a dollar. Her father must be picking the wrong ponies these days.

Swinging the briefcase, Maxie went back to the great

hall and ran lightly up the stairs to her bedroom. The canopied bed and jeune fille dressing table were unchanged. She pulled out the pink upholstered stool and sat down. Reaching behind a jumble of cut-glass bottles, she brought out a little cedar box, *Maxie* crudely woodburned on the lid. This was where she kept her mementos. The second-class Girl Scout badge she'd earned with projects in hostessing and agriculture was buried under a jumble of dried flowers, old notes, her class ring from Miss Gratton's, and a locket. Maxie unfolded a creased piece of notebook paper. *Maxie darling, meet me in the third-floor storage closet, midnight sharp! C.W.* Who was C.W.? Maxie couldn't remember. She put the cedar box back and looked around the room. Was there anything else she needed? She started at the sight of herself in the mirror, hair tousled, face streaked with sweat and dirt. *I look like an interloper.*

She picked up the briefcase and tiptoed down the hall to her mother's room. Cautiously she eased open the door and stepped inside. For a second she inhaled the familiar scents of Vandovar face powder, Bonne Souvenir perfume, and cigarettes, which mixed together spelled *Mother* as clear as writing on the wall. The drapes were drawn and the room was cool and dim. Maxie went to the carved mahogany dressing table and looked for the little lacquered box. It wasn't there.

She sat on the foot of her mother's massive mahogany bed in bewildered frustration. Had her mother taken precautionary measures? *Well, really!* Maxie thought indignantly. Imagine, treating your own daughter like a thief! She went back to the dressing table for another look. A rhinestone brooch twinkled mockingly from the silver tray of costume jewelry. The real jewels, of course, were locked in the safe in the closet.

*Not that I would steal her jewelry,* Maxie told herself virtuously, as she pulled out her mother's glove drawer and felt around for the lacquered box. Would it be stealing though, if she took the amethyst set that had been given to her, Maxie, on her eighteenth birthday?

Maxie was on her knees before the safe, trying to remember the combination when she heard footsteps outside. In a split second she had shut the closet door and burrowed behind her mother's sheared beaver.

It was Mumsy, she knew instantly. The quick impatient tap of heels across the floor, a drawer being pulled out and shoved in, rustling sounds that might mean she was taking off her hat. Was she changing clothes? Would she open the closet door? Maxie dug herself deeper into the wall of fur.

She heard the bedroom door open and close again. After a few seconds, Maxie emerged from the closet. She tiptoed to the door and opened it an inch.

"We'll have lunch on the terrace," she heard her mother say, as she descended the curving staircase.

Her guest responded with some indistinct pleasantry, and Maxie drew back.

What on earth was her mother doing home? She should be sitting in the Bay City Women's Club dining room having the half melon filled with chicken salad, just as she did every Friday after her session at Countess Elfi's.

It was time to take a powder. Maxie picked up the briefcase and then cursed, silently. Her pocketbook. She'd left it in the library. She had to get it. Not only did it contain her return ticket to Bay City and all her money, but it belonged to Lois!

Creeping down the stairs, feeling as conspicuous as a horsefly on a bride's bouquet, Maxie made it to the library unseen and picked up the pocketbook. The French doors to the terrace were ajar, and her ears perked up when she heard her own name.

"And your daughter, Maxine, does she also do charity work?" The voice was female—cultured and suave. Whoever it was, she was important enough to make Mumsy miss her morning at Countess Elfi's salon.

"Maxie has many interests," her mother answered curtly. "Now, your main rival for the Beautification Committee is Hazel Houck—"

Maxie couldn't resist peeking through the French doors at the unknown visitor. The table for two was set by the lilac bush. Opposite Mumsy was a woman in her thirties, Maxie thought, not quite the clubwoman type. Her air of brisk confidence reminded Maxie of Pamela's boss, the head buyer at Grunemans—only this woman was a lot better looking. Her hair was platinum, and she wore a simple cream-colored suit that set off her tan, shapely legs to advantage. "The Houck woman should be easy to handle," the stranger said briskly, as she unfolded her napkin.

Selma appeared with a plate of popovers, and Maxie lost interest in the conversation. Her stomach grumbled so loudly she was afraid the women on the terrrace would hear, and she drew back into the shadows of the library. She was starving, she realized. Walking three miles and scrambling around the ravine had really given her an appetite.

Her father's copy of *Hard Times,* her mother's lacquered box, the jewelry safe—they'd all failed her. A raid on the refrigerator would help balance the books. Maxie was pushing open the door to the service corridor and heading for the kitchen almost before the idea had fully bloomed.

"You! You're not supposed to be here!" Selma snapped.

She was returning to the terrace with a tray full of avocado salad.

Maxie was beginning to perceive that the deference the servants had once shown her had melted away, like a thin crust of ice that had been concealing a dark pond of resentment. "Mumsy won't want you to make a scene," she called after the departing maid.

Hoping Selma would heed her advice, Maxie crept through the kitchen to the big pantry. Mrs. Grimes, the cook, who had terrified Maxie for as long as she could remember, was stirring something on the stove. Maxie looked around at the well-stocked shelves and gleaming refrigerator. Someone had sliced brioche bread and put it on a platter with smoked salmon—mmmm. Maxie had to make herself a little sandwich. Where were the capers kept?

"You put that down, you child of Satan! What the hell are you doing in my kitchen?" The cook advanced on Maxie threateningly, a meat tenderizer in one muscular hand. Maxie swallowed half the sandwich hastily. "Your soufflé is sinking, Mrs. Grimes!" she managed to say, just as the fearsome woman grasped her arm. The cook sniffed the air, her beady eyes never leaving Maxie.

"I'll settle with you, you little brat," she growled as she backtracked to the stove. Maxie seized a string bag hanging from a hook and snatched provisions at random from the refrigerator and pantry shelves, hurling them pell-mell into the bag. She tucked Lois's pocketbook under one arm, picked up her father's briefcase with her remaining free hand, and ran from the kitchen, down the service corridor, into the great hallway, past the suits of armor and under the faux medieval tapestry, which depicted Great-grandpa Mainwaring on a hunting trip in Loon Lake, and burst out of the front door, not bothering to close it behind her.

"See you, Pat!" she panted as she ran past the astonished groundsman and down the curving drive. At the granite pillars she turned back. Mrs. Grimes was a tiny figure, shaking her fist from the steps while Patrick stood indecisively, clippers hanging from one hand.

Maxie raised the hand that held the string bag in mock salute. "So long, old homestead!"

# Chapter 8
## A Writing Assignment

It was on the train ride home, munching a brioche-bread-and-smoked-salmon sandwich, that Maxie got her bright idea: She would write something for *The Step Stool,* earning money and acquiring a writing sample for the *Sentinel* at the same time!

She'd been flipping through her old report cards as the trees and half-timbered shopping centers flashed by outside the train window, looking at her Evaluations from Circle School. She'd attended the progressive school for wealthy girls with problems after her expulsion from Miss Gratton's, a blurry year of free reading, automatic drawing, and sitting in the eponymous circle, discussing school rules in a democratic decision-making exercise that never seemed to end. At the Circle School, there were no letter grades, just Evaluations.

*Enormous creativity . . . a talented writer, if only . . .* Maxie read. *Real potential as a leader, but . . . A delightful girl, although . . .* Maxie ignored the quibbles and focused on the praise. She had writing talent. She had potential!

Of course *The Step Stool* probably couldn't pay much. The little homophile newsletter had struggled to stay afloat since its inception, and Pamela was always dragging Maxie to a "Save *The Step Stool*" bowling match or bake sale. But still, Maxie reasoned with newfound frugality, every little bit would help.

And wouldn't it be nice if Pam picked up her precious newsletter and saw Maxie's name in print? Then she'd realize that the ex-deb was capable of more than "shopping and chasing girls!" Maxie imagined a humble Pam, climbing the stairs to the ex-deb's fifth-floor room, where she would be busily typing away. "I underestimated you," Pamela would say. "Louise tells me you're the backbone of *The Step Stool*!"

Maxie made a mental note to get hold of a typewriter, as she descended from the train in Bay City. Let Mumsy hide her lacquered box! Maxie didn't need the Mainwaring money—she was creative and talented, and had the teacher's comments to prove it. Between Miss Watkins and the gang at the Arms, the perfect position was bound to present itself.

The ex-deb made a stop at Central Station's washroom to tidy up before visiting *The Step Stool*. A wetted comb put new life into her Fairweather Flounce, and a friendly traveler with some spot cleaner helped her remove the worst of the grass stains and dirt streaks. "Rinse with a little hydrogen peroxide when you wash it," the woman advised. A brush from the washroom attendant and a quick polish at the shoe stand and Maxie was back in business, swinging her string bag as she walked down Lake Street. She was glad she'd pocketed the dollar bill from *Hard Times*. At least her parents had paid for her good grooming!

She hopped on board the 153 bus to the Olsenville district, and dropped her twenty cents in the coin box, feeling pleased with her economy; that was twice today she'd resisted the taxi temptation. "Transfer?" the driver asked her. "No thank you," said Maxie politely, wondering what a transfer was.

Getting off at Loomis Boulevard, Maxie rang the worn buzzer above the label SOS. *The Step Stool* office was on the third floor of a narrow brick building half a block from the interurban tracks. There was a delicatessen on the ground floor, and Maxie looked at the liverwurst longingly as she waited to be buzzed in.

*Bzzt!* Maxie entered and started up the stairs. "Who is it?" Louise Elward, the managing editor, was peering suspiciously over the bannister as Maxie climbed.

"It's just me, Maxie." She came up the last steps and followed Louise through the worn door, which had S.O.S. painted on the pebbled glass. "S.O.S." stood for "Sisters of Sappho," but everyone always used the innocuous acronym.

The room was crowded with filing cabinets, two desks, and a long table where Maxie had once helped assemble and staple an issue of *The Step Stool* in its early days. At the far desk, a round-faced, curly-haired girl was tinkering with a camera. At the desk inside the door stood Louise's right-hand woman, Donnie, obviously waiting for the managing editor.

"What can I do for you, Maxie?" Louise asked with a preoccupied air. When Maxie told Louise she'd come to offer her services as a freelance writer, the editor dismissed her: "Talk to Stella, she's in charge of features now," she said, pointing at the curly-haired girl before turning back to Donnie.

The features editor's response was more enthusiastic. "Sure, we can use you!" she exclaimed. "Gosh, and you work with Mamie McArdle at the *Sentinel*! That's just terrific!" She put down the camera, and Maxie sat in a straightbacked chair. "I'm Stella McSweeney, and I've just taken over the features department. I think I've seen you before, maybe at that bowling party in January? Oh, and weren't you at Francine's the other night? Wasn't that awful? Louise and Donnie are planning an editorial. Now, where's my notebook. . . . Gosh, this is great—I was worried I'd have to practically write this whole issue myself!"

While Stella chatted away, Maxie studied the peppy new features editor, who wore a blue-and-white-striped sailor shirt and matching blue capris. She was glad she wouldn't be submitting her articles to humorless Louise!

"Here we are." Stella unearthed a notebook and opened it up. Maxie got up to look over her shoulder at the "Feature Ideas" list: *Married Lesbians, Medical Est., Biblical Evidence*—the items filled the page.

"Movie round-up—that sounds fun!"

"I've already got someone lined up for that," Stella told her. "How about something in the 'Working Girl' series I've planned? You know, advice, analysis—"

"What the working girl wears?" Maxie suggested.

"Sure!" said Stella. "Just be sure to give it that Sapphic-specific slant our readers expect—you know, 'businesslike but not butch.'" She winked. "That always gets the letters coming in!"

She'd not only gotten an assignment, she'd made a new friend, Maxie realized as she left. And she'd lightened her load, leaving *The Step Stool*ers the big cannister of lemon drops she'd grabbed from the Mainwaring pantry in her haste.

Filled with zeal, she decided to get right to work. She stopped at a nearby newsstand to purchase a stack of the latest magazines for some fashion background, tucking away the receipt carefully—Mamie had been a stickler about saving receipts for her expense account, and Maxie suspected *The Step Stool* would be the same.

*Now I need to observe the Lesbian in her natural habitat.* Francine's would be dead this early, especially after last night, but the Blue Danube wasn't far. A bus lumbered up, and Maxie boarded it. "Transfer?" the driver asked, and Maxie said again, "No thank you." *I should really find out what this transfer business is about,* she thought.

She got off in front of the Blue Danube, in the heart of Little Bohemia. Peering in at the late lunchers, she spotted Barbara Babcock, the star of the television drama *A Single Candle,* deep in conversation with her "masseuse." A table over, lyricist Louis van Heldt was consuming the restaurant's famous *kartoffelpuffer* with gusto. Other less famous but equally artistic types chatted over schnapps and coffee.

*Back to business,* Maxie ordered herself. *I'm not here to gawk at celebrities.* She surveyed the crowd, focusing on apparel. Too bad she wasn't writing for *If, The Step Stool's* fraternal publication. She could do a whole paragraph on pocket squares. Her eyes lit on a knock-your-eyes-out number: bold polka dots, bracelets up to the elbows, and the giveaway low heels that said "Sapphic" to those who spoke the lingo of the shadow world. *False eyelashes a foot long,* Maxie scribbled in her notebook. She noticed her subject was waving vigorously, gesturing for Maxie to come inside.

"Dolly!" Picking up her briefcase and string bag and tucking her reporter's notebook and pocketbook under her arm, Maxie pushed open the door to the Blue Danube, and wound her way through the tables to her polka dot–clad friend.

"Dolly, what are you doing here, besides having schnitzel?" asked Maxie as she joined her friend.

"Hoping for a break," Dolly told her glumly. "I've just

finished making the rounds. Nothing, *nada, nichts!* But
there's always the chance I'll catch someone's eye here."
She looked around hopefully.

A waitress in an alpine outfit handed Maxie a menu.
"The soup today is sausage and pea, and our special is
broiled Loon Lake trout with spaetzle."

"Just coffee," said Maxie hastily. "I've had my lunch."
There it was again, that rebellious desire to order a whole
meal, just because she shouldn't! "And some apple
strudel," Maxie amended her order. Then her conscience
got the better of her: "Hold the ice cream."

"But what really got me down," Dolly continued, un-
aware of Maxie's seesaw struggle not to spend, "is that
my agent told me the *Jarvises* are going off the air—no
more residuals!"

For years Dolly had depended on the residuals from
*Meet the Jarvises,* the television show that had made her
a child star, to round out her erratic income. Now she
told Maxie despondently, "I'll be in your boat, Maxie—
this is just like losing my allowance."

"Don't worry, Dolly," Maxie consoled her. "You're
creative and talented—you're bound to find something!"

Dolly looked dubious. "More likely I'll be asking for a
handout." She nodded at the bag Maxie had set on the
table. "Looks like quite a haul."

"I raided the Mainwaring Manse, and with these eats,
I won't have to buy a meal for a week!"

Dolly sorted through the contents of the string bag.
"Mmmm—smoked salmon! Too bad there's not more."

"I ate most of it on the train."

"Look at this sausage! You could feed an army. But
where are you going to cook it? And applesauce—this'll
last you a while." Dolly looked at the giant jar she held in
her hand in awe. She put it down and pulled out a pack-

age wrapped in wax paper. "Oh, lemon pound cake! Yum. What's this?" She held up a small tub.

"Farmer's cheese, from Loon Lake."

"I'm seeing a lot of applesauce-and-cheese sandwiches in your future," Dolly predicted. "I'm heading back to the Arms for my beauty nap. Do you want me to take the groceries? I'll stick 'em in the icebox so's we don't die of ptomaine poisoning."

"Dolly, you're an angel." Maxie hadn't thought about refrigeration.

"I'll take any available role," quipped Dolly, departing.

Maxie made notes as she ate her strudel. *Saddle shoes and cuffed linen pants,* she wrote, eyeing a girl lunching alone. Unbidden, the image of Lon came to her. What had she been wearing last night? *Men's sport shirt, open at the throat,* she wrote from memory. *On the right girl, the mannish look can convey a certain devil-may-care flair.*

She should be concentrating on her assignment, Maxie scolded herself. Not reminiscing about Lon's good looks. And she'd forgotten to call Sookie, as she'd promised Mamie. She went to the bar to phone.

The call to the Carmichaels was a toll call, and she had to get change from the bartender. After all that, the Carmichaels' maid told her Sookie was gone for the weekend. "No message." Maxie hung up. Sookie was undoubtedly off on one of those leisurely weekends that were now part of Maxie's past.

*I'm a working girl now,* the aspiring writer reminded herself, squaring her shoulders as she stepped from the phone booth. She'd make the Knock Knock Lounge her next stop. She could observe deviant dress while satisfying her curiosity about last night's brouhaha. Hadn't Lon suggested there was a connection between the seedy Dockside dive and the raid on Francine's?

Maxie waved down a taxi. After all, it made no sense to risk her safety in the dangerous Dockside district just to save a dollar. *And I can expense it!* she told herself.

The cab rolled past dilapidated brownstones, where unshaven men in shirtsleeves sat on the stoop, smoking. A flashy fellow in two-toned shoes climbed out of a double-parked Cadillac, while an artist in paint-spattered pants smoked a pipe, his portfolio under his arm. They turned down Pingst Street, and two girls in black tights and turtlenecks came out of a bar. Beatniks? B-girls? Both?

Maxie paid the driver and hopped out at the Knock Knock. The neon sign that dwarfed the sagging storefront was unlit, giving the bar the air of an aging star who hasn't put on her makeup yet. Maxie blinked, momentarily blinded as she came out of the bright sunlight into the dim interior. When her eyes had adjusted, she looked around. The bar was almost empty—just three hardbitten women at the circular booth in the back, a tableful of empty glasses in front of them. Two young men in tight trousers were having an earnest conversation at the far end of the bar while the bartender served a bleached blonde.

Maxie pulled out a stool at the other end of the bar. There was a pause while everyone eyed her suspiciously. The girl reporter knew she looked out of place in her office-girl attire, carrying her father's briefcase.

"Beer," she said. The bartender drew it without a word and set it down in front of her. "Fifty-five cents." That was a dime more than Francine's charged. But Maxie paid it meekly and the bartender went back to her conversation. Maxie leafed through one of her fashion magazines and eavesdropped. The bleached blonde with the heavy mascara was some sort of performer, Maxie gath-

ered. She was complaining about disrespectful audiences
and small tips. "The kids today just come for a laugh,"
she said bitterly. "And they're cheapskates to boot. I
don't like this new generation. Think the world owes
them a living!" One of the boys from the far end of the
bar piped up, "The world's a mess and we're just trying
to fix it, dig?"

Maxie sipped her beer and wondered if the visit was
going to be a bust. She admired the boy's narrow, Italian-
cut pants, but she couldn't work them into her article.
The fashion magazines weren't very useful either. One
feature was about "Fun in the Sun." Swimsuits were no
good to her—not unless she covered the lifeguarding profession.

"And now there's this new boss and the business at
Francine's." The bartender lowered her voice, and Maxie
pricked up her ears. She felt rather than saw the bartender's wary glance around as she kept her eyes glued on
a photograph of beach cover-ups. "I've got no beef with
Francine. She has her customers, and we've got ours."

"She should know better than to squawk." The blonde
shook her head. "We've all had to pay—" Abruptly she
broke off. A shadow fell over the blue batiste beach
cover-up Maxie was pretending to study. "Slumming?"
said a familiar, velvety voice.

Maxie looked up, skin prickling, directly into Lon's
eyes. They were Viking blue in the daylight, and her hair
was a tousled golden blond. The handsomest girl she'd
ever seen, Maxie had to admit. Like Paul Newman in
*Hud*.

"Can't a thirsty girl get a drink?" the ex-deb parried.
"It's been a busy day."

The bartender brought Lon a beer and Lon nodded at
Maxie. "She's on my tab."

"Thanks," said Maxie. The woman with the bleached-blond hair had left. Was it the sudden appearance of the beautiful butch that had frightened her away?

Lon leaned on the bar as if she had all the time in the world. "Busy doing what?"

"Oh, shopping, getting a manicure—rich-girl things," Maxie told her. "What have you been doing since I saw you last? Bribed any more cops?"

Lon smiled at the taunt. "What department?"

"And what's next on the agenda for the new boss in town?" Maxie tried.

"New boss? Is that what I am?"

"Aren't you?"

"Do you want me to be?" Lon's voice was a purr.

"Could you please stop answering my questions with a question?" Maxie begged.

"Is this an interview, or are we off the record?" Lon sounded serious.

"What do you mean?" It was Maxie's turn to evade.

"I hear you do some digging for Mamie McArdle—are you here on her account?"

"How do you know so much about me?" demanded Maxie.

"Maybe I've done some digging of my own." Lon's blue eyes darkened as if a cloud had covered the sun.

"Business or pleasure?" *Damn!* Maxie thought with dismay. *I'm flirting again!*

"Maybe a little of both," Lon answered with a cryptic smile. She glanced down at her wristwatch and slid off the barstool. "See you," she said, and vanished as suddenly as she'd appeared, while Maxie sat and tried to decide if she'd learned anything at all from their interchange. Not really, she decided. She'd only confirmed her hunch that Lon was criminally attractive!

# Chapter 9

## Blind Item

Saturday morning Maxie was sitting up in bed, impatiently filing her nails. At a discreet tap she cried, "Finally!" and throwing back the wadded rose satin coverlet, she leaped out of the bed to open the door. Lois entered, carrying three cups of coffee, while Phyllis, behind her, bore a plate of toast and a bowl of hot cereal.

"Darlings!" exclaimed Maxie. "I was about to expire! Lois, you remembered cream and sugar?"

"Yes, Maxie," said Lois. "But I don't think we can do this every day. Mrs. DeWitt nearly caught us before the elevator door closed."

Lois had been grumpy ever since she'd seen the state of her new spring ensemble. Maxie had waded through the weedy garden and climbed the rusty fire escape to avoid Mrs. DeWitt last night, snagging the borrowed skirt as she came through the hall window. If only Lois hadn't spotted her, before she had time to at least brush herself off! Since then she'd been harping on Maxie "coming clean" with Mrs. DeWitt.

"Just as soon as I have money coming in, I'll stop hiding from Mrs. DeWitt," she promised Lois now. "I'm going to have another go at Mamie on Monday."

"Speaking of which, I brought the *Sentinel*," Phyllis said, as she and Lois settled on the pair of pink slipper chairs with their own cups of coffee. Phyllis kept the front page, and handed Maxie the local news with Mamie's "Confidentially" column. Lois leafed through the rest, looking for her agency's advertisements.

"Mrs. Johnson's visiting Kentucky," Phyllis reported. "She wants to examine the poverty situation from up close."

Lois held up a page for Maxie to look at. "What's the first thing you notice?"

Maxie studied the page as she spooned up her Cream of Wheat. "The special offer for stainless-steel silverware in a Danish Modern design?"

"Oh, you're just saying that!" Lois turned the page, pleased.

Phyllis read, "Unrest increases in second week of civil rights push." Lois looked up in alarm, and Phyllis added reassuringly, "In St. Augustine."

"Netta wrote me that someone threw a rock through their window," Lois told them in a worried tone. "But does that make the news? She'll have to be dead before I hear anything!"

Maxie wiped the bottom of her bowl with the last crust of toast. "Nothing will happen to Netta. Didn't she say she's having the time of her life?" She picked up the paper and turned to "Confidentially." She'd felt badly about not getting the story on Elaine from Sookie the other day, and wondered whether Mamie had used the engagement item.

*A gay gathering of the finest hens in Bay City's flock . . .* Maxie read. Mamie had evidently decided to do the DAP tea, dull as it was.

Suddenly Mamie's assistant sat up straight. The coffee

sloshed in her cup as she set it down hard on her bedside table. "Mamie used *me!*" she squeaked.

Her two friends looked up as the unemployed heiress read in a shaking voice:

"'. . . speaking of fancy plumage, a certain bird of paradise in the aging debutante set has gotten her wings clipped after a sexsational pas de deux in the Bay City Women's Club powder room left the fine-feathered Daughters of the American Pioneers all aflutter. Can this *Main*stay of Bay City society learn to feather her own nest? A little bird told me that Mama and Papa Peacock have cut off the birdseed after this latest shenanigan.'"

Maxie put down the paper, horrified. This wasn't the way she'd hoped to see her name in the *Sentinel*!

"I don't think you're an aging debutante," Phyllis tried to console her. And Lois added, "Lots of people won't know it's you. The ones who don't know you already, I mean."

Their attempts at comfort were fruitless. Her erstwhile employer had hung her out to dry! The columnist had never taken her seriously, Maxie saw now. She was just so much grist for the gossip mill, no different from the silly society types Mamie twitted behind their backs!

"I'm through with Mamie!" she declared.

"Finish your coffee." Lois tried to pacify the irate ex-deb. "Don't go off half-cocked!"

It crossed Maxie's mind that if she'd come through with the goods on the Ellman-Driscoll engagement, Mamie wouldn't have been short on copy for the column. But no—that was no excuse. Mamie had paraded Maxie's private problems for the entertainment of her gossip-hungry public.

"No one makes a blind item out of me," she told Lois, crumpling the column and throwing it into the corner. "It was a dead-end job anyway."

First Mumsy, then Pamela, now Mamie. She was cutting ties so fast she'd soon be completely adrift!

She was still fuming when her door was flung open. "Is it true?" Mrs. DeWitt intoned, in the voice she reserved for recitations of Lady Macbeth's famous monologue. "Are you, indeed, destitute?"

The three girls were open-mouthed at this sudden apparition. Rumor had it Mrs. DeWitt hadn't been above the first floor in twenty years. She stood in the doorway, her gray hair trailing down her back in a disordered braid. She wore a moss-green wool cardigan over a bias-cut, lace-edged, lavender satin nightgown.

And Maxie saw, with a sinking feeling, that she clutched a copy of "Confidentially" in one hand.

"Mrs. DeWitt, you shouldn't pay any mind to Mamie." Maxie scrambled out of bed. "She's always exaggerating and getting details wrong, and anyway, I'll come into my trust soon, a few birthdays from now, practically right around the corner—"

Mrs. DeWitt swooped down and enveloped her startled tenant in a smothering embrace. "You poor girl!" Her voice throbbed with passionate sympathy. "You poor rejected child!"

Maxie struggled to breathe through the combined scents of gin, tobacco, and violet water. Mrs. DeWitt finally released her, but kept a grip on her shoulder as she gazed down at her tenderly.

"I, too, was once expelled from my happy home," she told the astonished girls. "I, too, have been reviled by society!" In a ringing voice, she recited:

> *"Cursed be the social wants that sin against the strength of youth!*
> *Cursed be the social lies that warp us from the living truth!"*

Then, from the pocket of the wool cardigan, she withdrew an old photograph of a little girl with a large ribbon in her hair, sitting on a pony in front of a many-gabled mansion. "Before!" she intoned. She pulled out another photo. "And after," she added sepulchrally. The second photo showed a laughing girl with bobbed hair surrounded by soldiers and beer steins.

Maxie was weak with relief, once she understood the Magdalena Arms' housemother had seen a parallel in their lives. "Gee, Mrs. DeWitt, you were a looker!" she complimented their landlady.

"I was one of the most popular chorus girls at Die Schwarze Katze," the old woman declared with pride.

"Was it hard—being on your own, at first?" Maxie was eager for advice from one who'd been through her ordeal.

"I nearly starved," Mrs. DeWitt stated solemnly. "My clothes were in tatters. I subsisted for one whole winter on nothing but cold soup." Maxie started. "I lined my shoes with cardboard, which soaked through every time it rained. I lived in an unheated room. I pawned every piece of jewelry I owned, even down to my baptismal bracelet, just to pay the rent. Which reminds me . . ." Mrs. DeWitt stopped projecting to the balcony, and her voice became pleading. "Do try to get me a little on account. I hate to hound you, but the Magdalena's finances aren't as flush as they were in the days when our benefactress was alive."

The Magdalena Arms had been founded by Mrs. DeWitt's childhood friend Mrs. Payne-Putney to provide a respectable and affordable place for actresses and other independent-minded young women to live, but it had lost its popularity as other options for single girls appeared.

"I'll scrape up something," Maxie vowed. She might

be capable of robbing her rich mother, but she'd never do anything to hurt the Magdalena Arms!

"Fortunately I've finally rented Jeannette's old room." Mrs. DeWitt meant "Janet." "So you'll have a new neighbor. A lovely girl—very studious. Kelly Connor. She'll be here at least for the summer. Do make her welcome to the Magdalena family."

Maxie hoped this Kelly, or whatever her real name was, would fit in with her neighbors. The fifth floor had a certain reputation to maintain.

"I'm glad that's straightened out," said Lois after Mrs. DeWitt departed. She was clearly relieved that her wardrobe was safe again. "I told you Mrs. D. would understand!"

"Mrs. DeWitt is the perfect example of a real progressive," Phyllis declared.

Their landlady had drifted to the stairs and begun her slow descent. "Hello, Priscilla," Maxie heard her greet someone on the way up.

Priscilla—that's what Mrs. DeWitt always called Pamela!

And then Pamela herself appeared, out of breath after the climb, but looking wonderful in her weekend uniform of white shirt and plaid pedal pushers. "Pam!" Maxie breathed. Phyllis and Lois evaporated discreetly as Pamela approached.

Pam paused uncertainly in the doorway. "Hello, Maxie." Her greeting was stiff, but Maxie pulled her into the room and closed the door. She slipped her arms around Pam's waist, inhaling Pam's clean, spicy smell. "Mmmm—I've missed you."

"It's only been two days." But Pam's arms encircled Maxie tightly.

"Two nights and a day and a half," Maxie corrected.

"You're still in your pajamas." Pam's voice was muffled in Maxie's hair.

Maxie kissed Pam's neck. "All ready to crawl back into bed. Want to join me?"

She felt Pam sigh. "Maxie, what am I going to do with you?"

Maxie had a number of suggestions, and soon the two girls were in the nest of satin quilts, and Maxie was unbuttoning Pamela's crisply ironed blouse. Pamela told her, "The reason I stopped by is that I heard from Louise at *The Step Stool* that you're going to do an article for them—that's just swell, Maxie!"

Maxie shrugged off the compliment along with her pajamas. "Well, Mamie was twitting me about my lack of writing samples, and so I figured . . ." Maxie's lips grazed Pamela's throat as she helped the Junior Buyer wiggle out of her plaid pedal pushers.

"It shows real initiative." Pamela's breath came faster. "I always said that you could do anything you wanted if you just put your mind to it!"

"Anything?" Maxie panted, as Pamela did that thing to her left nipple that she always liked. And then the two girls abandoned the conversation about Maxie's prospects to give themselves over to a more basic form of communication.

But later Pamela returned to the topic. "Initiative has never been your problem; it's stick-to-itiveness you lack!" The hardworking girl was tucking in her shirt, while Maxie lit a cigarette.

Maxie squirmed as she lounged back in bed. This sounded like the beginning of another lecture. While she was content to bask in bed, Pamela had put on practicality with her penny loafers.

"Stability—the ability to be there for the long haul," Pamela continued. She picked up Maxie's brush and brushed her hair with quick decisive strokes. "That's what counts!"

Maxie had a presentiment they were no longer talking about her employment prospects.

"This quarreling and making up—it's getting to be as predictable as florals in spring."

"Well, that's a kind of stability, isn't it?" Maxie argued, tapping her cigarette in the ashtray. To distract her improvement-oriented girlfriend, Maxie adroitly switched subjects. "Say, would you look at my piece for *The Step Stool*? I knocked together a rough draft last night, but I need a fashion expert's opinion."

The ploy worked. "Of course," agreed Pamela. She read through the looseleaf pages while Maxie got dressed. The ex-deb couldn't help hovering over Pam as her girlfriend finished her article. She was quite proud of her first piece of real writing.

"'What to Wear While Cruising.'" Pamela returned to the title. "I think that's a little frivolous, when it's supposed to be about working women!"

"I wanted something attention-getting." Maxie defended her choice. She was disappointed Pamela hadn't laughed at any of the quips Maxie had been so pleased with last night. She hadn't even cracked a smile.

"Well." Pamela was visibly hunting for something to praise. "It certainly is peppy. But I wonder if *The Step Stool* will be expecting a more, well, *serious* piece."

"Didn't you like the part where I wrote, 'It's not about what a girl wears but what she wore'?"

"Cute," Pamela admitted, "but—"

"What about the part about pants and women's figures—the 'what shape are you?' They could even illustrate with drawings of the different body types, you know, narrow-hipped but femme—"

"Good lord, Maxie!" Pamela burst out. "Haven't you

ever read *The Step Stool*? They have a policy on pants! Louise once wrote an editorial about how inappropriate attire sets back the movement!"

Dimly, Maxie remembered Stella saying something along those lines. But Louise had herself been wearing pants! She should practice what she preached and not go around confusing people, the would-be writer thought indignantly.

"Fine, you think it's a flop," she said, trying to keep her temper. "Maybe Stella will think differently. And if she doesn't, I'll rewrite it. I *am* a professional, and I'm ready to earn my pay."

Pamela looked at Maxie, aghast. "Pay! *The Step Stool* doesn't pay its writers!"

Maxie's jaw dropped. "Not even a kill fee?" she managed to ask.

"What's a kill fee?" Pamela asked blankly. But Maxie was too jolted to take any pleasure in explaining the term to her know-it-all girlfriend. The bottom had certainly dropped out of her writing career!

"I must say, Maxie." Pamela kept her voice even with an effort. "I think you should have found out about payment before you took that assignment. It just proves that you have a lot to learn about the working world. Be realistic and let me get you a job in the packing room—I'm sure you'll be promoted to stocker before the year is out!"

The prospect sounded unbearable to Maxie. "Stop trying to push me into the packing room, Pamela," she begged. "Being cooped up in a windowless room all day would give me the heebie-jeebies." On a hunch, she accused her practical girlfriend, "You just want me someplace you can keep an eye on me!"

Pamela flushed, and rose from the bed. "I'm not going to quarrel with you, Maxie. But I'm not going to see you anymore either—not until you prove you're more than a fly-by-night in both work and love!"

"Fine," Maxie said, as panic mixed with anger. Pamela's threat sounded serious this time. "Suit yourself!" She couldn't help following Pamela to the door, and calling after the disappearing girl, "But would you rather take your pants off with me, or discuss pants policy with Louise?"

The door of the room down the hall closed softly, but not before Maxie caught a glimpse of a mousy-looking girl, retreating hastily into the room. Oh dear! What a welcome for her new neighbor!

# Chapter 10

## A Job for Maxie

The following week found Maxie tied to the phone on the first floor.

She was waiting for a call from Miss Watkins. She'd told the career counselor when she dropped off her records that she was ready to do anything, really, *anything!* But Miss Watkins merely counseled patience. "Which I know from your PPA will be difficult," she said sympathetically.

Maxie didn't even have her work for Mamie to occupy her. She'd written the columnist a resignation letter. Pamela would be pleased, if she knew, Maxie thought, but Pamela wasn't calling her up these days either.

When the phone did ring, it was usually the Tip-Top Tailor Shop, with an inquiry about the overdue bill for the alterations she'd had done in April; the billing department at Grunemans, where her charge account had gone unpaid this month; Countess Elfi's, where she owed for her favorite face cream.

And even though she was sure Luigi didn't read Mamie's column, she couldn't show her face at her favorite neighborhood restaurant until she could pay her tab there. Instead, she ate the cream-cheese-and-applesauce sandwiches she'd grown to hate. She'd rather drink cold soup!

"It turns out I haven't just lost my allowance," she told Dolly dolefully. "I've acquired a pile of bills!"

Dolly was a blessing—listening for the phone so Maxie could escape the confines of the Magdalena Arms from time to time, or keeping her company as they discussed their employment woes. They spent hours playing Ping-Pong in the lounge, listening for the phone. Maxie had become quite expert at the game.

Sometimes she listened to Dolly practice a new monologue, or helped her pick out an eye-catching outfit for "making the rounds," as the actress called it. Then Maxie would be alone again, biting her nails, adding up figures on scraps of paper again and again, hoping the results would change, or looking through her possessions and trying to decide which piece of jewelry or clothing she could part with.

She wasn't quite alone; there was the new girl on the fifth floor, whose name turned out to be Kitty Coughlin. She was a thin-faced girl with dark crinkly hair and intense green eyes under heavy brows. While Maxie and Dolly played Ping-Pong, Kitty usually sat in a corner of the lounge poring over a thick textbook. She was studying psychology, she'd told the two girls, working on her thesis. At night Maxie could hear the new girl's typewriter rattling away.

For all her study of the human psyche, their new neighbor seemed oddly naïve. She still dressed like a high school girl, in full-skirted pastel dresses or gingham middy blouses and skirts. She was wide-eyed when Dolly and Maxie explained the Magdalena Arms message system.

"This is the only phone?" Kitty said, when they showed her the phone at the first floor's front desk. "And it's all right for anyone to answer it? None of the girls has a phone in her room?"

"Mrs. DeWitt is a little old-fashioned," Dolly told her, going on to explain that the practice of having the girls take turns as front desk receptionist for a reduction in rent had ended the previous year. "So if you hear the phone ring, answer it and take a message. We take turns sorting the mail too."

The new girl seemed a little shocked. "That's certainly a casual way to treat the U.S. Mail!" she exclaimed.

"Do you know," Dolly reported to Maxie in a low voice as they rested after a hard-fought game, "I saw her down the street the other day, making a call from the luncheonette. She just can't adjust to the catch-as-catch-can Magdalena Arms way of life." She glanced at Kitty, bent over her books in the corner as always.

"Maybe she's got a whatamacallit, fetish for privacy." Maxie thought about her old psychiatrist, Dr. Ridgeway. "These psychological types are usually a little off."

The word "fetish" reminded Dolly that she was booked for a photo shoot that afternoon, and she left the lounge, saying she'd better do her hair and makeup.

Whatever her fetishes, Kitty was certainly friendly. She was interested in everything Maxie did and was always asking her questions—what did Maxie do for fun? Where did she go? How did she get along with her mother? "I'm awfully interested in the mother-daughter relationship," she explained.

Once the phone was for Maxie and it wasn't a bill collector. Stella at *The Step Stool* asked cheerily, "How's the fashion piece coming?"

Maxie was so happy to hear a friendly voice that she forgot how furious she was at *The Step Stool* over their no-pay policy.

"I've got a rough draft," she told Stella instead. "Although Pa—some people think it's a little frivolous."

"I'm sure it's terrific!" Stella enthused. "When can I get a look at it?"

"This week," Maxie heard herself promising. She would have a sample, she reasoned, the next time she was asked. And it would certainly help fill the empty hours!

The unemployed heiress's other occupation was budgeting with Phyllis. She'd agreed to the nightly sessions out of sheer boredom, but soon found Phyllis's tutorials were not as dreary as she'd expected. The mild-mannered statistician was a fecund fund of money-saving tips. Maxie had always made affectionate fun of the earnest ideologue; now she felt a new respect for her friend, who knew how to stretch a dollar until it screamed.

"Should I mail my article, or walk it over to the *Step Stool* offices?" She asked Phyllis's advice the next evening, after she'd finished her piece and had typed it as best she could on Lois's machine.

"Shoe leather is more expensive than a stamp," Phyllis said instantly. "And a stamp is cheaper than the bus."

Phyllis had even explained the mysteries of the transfer to Maxie: "They let you ride on any number of different buses within a given time limit," Phyllis told her, without upbraiding her for her ignorance as Pamela so often had. "So you see, you might even be able to go somewhere and come back on one fare!"

That seemed to Maxie a very generous system compared to cabbing, where you paid by the mile. "Why, I could explore the whole city for under a quarter!"

One evening Phyllis took the ex-deb to the public library. "You can borrow books and read magazines and newspapers for free," she said, as they toured the periodicals room of Bay City's main branch.

"Why does anyone bother to buy a newspaper?" Maxie asked in wonder.

The statistician showed Maxie how to polish her own shoes, and was teaching her to iron. Dolly could do her hair as well as Henri, the number-cruncher assured the doubtful ex-deb; and besides, Phyllis thought Maxie looked better without a bouffant.

Under Phyllis's tutelage, Maxie was now recording all her expenditures in a little black book, putting them in categories like "food," "clothes," "sundries," and "beer." "This will help us build your budget," Phyllis explained.

Looking over the list, Maxie was appalled at how fast the costs mounted up: the breakfast with Mamie, the trip to Waukesset, the apple strudel, the toll call to Sookie, the cleaning bill for Lois's outfit, and even the cigarettes from the corner store. "Why, I spent a fortune in three days!" she said in dismay.

Phyllis didn't scold Maxie for her spendthrift ways, as Pamela had. She simply pointed out the many ways by which Maxie could save money in the future: eat the Magdalena Arms breakfast, which was included with her board; make all toll calls person-to-person or collect; no cabs, not even in so-called "bad" neighborhoods—the intrepid statistician insisted you could travel safely anywhere by bus.

"I can show you how to cut down on cleaning bills," Phyllis added as she studied the list. "And we'll take up in-room recipes—there's absolutely no need to dine out!" She tapped the last item. "You could save a bundle if you gave up these."

"Give up smoking?" Maxie recoiled a little. "What if I just stopped tipping so big?"

"Do you realize what you spend on cigarettes in one year?" There was a zealous light in the social scientist's eyes. "In addition, several scientific studies show they're bad for you—you'll be sleeping better, breathing deeper, and saving on medical bills in the future!" she concluded triumphantly.

"Oh, those scientists always have some bee in their bonnet." Maxie discounted Phyllis's studies. "Why, the army gave Uncle Karl cigarettes in the service, along with his chocolate ration and the condensed works of Nathaniel Hawthorne!"

"It's true, cigarettes *are* bad for you," a new voice piped up. It was Kitty. She'd been hidden behind the bookcase, and Maxie hadn't even realized she was there. *She's always eavesdropping!* Maxie thought, irritated.

Maxie was smoking a cigarette the next day, leafing through a magazine—borrowed from Lois—and pondering her pearls and their potential price when the phone rang. She jumped up to answer it, and when she heard Miss Watkins's "Hello, Maxie!" lilting over the wire, she knew it was the call she'd been waiting for.

"Do you have my results?" Maxie asked eagerly. "Have you found me a job?"

"No results quite yet." Miss Watkins explained that she'd sent Maxie's tests and educational records, from her kindergarten attendance sheet to her Oil Portraiture Completion Certificate, to Mrs. Spindle-Janska at the Institute of Applied Technology, where the inventor of the Personality Penchant Assessment was Professor of Personnel. "She's going to feed the information into the OCIVAC, a computer specially designed for personality assessments," burbled Miss Watkins excitedly. "It's something very new in our field. You're a fortunate girl, Maxie, to get this kind of attention from Mrs. Spindle-Janska herself!"

Maxie didn't feel fortunate. "But, Miss Watkins, my rent won't wait for your results," she said desperately.

"I found something," the career counselor said a little hesitantly. "It would be purely for pay, I'm afraid. Your lack of experience *is* a stumbling block. How do you feel about recreational work? There's an opening in the Bay City Summer Recreational Program for Disadvantaged Youth."

"Miss Watkins, that sounds like heaven!" Maxie exclaimed. Anything that got her out of the Arms and put a little cash in her pocket would suit her, she felt like adding.

"Good!" Miss Watkins sounded relieved. "I'm glad you're so open to new experiences. You can start tomorrow—they need a Recreational Aide urgently in the Dockside neighborhood. Do you know where the Eleanor Roosevelt School for Troubled Girls is located?"

Maxie assured her she did. "Netta teaches there," she reminded Miss Watkins.

"Oh, of course! Report there tomorrow at eight A.M. Your supervisor is Miss Santucci. And, Maxie—" Miss Watkins paused. "May I give you a word of advice?"

"Shoot!"

"My preliminary analysis of your PPA shows signs of impulsiveness, recklessness even, that might—"

"I got you," Maxie interrupted. "I'll try to keep my impulses under wraps. Thanks again, Miss Watkins!" Maxie hung up the phone jubilantly. Turning around, she saw Kitty. Why was that girl always at her elbow?

"Sounds like you got a job." Kitty didn't even try to conceal her curiosity. "Where will you be working? What will you be doing?"

"I'm an aide!" Maxie announced. "In the Bay City Summer Rec Program. I guess I'll be helping the kids make sit-upons and so forth."

Kitty looked thoughtful. "That Miss Watkins must have connections. Those rec program jobs are all patronage positions."

It was Maxie's turn to be curious. "How do you know?" Kitty often displayed odd bits of esoteric knowledge, but this was interesting information.

"Oh . . ." Kitty turned vague. "I just heard that somewhere. But gee, Maxie," she added with little-girl enthusiasm. "I'll bet you'll be a whiz at the job! The campers will love you!"

Dolly had come back from her photo shoot and was in time to hear Kitty's last comment. After the studious girl went back to the lounge, the unemployed actress told Maxie with an air of discovery, "I know what's making that psych student act so strangely—Kitty has a crush on you!"

# Chapter 11

## Recreational Aide

"How was your first day?" Kitty was hanging around the front hall the next afternoon when Maxie wearily stumbled up the steps.

"Fine!" Maxie managed a smile. She was too tired to care about Kitty and her crush, but she didn't want to admit to the psych student that this Recreational Aide business was more complicated than she'd realized.

"Did something happen to your handbag?" Kitty called after her, as the exhausted aide began to climb the stairs to the fifth floor. The elevator was out again. Maxie's legs were like Jell-O and she leaned heavily on the bannister.

"Just a little accident," she said faintly. An errant ball had bashed in her white wicker purse during the chaotic game of dodgeball she'd refereed that morning. But that was only a sample of the damage she'd suffered. Her matching white shoes were streaked with black. Her burnt-orange linen was smeared with bits of clay, and she'd lost her hat. Her effort to appear employment-worthy had been for nothing. She'd gotten a surprised look from her supervisor, Miss Santucci, and had overheard the other

Recreational Aide, Pat Pressler, referring to her as "Miss Society."

*Supervisor—that's a laugh!* Maxie thought bitterly as she reached her room and collapsed on her bed. Carmine Santucci had provided Maxie with a whistle and a smeary, mimeographed sheet of suggested activities and then abandoned her to her fate.

Of course Carmine had her hands full as much as Maxie. The three girls divided the kids into three "tribes"— Carmine was chief of the Choctaws, Pat managed the Menominees, and Maxie spearheaded the Sioux. The Recreational Aides rotated their tribes around the asphalt courtyard for outdoor games; the gym for basketball, rope climbing, and the like; and the cafeteria, which was used for crafts. Today's craft had been clay modeling.

*How am I going to survive another day?* Maxie wondered in despair. There was so much more than sit-upons involved in this new job. A constant stream of activities was required to keep her charges occupied. When boredom set in, the hard-bitten nine-to-twelve-year-olds turned to violence, attacking each other at the drop of a hat, especially if the magic phrase "your mother" was invoked. Maxie was bruised from separating the fighting preteens. Wasn't there an easier way to earn her living?

*I'll think about it tomorrow,* Maxie decided, closing her eyes without even shedding her soiled clothes.

Somehow, she managed to get up at the crack of dawn the next day—and the day after, and the day after that; she arrived at the Eleanor Roosevelt School in the dismal Dockside district at eight A.M.; she trudged through the grueling round of sports, crafts, and games until the buses collected the howling Indians at two. The gang had told her it was good she was entering the work world gradually, with a thirty-hour week. Maxie shuddered to think what forty hours a week of recreation would do to her.

One benefit of her new job was that the ex-deb was too tired to do anything when she got home. Gone was her desire for gay evenings out; she barely missed the amorous interludes she and Pamela had shared. Any alert moments before her collapse into heavy slumber were spent poring over books borrowed from Netta's room—*Games for All Ages, Stories from Folklore,* and *The Disturbed Child*—in an effort to arm herself with enough time-filling activities to keep her wild Indians from committing mayhem.

She'd hoped Mrs. Olssen, head of the whole Summer Recreation Program, might offer some guidance during one of her weekly visits. But when introduced to Maxie, she'd only reminded the new employee to include a weekly "enrichment activity" before disappearing into the kitchen with Mrs. Atkins, the cook, leaving Maxie wondering what an enrichment activity was.

Maxie supposed the administrator and cook were conferring about lunch menus—with poor results, in Maxie's opinion. The debt-ridden girl had hoped to take full advantage of the free lunch that was one of the few job perks, but the food Mrs. Atkins dished up was disappointing. Her sloppy joes had more tomato sauce than meat, and were unappetizing poured over mushy white buns. The apples were bruised, and even the gingersnaps that alternated with Jell-O for dessert were stale. Maxie supplemented with sandwiches from the deli.

However, the exhaustion, the bruises, and the bad food were all worth it when at the end of the second week she was able to pay off her May rent and give Mrs. DeWitt something toward June. By the next week Maxie felt like she'd gotten her second wind. Pat no longer called her "Miss Society," and even took her out for a beer one afternoon, explaining to Maxie what enrichment activities were—"she means taking them to the museum or something"—and why the kids found "your mother" such a provocative phrase—"classic Freudian psychosexual confusion," she said confidently. She told Maxie the only reason she'd returned for a second summer in the Recreational Program was to collect data for the thesis she was writing, "The Wild Child."

The children, too, who had once seemed a frightening, faceless mob were now becoming individuals to Maxie. Some of them, Maxie discovered with surprise, she even liked!

Nadia Nemickas was undisputed queen of the playground—her father had been a champion wrestler in the Ukraine, and had taught his little girl everything. After Nadia showed Maxie several simple holds, the Recreational Aide found breaking up fights much easier.

She was intrigued by Roseanne Jones, a small girl with a fast mouth, whose casual references to hot-wiring cars and hijacking hubcaps made Maxie glad she had nothing worth stealing. One day, when Roseanne mentioned "the new mob in town," Maxie asked the girl in astonishment, "How do you know there's a new mob in town?"

The ten-year-old rolled her eyes. "*Everyone* knows about the new mob! There are new people running the numbers racket!"

Roseanne returned to mending Maxie's torn taffeta cocktail gown—it was craft hour, and Maxie's latest bright idea was to bring in garments in need of mending for the kids to work on. *Terrific,* the ex-journalist thought. The *Sentinel* refused to print a story even little girls on the street were talking about. *All because those DAPs think it will be a black eye on our town's reputation!* Maxie snorted. Rich people made her sick!

Maxie even had a certain fondness for Fernanda Ruiz, although the underweight girl had a weak stomach, and had upchucked on Maxie's shoes her first week. But every morning Fernanda cried, "Oh, Miss Maxie! You look so pretty today!" even when the chief of the Sioux was wearing a faded cotton from three years ago. The young girl's unfeigned admiration brightened the aide's day, Maxie had to admit.

"Miss Maxie, there's someone watching you," Fernanda told her leader one morning. The Sioux were playing softball in the courtyard, and Maxie had sent Fernanda to the sidelines as soon as the delicate girl said she felt unwell.

Roseanne dropped the ball and came to look. "Are the fuzz after you?" she asked Maxie with new respect.

Maxie looked across the street. Kitty Coughlin was standing in front of the shoe repair shop. When she saw she'd attracted the attention of Maxie's tribe, she crossed the street and called, "Hi there" through the wrought-iron bars that caged in the courtyard.

"I've just been getting my shoes resoled," she explained. "So this is where you work!"

The children were crowding around the fence curiously. "Are you a cop?" Roseanne asked.

Kitty gave a high-pitched laugh. "No, I'm a psych student."

Maxie shooed the kids back to their game. "If no one's bleeding at the end of the inning," she promised, "I'll tell you more 'Stories from High Society.'"

"You certainly know how to handle children," Kitty said, as the kids pounded away.

"I'm learning," Maxie said modestly. She wondered what the psych student was doing in this part of town. Weren't there any shoe repair places closer to the Arms?

"Would you like to join me for lunch?" Kitty asked. "My treat."

"I'm sorry, I can't," Maxie said regretfully. She would have enjoyed a feed at someone else's expense. "I have to eat with the kids."

"Oh well." Kitty backed away from the bars. "Perhaps another time."

Maxie turned back to her tribe, puzzled. There'd been a queer flicker of relief in Kitty's eyes when Maxie had refused her invitation. Was Dolly correct in thinking Kitty had a crush? Or was the psych student still working out her own traumas about same-sex romance?

Maxie had no time to speculate. It was shaping up to be one of those days. Roseanne cut off Barbara's braids instead of making stencils during craft hour, and Fernanda threw up just as lunch was served, starting a chain reaction of stomach sickness among the rest of the Sioux.

"The milk makes her sick," Nadia informed Maxie.

At the end of her rope, Maxie turned on the Ukrainian girl. "That's not true, Nadia. Milk is good for growing girls. It's full of vitamins and nutrients—in fact, it's the most wholesome beverage you can consume!"

After all, this was Mainwaring milk the disadvantaged girl was maligning. Maxie had seen the Sunshine Dairy truck delivering its load to the Eleanor Roosevelt School just the day before, and felt a trace of pride, thinking of her canny great-grandfather, who had founded Sunshine after the wheat failure, and become a leader of the state's dairy industry. The ex-deb dimly remembered that her parents had received some kind of good citizen award for providing fresh milk to the Recreation Program at cost.

"No it's not, it's nasty!" Nadia declared now.

"If you like it so much, you drink it," challenged Roseanne, making a gagging noise.

Maxie snatched Roseanne's cup, intending to set a good

example for these irritating girls, but she stopped short at the sight of the thin, bluish liquid. This wasn't the milk of her childhood!

"Someone must have tampered with the milk supply," Maxie stammered. "Honestly, it isn't supposed to look like this!" *That Mrs. Atkins!* she thought. *But why?*

Whoever and whyever, the Recreational Aide intended to get to the bottom of the mystery, especially if it would solve Fernanda's upset stomach!

It was easy to snag Mrs. Atkins's keys—Roseanne had demonstrated the finer points of picking pockets earlier that week. As soon as everyone was gone for the day, Maxie tried the keys until she found the one that fit the storeroom door.

Her mouth fell open and her eyes widened as she beheld the cornucopia of comestibles that filled the room to the bursting. Canned delicacies like oysters and pineapple chunks lined the shelves. There were flats of strawberries, and red, ripe tomatoes. Wandering into the walk-in cooler, Maxie found whole chickens, boxes of bratwurst, orange rounds of cheddar, and even slabs of smoked salmon. And milk! Crates of wholesome whole milk labeled SUNSHINE DAIRY were stacked high.

None of this had made it to the mouths of the disadvantaged youths, Maxie realized. Inspecting further, she found on the other side of the storeroom burlap sacks of musty potatoes, cans of spaghetti and beans, bruised apples, and boxes of gingersnaps—the familiar fare she'd seen served each noon. And, yes, there was an enormous plastic tub of white powder. Maxie pinched a little between finger and thumb and sniffed it. Powdered milk! Her mouth twisted in disdain.

*Mrs. Atkins must be making a mint,* Maxie thought, *cheating those poor kids to the point of sickness!*

Then, "That dumb dame left the door open!" The

raspy voice came from outside the storeroom. Instinctively Maxie ducked behind the wall of milk crates.

"I'll speak to her," said a second voice.

*Mrs. Olssen!* The corruption evidently extended to the highest reaches of the Summer Recreational Program.

"Start with the perishables," ordered the unseen Mrs. Olssen. There was the rattle and thump of a hand truck. Before Maxie could react, the stack of milk crates concealing her was removed and the flustered Recreational Aide stood revealed.

"You! What's your name?" Mrs. Olssen snapped her fingers. "Miriam, Minnie—what are you doing here?"

"It's Maxie," said the dairy heiress with hauteur. "Maxie Mainwaring. And, apparently, I'm witnessing grand larceny!"

"Don't be silly." Mrs. Olssen was unfazed. "You haven't seen anything."

"The police may not think so!" Maxie moved toward the door, but the man with the hand truck blocked her way. He was a burly fellow, with a curiously deformed ear and small, beady eyes beneath a brutish brow. He wore a shirt that read, Sunshine Dairy.

"You ain't going nowhere," he told Maxie menacingly.

"You don't dare do anything to me!" Maxie was indignant. "Don't you know who I am? My father owns Sunshine Dairy!"

To her amazement, the thuggish dairyman laughed contemptuously. "Mr. Mainwaring ain't the one running things. He don't give me my orders."

Darn Dad, and his lackadaisical attitude toward the family business! Why couldn't he pay more attention to milk, and less to polo?

"Maxie Mainwaring, the disinherited heiress," Mrs. Olssen said thoughtfully. "I read about you in Mamie McArdle's column. Don't worry, Sami," she told her henchman. "She can't even get her parents on the phone." She took out a large roll of cash, continuing, "I think she'll see reason. No one's going to believe the story of a disgruntled employee who was fired for incompetence and chronic lateness!"

"I was only tardy twice," Maxie protested.

"Here, dear." Mrs. Olssen peeled off a few bills and held them out. "Some severance pay, to soften the blow."

Maxie was mesmerized by the money in Mrs. Olssen's hand. She hadn't seen that much cash in more than a month! She glanced at the dairy thug, who cracked his knuckles meaningfully.

"Grab it while you can, dear." There was just the hint of a threat in Mrs. Olssen's friendly voice.

Maxie knew when she was beat. She reached for the money.

## Chapter 12
## Table for One

It was better to run from the lion and live to hunt another day, Maxie told herself as she walked away from the Eleanor Roosevelt School for Troubled Girls, unemployed again. She'd learned that maxim at the Circle School.

Maxie wondered if the Sioux would miss her the next morning when she didn't show. She'd never had the true teaching bug, not the way Netta did, but in her own way she'd been fond of those disadvantaged youths! Besides, she disliked the way Mrs. Olssen had checkmated her.

And how was being laid off for lateness going to look on her resume? She'd appear more unreliable than ever!

Maxie had been walking without direction, driven to movement by her restless thoughts, but now she stopped and looked around. She was on the edge of the posh shopping district along Linden Lane, with Grunemans on one end and Countess Elfi's on the other. Around the corner was Le Cheval Blanc, where Maxie had lunched in her plush days.

There's an upside to unemployment, Maxie realized. Particularly when you have money in your pocket!

Here she was with no crafts to clean up, no need to review the rules for the next set of games, no fights to break up. Unconsciously she rubbed her rib cage, bruised a permanent purple these last few weeks from constant contact with flying fists. How much money had Mrs. Olssen given her anyway?

Standing outside the House of Henri, Maxie counted her take. Almost fifty dollars! Why, she could pay off the rent and have a little left over. Maxie thought of today's ruined lunch, and suddenly longed for a leisurely meal, something she hadn't concocted in her room out of odd ingredients, something eaten at a table, something with courses, even.

She knew she shouldn't, but she sauntered around the corner to Le Cheval Blanc, telling herself she'd just glance at the menu for old-time's sake. The dubious look of the maître d', as the disheveled girl in the faded, stained dress approached him, did the trick. No one told Maxie where she could or could not eat! "Table for one," she said, in her best Mainwaring manner.

After all, didn't a girl need a little pick-me-up after being threatened by some milk-fed goon?

Just one martini, Maxie pledged, after the maître d' had seated her at the remote end of the banquette. Now, should she have the lobster salad or the steak sandwich?

She tried not to think of what Pamela would say about this latest episode of unemployment. "No stick-to-itiveness—no stability!"

A shadow fell over her menu, and Maxie murmured, "I'm still making up my mind, but I'll take a martini."

A laugh tinkled out. "Maxie, darling, you haven't forgotten me that thoroughly, have you?"

Startled, Maxie looked up—right into the big brown eyes of Elaine Ellman.

Elaine was the picture of polished perfection in a summer sheath of the palest possible pink linen. *She finally got in some sunbathing at Loon Lake,* Maxie thought, noting the bicycle heiress's deep tan, *while I've been sweating my days away in dreary old Dockside!* Elaine's lustrous locks were molded into a glossy half-moon hairstyle that had Henri's fingerprints all over it. Maxie hadn't visited the House of Henri since the day before that fateful DAP tea. Elaine put down her patent white clutch next to Maxie's bread basket and pulled off her gloves. Maxie hadn't worn gloves in weeks.

"You!" said Maxie with distaste.

Elaine sat down, ignoring Maxie's truculence. "I feel terrible about that . . . contretemps in the powder room," she confided, pulling out a compact and examining her makeup. "I've been wanting to tell you, but of course I didn't dare be seen with you after what happened." She looked warily around the deserted restaurant.

"You threw me to the wolves, you two-faced temptress!" said Maxie hotly. "And ruined my life in the process!"

"Am I so tempting?" Elaine smacked her lips in the mirror and shut the compact with a decisive click.

Maxie hated to admit it, but Elaine was still a dish of dessert that she'd like to taste. But would the taste be worth those extra calories she could no longer afford?

The waiter finally appeared. "Madame?" He bowed at Elaine, pencil ready, increasing Maxie's ire.

"Oh, I'm just visiting," Elaine told the waiter sunnily. Turning to Maxie she added, "I'm sorry, I have a date already."

"Martini and a lobster salad." Maxie handed the waiter her menu and glared at Elaine. "And I didn't *ask* you to lunch with me. You're the girl who lost me my allowance!"

"We all have to cut back, these days," Elaine told her chummily. "Daddy had to close five stores in Indiana alone!"

"I had to get a job as a Recreational Aide!" Maxie lashed out.

"I used to be a candy striper, but it was too much for me," Elaine confided. She lit a cigarette, and suddenly Maxie noticed that Elaine, too, had lost something. She was missing the big diamond that had once twinkled on her left hand.

"And you've cut back on fiancés as well." Maxie nodded at the ringless hand. Elaine blushed faintly.

"Daddy's finally letting me go to Europe this fall," she said, as if this explained everything, and Maxie would understand the debutante accounting by which a fiancé could be exchanged for an airplane ticket abroad. "He doesn't think Ted's such a good catch anymore."

Elaine hadn't the faintest clue about managing money or the difference between a dollar and a dime, Maxie realized. She wouldn't recognize a budget book if Maxie bopped her on the head with one. *She may have a hairdo from Henri,* Maxie thought with a growing feeling of superiority, *but she'd be like a sheep without a shepherd if Daddy pulled the plug!*

Elaine was rising. "There's my date. I'm co-sponsoring her for the DAP, isn't that a scream? Oh, you probably know that already since—"

"Since Mumsy's the other sponsor," finished Maxie as she watched the platinum blonde approach their table. It was the woman whose unexpected luncheon with her mother had ended her raid on the Mainwaring Manse.

"Velma Lindqvist, may I present Maxine Mainwaring." Elaine made the introduction in her best style.

The woman Maxie rose to shake hands with wasn't as youthful as the ex-deb had first thought. There were tiny wrinkles in the corners of those gold-flecked brown eyes, and her platinum hair was too perfect to be natural. It curved in short, becoming waves around her square jaw. Today she wore a silver shantung suit.

"Maxie Mainwaring—I've heard a lot about you." The Lindqvist woman smiled as she clasped Maxie's hand. "Your mother, Mabel's, been one of my staunchest friends since I arrived in Bay City."

Her grip tightened, and Maxie felt her eyes widen. Was it her imagination, or did the warm brown eyes mirror her startled expression?

Maxie had always prided herself on her ability to pick out a sister from a crowd of girls. The talent had fueled her reputation as a flirt and caused many a fight with Pamela. She wasn't collecting scalps, she'd tried to convince her angry girlfriend. But once she got the signal from someone, she simply had to find out if her instinct was on the money.

Shaking hands with Velma Lindqvist had set her Sapphic geiger counter clicking madly. She'd struck variant paydirt with this one, for sure. Maxie glanced at Elaine with renewed interest as she murmured automatically, "Any friend of Mumsy's—" Was this why Elaine had ditched Driscoll Dry Cleaning?

Velma loosened her clasp, and Maxie made herself drop the older woman's hand. The signal was lost. "You live in Bay City, I understand," Velma continued as if nothing had happened. "Your mother tells me you're interested in the arts."

"I don't have much time for art anymore," Maxie replied. "I have a job."

"Maxie's a Nurse's Aide," Elaine put in.

"A Recreational Aide," Maxie corrected, "at the Bay City Summer Recreation Program for Disadvantaged Youth." There was no point in going into her unemployment with these two.

"Ah, a working girl." Mrs.—Miss? Lindqvist nodded

approvingly. "You have my admiration. It's all too easy for those of us privileged with the means to do nothing, to do just that! But I've always found work is its own reward." She gave Maxie a card. *Amalgamated Enterprises,* Maxie read. *Velma Lindqvist, Vice President of Sales.*

Had Maxie imagined the suggestive pressure as Velma's hand brushed hers? There was no way to find out—already the maître d' was standing by, ready to lead Elaine and Velma Lindqvist to their table. After a round of polite good-byes, Maxie sat down and sipped her martini, watching the pair covertly as they were seated across the room. Elaine's attraction was like a feeble campfire compared to the glow Velma gave off.

Maxie couldn't help wishing she was on better terms with Mamie. Her old boss would be sure to have the Who, What, and Where on the platinum blonde. But the ex-deb still wasn't ready to forgive and forget, even though the other week Mamie had sent her a bonus check and a long, philosophical letter on the nature of news. Maxie had softened at the sight of her money—and then boiled over again, realizing it was the same kind of payout Mamie made to bellhops and cigarette girls who passed on hot tips.

Anyway, she had no time to research every platinum blonde that passed her way, not even if they did radiate a certain invert energy. She had to find another job!

# Chapter 13

## A Visit to the Pawnshop

Yet the ex-deb was still thinking of her mother's new friend when she returned to the Arms. The preoccupied girl nearly bumped into Dolly. Right behind her, to Maxie's surprise, was Stella McSweeney from *The Step Stool*, camera in hand. The pair of them was giggling and giddy.

"What gives?" Maxie greeted them. "You act like you've been drinking poverty punch." Poverty punch was a concoction Dolly had devised, which involved all the girls pouring their leftover liquor into a bowl and adding boiled and strained applesauce. "I didn't know you kids knew each other," Maxie said, looking from one to the other.

"I came here looking for you," Stella explained. "I was hoping you'd write another piece for *The Step Stool*. And then Dolly here told me how busy you were—"

"And I told her how busy I *wasn't*," Dolly put in. "And she told me about being a photographer—"

"I'm just a camera nut, really," Stella said self-deprecatingly.

"And so I'm going to show her the art photography ropes, and we'll split what I can sell fifty-fifty!"

Eagerly they described the theme they'd hit upon for their first series. "We're calling it 'Around the World, Through the Seasons'—kind of a calendar-type thing," Dolly explained. "We're off to collect some props now."

"Good for you!" said Maxie heartily. But she couldn't help feeling it wasn't fair—she'd spotted the curly-haired, curvacious camera girl first!

She scolded herself mentally. *What kind of dog in the manger am I? Panting after platinum blondes, pining for Pamela, and now begrudging Dolly a new friend?*

"So we're off on the road to fame and fortune," Dolly finished.

"Send me a postcard when you get there," Maxie murmured as the pair headed out the door.

She sighed as she climbed the stairs. She missed Pamela. Not the quarrelsome, critical girl of recent vintage, but the passionate Pamela of the early days, who had pursued Maxie and paraded her proudly around Francine's. She missed the companionable Pamela who had brought her designer samples from work and shared the Waldorf salad for two at the Blue Danube; the girl who had driven with her to Loon Lake for picnics, or curled up in the opposite corner of the couch, studying clothing catalogs while Maxie read the *Sentinel* or perused *You Can Paint!* or *Finnish for Beginners*.

She even missed the committed Pamela, who dragged her to *Step Stool* fundraisers, who pestered her to move in, and who gave her the bracelet engraved with the Millay quote "Here such a passion is." Would any of those Pamelas ever come back?

Phyllis was in Lois's room, and both girls called to Maxie as she passed. Lois was sitting on the scarlet-and-white patchwork quilt that covered her bed with a letter in her hand. She'd evidently been reading it to Phyllis, who sat in the rocking chair. A faded Walnut Grove High

School pennant hung over the desk, where a studio portrait of Netta held pride of place.

"You need another room, just for your filing cabinets," Maxie observed, as she entered and dropped on the foot of the bed.

"I know." Lois glanced at the wall of gleaming metal cabinets. "I can't wait until Netta and I are settled in our own place this fall. I've been writing her about some of the possibilities, but it's hard to pin down her preferences—she's so preoccupied with that voter registration drive." She scanned the letter with professional rapidity. " 'Uphill struggle . . . new arrival, so we're overcrowded . . . another bomb threat . . . Gwen was jailed briefly. . . .' Here, all she says is: 'It's hard for me to imagine life in Bay City right now, and those apartments you describe sound off-puttingly luxurious when I think of the harsh realities of life down here, so I'll leave it up to you.' " Lois sighed. "That's not very helpful, is it? And the apartments aren't so luxurious, really—the two-bedroom on Forty-ninth, just around the corner, or the one-bedroom with the huge living room and darling fireplace that's closer to Pamela's place."

"Read Maxie what Netta says about the Summer Recreation Program," Phyllis suggested.

"Oh yes." Lois shuffled the sheets in her hand. " 'Tell all the gang hi for me—they seem like a mirage at times.' " Lois looked up to remark, "That's her big theme these days—how life in Bay City is a big mirage. 'And kudos to Maxie for getting a job, even if it's just Recreational Aide. Tell her from me that the hardest jobs are always the lowest paid. This is the most difficult thing I've ever done, and none of us are getting paid a dime. . . .' "

Maxie decided it was time to make her big announcement. "Well, here's hoping that my next job is easy and highly paid," she said in her blithest way. "And if any of you have the inside scoop on the perfect position, tell me now—I was let go today."

"Let go!" her friends cried. "Oh, Maxie, no! What on earth happened?"

"It wasn't my fault," Maxie lied. "Mrs. Olssen has a niece who needed the job, and so I got eased out. Bay City politics."

She'd decided on the way home that she needn't share the blackmail and threats with the gang on the fifth floor. It was a nasty business. And the truth was, she felt a little ashamed of taking the money, even if she hadn't had much choice.

Phyllis urged, "You should report this to the Good Government Commission! Why, this is the very kind of corruption they're trying to stamp out in Bay City bureaucracy."

*If only you knew,* Maxie thought as she begged, "Can't we just forget about it for now? Honestly, I just want to go to Francine's and have a beer and not think about jobs, lost or found."

"Of course, Maxie," said Lois immediately.

"Whatever you want," Phyllis echoed.

"Only, isn't there someplace besides Francine's?" Lois wondered. "It's just not as much fun, knowing the boys in blue may walk in!"

The three girls pondered the lack of places a girl and her friends could get a drink in Bay City without being bothered by men, in or out of uniform.

"We really ought to go to Francine's," Phyllis finally declared. "Show them they still have loyal customers."

Lois looked down at her letter. "Netta said the time has come for every American to stand behind his principles," she murmured.

This was beginning to sound more like a crusade than a night out to Maxie, but at least there was a cold drink involved. "Let's go then!"

The jukebox echoed loudly in the mostly empty room as the three girls hesitantly descended the familiar stairs and entered their old hangout. "Look," whispered Lois, clutching Maxie's arm. There was a stranger behind the bar, an acne-scarred woman reading a magazine. Maxie asked her, "Is Tobey off tonight?"

"Retired," said the new bartender laconically. She drew their beers and returned to her reading—*True Adventure* magazine, Maxie saw.

They took their beers to a corner table and conversed in hushed voices. The other patrons had either drunk themselves into a state of oblivion, or wore the same strained, alert expressions Maxie felt on her own face. They all flinched simultaneously at the squawk of a siren, and relaxed as it receded into the distance.

"There's the new girl." Phyllis nodded toward the end of the bar. Lois and Maxie turned. Sure enough, there was Kitty with an untouched glass of beer and a notebook, listening intently to barfly Terry, who was undoubtedly holding forth about her love life. When she saw them looking at her, she gave a little wave. Maxie wondered irritably if she'd followed them.

"I didn't realize she was one of us," Lois said, turning back.

"She told me she's just doing research on her thesis—'The Maternal Urge and the Consequences of Its Suppression,'" Phyllis reported.

"There's something funny about that girl," Maxie declared. "Sometimes I wonder if she's really a student of psychology at all!"

"Oh, Maxie!" Lois scolded. "You're suspicious of everyone these days."

Maxie couldn't defend her sudden conviction. It had sprung into her mind full blown. Maybe Lois was right, and it was just the sense she had these days that nothing was as it seemed. Everything was a cover-up for some other activity.

"Call it a hunch," she insisted stubbornly. "But I say there's something odd about her. This research bit could just be an excuse—"

"Some girls are shy and need an excuse." Phyllis made allowances.

"—for something sinister. Didn't she arrive the day after the raid?" Maxie raised her eyebrows meaningfully. "Maybe it's more than a coincidence! Maybe she's an undercover cop!"

"Now you're going too far," Phyllis reproved her. "You can't condemn her on such slim evidence!"

The conversation shifted to other topics, but Maxie kept her eye on Kitty. *Wasn't* it suspicious the way she sat there so serenely, while the other patrons started at the least noise or flashing light?

She was still sitting there when her three neighbors gave up and went home. Lois said she had a letter to write, Phyllis needed to darn some socks, and Maxie supposed she ought to outline a few job possibilities. None of them admitted what each was privately thinking— going to Francine's just wasn't fun anymore!

The next morning Maxie called Miss Watkins, who seemed to take Maxie's firing personally. "The supervisor's niece! I thought I had some pull at Parks and Rec!" Then her poise reasserted itself. "Well, let's look at the silver lining. While you're free, I'd like to do a Psychographic Recorder Interview. It's a new kind of test that Mrs. Spindle-Janska recommended I try."

Maxie agreed readily—she hated the thought of another inactive day at the Arms, without even a Ping-Pong partner. After the test was over and Miss Watkins was removing the electrodes from her temples and the pulsometer from the crook of her arm, Maxie begged the career counselor, "Can't you find something for me? If I have to sit home all day, biting my nails, sooner or later I'll succumb to the temptation to spend money I shouldn't. I need something to keep me busy!" Already in her budget book the unemployed girl had recorded the purchase of a perfectly unnecessary pair of espadrilles.

Miss Watkins counseled patience again. "I don't want to commit you to a full-time job until all the results of your tests are in, aggregated, and analyzed." She tried to cheer Maxie, adding, "And I have something brewing that might be just the ticket!"

On a whim, Maxie took out Velma Lindqvist's card and called the number for Amalgamated Enterprises. Hadn't Velma said she admired Maxie? Perhaps there would be a place for the ex-deb in the big company. But the attractive executive was away—"on a business trip," a secretary told her.

It was Lois who came to Maxie's rescue. The receptionist at Sather and Stirling was taking her vacation. With a little training, Lois thought Maxie might take her place.

Maxie brightened at the prospect. A pleasant office, no kids pelting her with clay, and good old Lois, who would wink at her mistakes. If only she didn't have to be there at eight thirty A.M., it would be perfect!

As it was, it wasn't bad. Repeating "Sather and Stirling, how may I direct your call?" all day long was a little dull, but at least no one threw up on her shoes.

Working for Lois was no cakewalk, however. Lois seemed to take on a new persona when she entered the gleaming advertising office. No longer the lovesick girl who pored over Netta's letters, she was brisk, business-like, and buzzing with efficiency. The secretaries jumped to attention when she moved through the office.

Maxie understood their zeal the morning she was late and found Lois covering the switchboard. She felt posi-tively cowed by the look Lois gave her; and even though all Lois said was, "Try not to let this happen again," Maxie began setting two alarms in order to make sure she wouldn't oversleep. If only Kitty wouldn't type so late every night, endlessly working on her thesis! Night after night, the ex-deb lay in bed, her worries about money taking on the rhythm of the pounding keys. And the wor-ries followed her to work, where between each call she asked herself again, *What will I do next?*

Her last day on the job, with nothing else in sight, Maxie decided it was time to part with her pearls. Her hush money was gone, and next month's rent was fast approaching. The calls from Grunemans about her over-due charge account had become positively threatening.

She'd thought about this moment so often that Maxie felt oddly excited when she walked into the pawnshop she'd picked out. It was between the old bus terminal and the office, so she could do the deed on her lunch hour. She looked around at the orphaned goods—a tuba, an old-fashioned fur coat, bicycles, more musical instruments, television sets, radios. The balding pawnbroker stood be-hind a glass counter that contained trays of brooches, rings, and bracelets—and ropes and ropes of pearls. Maxie laid hers on the countertop. "How much can you give me on these?" she asked.

The pawnbroker ran them through his fingers and

rubbed one of the pearls against his yellowed teeth. "Fifty dollars," he said.

"Fifty dollars!" Maxie was aghast and outraged all at once. "Why, it's worth several times that!"

The man shrugged. "That's my price." He waved at the stuffed jewelry case. "The law of supply and demand."

Maxie wasn't interested in his economic observations. "I'll try elsewhere," she said shortly, scooping the pearls back into her pocketbook. What kind of pawnshop was this?

"Sure, try your luck," he said indulgently.

There was a sound, as faint as a lizard rustling in the underbrush, and Maxie felt a curious prickle on the back of her neck even before she heard the velvety voice: "Fancy meeting you here."

She turned and there was Lon, lounging against an ancient armoire. Where on earth had she come from? The shop bell hadn't made a sound. Lon was wearing a striped polo shirt and faded Levi's, and her hair had gotten bleached by the sun, which had also freckled her nose. The all-American girl-boy looked as out of place in the seedy shop as a birchbark canoe in an industrial canal.

"Buy you a drink?" Lon held the door for Maxie and nodded at the pawnbroker. "See you, Pete."

On the pavement, Maxie found her voice. "You were there all the time!" she accused the handsome he-she. "Peddling stolen goods?" Maybe that's why the pawnbroker hadn't been interested in her pearls—he was a fence!

Lon smiled. "Pete does some appraising for me." Maxie wasn't sure if that meant she was right, or if Lon was kidding her. It was just so darn difficult to believe someone so clean-cut could actually be knee-deep in dirt!

Lon guided the suspicious girl into a dim bar down the street and they slid into a corner booth. The men at the bar looked them over and then turned back to the television overhead. Maxie realized with a start that she and Lon were being taken for a boy-girl couple! She felt offended, then uneasy, and, finally, rather deliciously naughty.

"So you need money," said Lon, playing with a toothpick.

The waiter came by to take their order, and Maxie asked for a martini, hoping it wouldn't fog her mind too much when she got back to work. Lon ordered a beer.

"Be careful, he might ask to see your driver's license," Maxie said. "What does it say, anyway?"

Lon took out her wallet from her back pocket and extracted her identification. The picture looked just like Lon, but the name read Yolanda Laney. Maxie turned it over hastily and slid it across the table to Lon. "Put that away!" she ordered.

Lon laughed as she pocketed her wallet. "Scared? I thought you were 'Madcap Maxie' who lived for thrills."

"Who's been telling you about me?" Maxie demanded. "Anyway, I'm not afraid. You're the one who'll get it in the neck if you're careless. I can just pretend I was taken in too." She thought of Elaine, pushing her away in the powder room.

"You wouldn't do that—they said 'madcap,' not 'mean.'" Lon slid over so she was right next to Maxie. "The bartender's looking at me funny—let's convince him."

Lon put her hand on the back of Maxie's neck and her lips on Maxie's. Maxie went still with shock, feeling the velvety stimulus through a layer of disbelief. Then, like a frostbitten pioneer rubbing snow on his frozen feet, sensation began to flow, a tingling that was half pleasure, half pain. As Lon's hand twisted into her hair, a shiver went through the temporary receptionist, and her initial coldness was completely cured—she was ready to kick over the bucket of snow and sink down in front of a raging fire on a bearskin rug. "Why, you're bound!" she murmured in surprise, as her hands traveled of their own free will around Lon's torso.

"Mmm." Lon was nibbling on her earlobe. Maxie had taken off her matching pearl earrings, but she'd forgotten to show them to Pete.

"Do you do that every day?" Maxie was intrigued.

"Only on special occasions." Lon began kissing her again. When they next came up for air, Maxie remembered to take a gander at the bar. No one was looking at them. The men were all riveted by the televised baseball game.

"Since your Pete wouldn't take my pearls, maybe you'll make me a loan," she suggested playfully. "I suppose you charge loan-shark interest?"

"Of course." Lon nuzzled Maxie's hair while Maxie tried to decide once again whether the beautiful butch was on the level.

"On the other hand, I've already made one shady deal this month. I think that's my limit," Maxie said, thinking of Mrs. Olssen and the milk money.

"What are you talking about?" Lon sat up.

"You mean, you don't know all about it already?" Maxie was pleased to discover a look of alarm in the other girl's eyes.

"Listen, Maxie—kidding aside—keep your nose clean." Lon seemed serious.

"*My* nose is as clean as a fresh handkerchief," retorted Maxie. "I'm working at an honest job and—oh!" She clapped her hand to her mouth in dismay. "I've got to get back!"

*Darn that Lon,* Maxie thought as she ran back to Sather and Stirling. That shady Sapphic sister had driven her substitute-receptionist job right from her head! Maxie didn't even want to think what Lois would say, or worse, how she'd look. Her fifth-floor neighbor might be lenient about a little noontime necking, but office manager Lois would call her on the carpet! The temporary receptionist quailed at the thought.

She flew into the office, breathless, the handkerchief she'd used to wipe away her smeared lipstick still in her hand. "I'm awfully sorry, Lois," she began. But to her surprise Lois was beaming at her.

"Good news, Maxie!" she said as the frazzled ex-deb slipped on the headset and settled herself at the switchboard. "Miss Watkins called—she thinks she's found you the perfect job."

# Chapter 14
## Polish

Maxie sat in the reception area of *Polish* magazine, trying to quell the butterflies in her stomach. Why hadn't she ever finished that secretarial course? Everyone said only the sharpest girls were considered for Bay City's most famous fashion magazine—the kind who typed ninety words a minute and brewed a perfect cup of coffee while answering phones with tact and style. When Maxie had told the girls at the Arms that she had an interview with dynamic young editor Harold "Hal" Hapgood, they'd wished her well, but urged her, one and all, not to get her hopes up. Only Miss Watkins seemed confident that Maxie and Hal would click.

"Stop thinking about what you can't do, and remember all you have to offer," she'd advised the anxious ex-deb. "You have some unique qualifications that will have Hal slavering to hire you!"

At least she looked polished, in new summer shoes and a buffed-up bouffant. She touched the Mainwaring pearls at her throat, glad she hadn't pawned them after all.

She looked around the office, with its modern furniture and fixtures, its vases of fresh flowers and the big windows lined with oyster-white drapes, which looked out over bustling Bay City. What a contrast to the grim courtyard of the Eleanor Roosevelt School! She bent her head to study the latest issue of *Polish,* which she'd picked up off the low cherrywood coffee table, polished, of course, to such a high gloss that she could practically check her lipstick in its gleaming surface.

> Who's going to be at the Gundersons' annual garden party? Why, practically everyone. The fete benefits Bay City's favorite charity, the Bay City Beautification Fund, and "beauteous" is the word for the festive array of flowers on the grounds of the Gundersons' famed country cottage. . . .

The column was called "Here and There" and seemed to be an excuse to stuff the page with as many names of Bay City movers and shakers as was possible.

Funny, how appealing the magazine made the Gundersons' flower fete sound, when Maxie remembered how dull she'd always found that particular party. She flipped to the fashion spread.

"Mr. Hapgood will see you now." A soignée secretary, her hair coiled in a smooth French knot, appeared before Maxie. The aspiring magazine assistant hastily put the copy of *Polish* back on the table, taking the time to align its edges with the five other copies. Then she followed the girl, who moved quickly through the busy office, picking up proofs and copy and passing on mysterious instructions like, "Mr. Hapgood wants the mood to be louche, not sordid—he says you'll have to salvage it somehow," without even stopping. She deposited the pile she'd collected on a desk outside a door that said HAROLD HAPGOOD in raised metal letters. Knocking on the door, she opened it without waiting for an answer. "Miss Main-waring, Mr. Hapgood." She waved Maxie in.

"Thanks, Lucille." Hal Hapgood rose from behind his desk as Maxie crossed the big office to shake his out-stretched hand. The door shut behind her with a quiet click.

"Maxie Mainwaring, welcome!" The editor was a slight man, under average height, with a high forehead, his sandy hair combed straight back. He was unexpectedly dandy in a striped summer suit with a forget-me-not in the button-hole. His eyes behind horn-rimmed glasses were sharp as they surveyed Maxie.

"So you think you can add an extra gleam to *Polish,* do you?"

"Well, I want a job here, if that's what you mean," the girl replied without thinking. She was trying to decide if she'd met Mr. Hapgood before or if he just looked like someone she knew.

The editor seemed amused. "And why is that?"

"It would be more pleasant than what I've been doing." Maxie decided that honesty was her best policy. Hadn't Miss Watkins told her to be herself?

Hal laughed this time, a short bark. "Don't be too sure," he warned her. "I'm glad to see losing your al-lowance hasn't stifled your spunky spirit." He eyed the ex-debutante to see how she reacted to this reference to the springtime scandal.

"The only thing it's affected is my pocketbook!" Maxie retorted.

"But do you know how to work?" Hal queried, sud-denly serious.

Maxie thought of all the different jobs she'd held and experiences she'd acquired. "I'll do anything you throw at me," she declared. "I can check facts, and even invent them! I can break up a schoolyard brawl, answer twelve phone lines, and speak a little Finnish. I've explained the facts of life to a four-year-old, and I know the difference between an ellipsoidal and a Fresnel!"

Hal seemed impressed. Then he asked the dreaded question: "Can you type? Take shorthand?"

"Not very well," Maxie replied lamely. "But I'm a quick learner!" However, she could tell she'd lost precious ground.

"I'll be honest with you, Maxie." Hal picked up a freshly sharpened pencil and twirled it between his two hands. "I was intrigued when Miss Watkins suggested I see you. I must admit I like your style. But I have dozens of applicants for this post, each of whom has top-notch secretarial skills. What can you offer, honestly, that could compensate for that lack?"

He was already beginning to get up, as if the question was rhetorical.

"I know where I know you from!" Maxie cried triumphantly. "You came home one Easter with Ginger's brother Greg! I forgot to say, I have an excellent memory for faces," she added modestly.

She'd known him only as Harold, but now she could see traces of Greg's soulful prep-school friend who wrote poetry, and had been altogether unlike Greg's rugby-playing crowd.

"Why, of course." Hal sat back down. "The two little girls, always underfoot. I'd forgotten it was the Mainwarings who lived next door. That was long ago, before I needed to know who was who in Bay City." The editor fell into a nostalgic reverie.

"We used to follow you, when you and Greg went walking in the ravines," Maxie reminisced. It had been her first observation of youthful passions. "Are you still friends with Greg?"

Hal spread his hands. "You know how it is. He's married now with a couple kids." He gave Maxie a look filled with meaning. "We take a fishing trip together, from time to time."

They sat a moment in comfortable cameraderie, two denizens of the twilight world, letting their hair down.

"I really would like to hire you, Maxie," the editor said regretfully. "But my second assistant *must* be able to—"

Maxie interrupted. She felt more confident now that she was talking to Greg's old friend Harold. "I bet you've got typists by the dozen here. But do you have someone who knows Bay City society like the back of her hand, the way I do? Who's visited the Houcks at home? Who's summered at Loon Lake since infancy? Can any of them ask impertinent questions of important people and get away with it? Do they know"—she leaned forward and lowered her voice—"*that half the flowers at the Gundersons' garden party are flown in from out of state?*"

"No!" gasped Hal.

"Yes," said Maxie with certainty.

"You're right," Hal decided abruptly. "You might be just what I need!" He stood up and held out his hand. "Welcome to *Polish*!"

Maxie danced out of the *Polish* offices in delight. Not only had she gotten the job, but she'd be making almost twice what she'd earned as a Recreational Aide!

She phoned Miss Watkins from the lobby to share her success. Her stalwart supporter was delighted by the news. "I'll put it with your dossier," she told Maxie. "When Mrs. Spindle-Janska returns from the Helsinki conference, and looks at the results of the OCIVAC . . ."

Maxie replaced the receiver, wondering when the indefatigable career counselor would realize her job was done. Maxie was positive she had finally found the perfect position.

And tonight was the party at Janet's to celebrate her

passing the bar exam, Maxie remembered. What an equally perfect way to celebrate!

As she hung up the phone, Maxie saw a familiar face—Kitty was dawdling on the sidewalk, looking in the windows of the jewelry store on the bottom floor of the building opposite. What on earth was she doing in this neighborhood? Bay City College was all the way across town.

Kitty glanced at the lobby, and suddenly hurried away. *Curious,* thought Maxie. *Didn't she see me?*

She followed the strange psych student around the corner and down the block. Her neighbor suddenly darted into a building. Maxie hurried after her. She had a feeling she was about to prove that the supposed psychology student didn't know an introvert from an extrovert!

Through the glass doors, she saw Kitty step onto an automatic elevator. She entered the empty lobby and watched the floor indicator until it stopped on the eighth floor. Then she turned her attention to the building's directory. A rare bookseller, something called Sociological Survey Editions, a literary agency—which one was Kitty visiting? Maxie frowned. Kitty could be visiting any of them, quite innocently.

Nontheless, she boarded the elevator and rode to the eighth floor. "Eeny, meeny, miney, moe," she whispered. Her pointing finger landed on IRA ABRAMOVICH, ANTIQUARIAN, RARE EDITIONS. But when she entered, the room behind the frosted glass door with the gold-leaf lettering held only an old man with a flowing white beard, bent over an illuminated manuscript. When he lifted his head inquiringly, Maxie backed out, saying, "Sorry! My mistake."

The elevator door was just closing. Darn it! Had she lost her quarry? Maxie looked at the literary agency. Was Kitty just another girl who dreamed of being a writer?

But why would she hide that? Maxie opened the door to Sociological Survey Editions, putting her money on the dark horse.

It was a publishing company, a small one. There was a rack of books in the reception area. Maxie picked one up. *In the Suburbs* was the title. *Wife-swapping! Dipsomania! Reefer parties!* ran the cover line. *Where boredom runs rampant and morals are trampled!* Maxie turned it over and read that the suburbs featured a host of problems she could learn about if she read the sociological study by Dr. Calvin A. Kilmer, Ph.D.

"May I help you?" Maxie looked up to find a gray-haired woman gazing at her suspiciously.

"I was supposed to meet a friend," fibbed Maxie. "Dark hair, Peter Pan collar?"

"You mean Miss Coughlin." The woman relaxed. "One of our authors. Are you . . . did you have an interview appointment with her?"

"Yes," lied Maxie, curious to see what would happen.

A man came out of an office in back, and shot Maxie a piercing glance. "Mr. Freitag, this young woman was looking for Miss Coughlin." She lowered her voice and murmured something.

"Won't you come with me, Miss, er . . . ?"

"Maxine," Maxie said. She followed the clean-shaven, gray-haired man, reasoning that she could always use one of Nadia's holds on him if he tried anything funny.

He led her to a small bare office and told her to sit down. Then he took out a portable recorder and placed it on the desk. "This is our Stellavox," he explained, noticing Maxie's startled look. "We record all our interviews." He attached a microphone and pressed a button. "Interview, Maxine," he said, and followed with the date and time. He turned his piercing gray eyes on Maxie. "When did you first enter the deviant life?"

# Chapter 15
## House Party

Maxie burst into the Arms full of her new job and her new discovery. "Hallooo!" she caroled, when she reached the fifth floor. "Where is everybody? I've got news!" How the girls would exclaim when she told them that Kitty, the new girl, was playing the innocent student while spying on all of them in order to write a supposedly serious sociological study of the Sapphic sisterhood!

"Just a minute." It was Dolly's voice, but it was coming from Netta's empty room.

Maxie put her ear to the door and heard another voice saying, "Lift your chin, just a hair—good! Hold that."

"Stella?" Maxie pushed open the door, and was momentarily blinded by a flash of light. She blinked and saw a nearly nude Dolly, stretched out on a polar-bear skin, complete with snarling snout.

"Maxie!" Dolly glared at her, while not moving a muscle. "You might have knocked. Was that okay?" she asked anxiously.

Stella was climbing down from a small stepladder behind a camera on a tripod, holding a strobe light in one hand. "Perfect!" she said cheerfully. "You looked genuinely surprised—as if you had seen Santa coming down the chimney."

"I'm sorry." Maxie remembered now that Dolly had written for, and received, permission from Netta to turn the absent teacher's room into a temporary studio. She and Stella had been hard at work on their photography project all last week. Now Maxie looked around the room, impressed by the transformation. Netta's bed had been pushed into a corner and the rest of the furniture piled on top. Dark cloth covered the narrow window and a roll of heavy paper was taped to the wall behind Dolly, painted soft smudges of pink and green and beige. "It looks like a real studio!"

Dolly had scrambled to her feet and was putting on a robe. "Not bad, huh? A little small, but we make it work!"

"Maybe the world doesn't need another girlie calendar," Stella apologized, a little shamefaced. "Not the way it needs, say, Louise's treatise, 'The Homosexual and Her Society.' But the money . . ." She sighed.

"I think it sounds exciting," reassured Maxie. "I'd love to help! I'll ask around the art department at *Polish* for photo-shoot tips."

Dolly stopped in her tracks. "You got the job at *Polish*?" She whooped. "No one thought it could be done!"

Stella's eyes were wide with admiration. "That's marvelous, Maxie, just marvelous!"

Their response was as satisfying as she'd hoped. "And guess what else," she began, ready to tell them she'd been right about Kitty.

But Dolly was saying, "I can't wait to see Pamela's face when she hears. She's going to be at Janet's party, you know."

Maxie's heart beat faster. She hadn't been sure Pam would show. *Would* Pamela be impressed by her prestigious new job? Was this the weapon that would win back her hardworking girlfriend?

"I'd better go change." The magazine assistant tried to sound casual.

Magazine publishing and gossip vanished from Maxie's mind like mist as she contemplated the contents of her closet. She pulled out the mauve sundress Pamela had gotten her at a sample sale last summer, wondering if Pamela would feel as sentimental at the sight of it as she did. She fussed over her makeup, and fluffed her bouffant. She wanted to look her best!

Janet's little studio was crowded when the girls from the Magdalena Arms arrived. Stella had tagged along, at Dolly's invitation. "I'd like to come," the amateur photographer confessed. "With Francine's the way it is, private parties are the only way to have any fun!"

Maxie surveyed the mob, wondering how many girls were here to cruise, and how many to celebrate Janet's success. The newly minted lawyer, flushed and happy, stood by the fireplace, with her certificate propped up next to her on the mantel. Maxie wiggled through the crowd to congratulate her. "Are you going to get a girl now?" she shouted over the din. Janet had always sworn she would avoid any entanglements until after she passed the bar. Now she shouted back, "After I find a job!" Then she pulled Maxie into the tiny foyer.

"Speaking of work, I took a look at that trust of yours," she said in a normal voice. "There are some irregularities that might be a weak spot if you decided to try to break it. Who is Alta Nyberg, for example?"

"That's my dotty great-aunt," said Maxie. "She's in a sanatorium out in the countryside now."

Janet nodded as if Maxie had confirmed a piece of evidence. "She's still listed as a trustee, despite being *non compos mentis,* which is quite improper," Janet explained. "If you could get the court to appoint a sympathetic trustee to replace her, that trustee could argue that the other trustee—your mother—was contravening the intention of the trust by cutting off your allowance."

"You mean I could get my allowance back?" Maxie was dazzled by the possibility.

"Don't depend on it too much," Janet cautioned. "And let me do a little more digging before we take it to court."

*Everything's coming up roses,* Maxie hummed to herself, as she headed back to the living room. If she got her allowance back, she wouldn't fritter it away on taxicabs and cigarette girls—not all of it, anyway. She'd save it for the things that mattered: nice meals out, a new camera for Stella, some shoes, a bookkeeping class . . . Her mind ranged over the possibilities.

It was as if the Friday night crowd at Francine's had packed themselves into Janet's little apartment. Maxie inched along the wall, craning her neck in an effort to see who Louise was talking to. Was it Pamela? No, a stranger. Maxie turned away, disappointed.

Stella wormed her way to Maxie. "Some party!" Her eyes were bright with enjoyment, her hair curlier than ever from the humid heat. "There's a bunch of us on the fire escape—come join us!"

"In a minute," said Maxie. "I'm going to get some refreshment first." She worried she might miss Pamela's arrival, out on the fire escape. On the other hand, she didn't want to look like she was lying in wait for her estranged girlfriend!

She headed down the hall to Janet's tiny kitchen. A redhead was there, an apron over her white shirt and gray slacks as she set Phyllis's hot-plate meatballs on a platter. For an instant she was a stranger, and then—

"Pamela!" The impetuous cry made the other girl whirl around, knocking the meatballs into the sink.

"Maxie!" the Junior Sportswear Buyer breathed. For an instant they ate each other up with their eyes, and then their arms were around each other, and Maxie felt the softness of Pam's lips and the steady pulse of Pam's heartbeat as they fit themselves into the familiar position, Maxie's head tucked under Pamela's chin. Greedily Maxie inhaled the scent of pinecones and mint. Was Pam thinner? She tipped her face back to look up at her steady. She'd gotten a haircut recently.

Pam was looking down at her, the same searching expression in her eyes. "I've missed you!" The same phrase burst from their lips almost simultaneously, and they both laughed. Pamela sobered immediately.

"Oh, Maxie, I was wrong—Lois told me how you've been working like a demon all these weeks—I'm never going to doubt you again!"

Trust Lois to give her a glowing report! "Did she tell you about my new job at *Polish*?" Maxie asked a little shyly.

Pamela's arms tightened around her. "No—really? Oh, Maxie!" The words meant nothing special, but the tone was music to Maxie's ears.

"I was wrong too," she said, her heart swelling with emotion. "I'm not going to give you a moment's uncertainty from now on, cross my heart and swear to God!" The thought of Lon crossed her mind, but she pushed it away. That interlude earlier this week had been an aberration. "No more visits to Kicksville!" she declared.

"I'm not going to dampen your natural vivacity with my dour predictions anymore," Pamela told her earnestly.

"I'm going to give you the stability you deserve," Maxie replied passionately.

Maxie could feel Pamela's strength as she grasped her

even more tightly. "These weeks without you have been hell!" she groaned, and the two girls kissed each other with a desperate hunger. Maxie wrapped herself around the junior executive like cellophane around a fruitcake.

"We're keeping the partygoers from the food," she panted.

Pamela pulled away from Maxie, but kept hold of her girlfriend's arm. "Let's squeeze ourselves out of this sardine can," she said masterfully. "We're going to my place!"

# Chapter 16

## Breakfast in Bed

Maxie rolled over to snuggle into Pam, but her hand felt only the empty pillow. Opening her eyes, she discovered she was alone. The room was empty.

"Pam?"

There was a clatter from the kitchen and the smell of sizzling bacon. "You stay in bed!" Pam's voice ordered her.

Maxie sank back, luxuriating in the sensation of being pampered. After spoiling her with a night of unparalleled pleasure, Pamela was making her breakfast in bed! Her old girlfriend knew better than anyone how much Maxie hated to get up in the morning.

How could she have quarreled with such a wonderful girl? She never, never would again, Maxie vowed to herself for the fortieth time since last night.

She pulled up the green-and-blue plaid bedspread. In spite of June's heat, there was a wonderful chill in the air. While they'd been separated, Pam had gotten an air-conditioning unit installed. *If I'd known that, I would have been in an even bigger hurry to make up!* Maxie thought.

"Ta-da!" Pam pushed open the door with her foot and entered, flushed and beaming, bearing a tray with coffee, orange juice, English muffins, scrambled eggs, and slices of crispy bacon.

"Here, have some cream." Pamela set down the tray and poured the cream from the blue pitcher with a flourish.

"Real cream!" Maxie breathed, watching her coffee turn golden brown. The Magdalena Arms only served milk at breakfast. She thought of the powdered milk concoction the Summer Recreation Program kids were drinking at the Eleanor Roosevelt School and felt a fleeting pang of conscience.

"Scootch over," Pamela ordered, climbing back into bed with Maxie. She lit a cigarette and picked up her own cup of coffee, which she drank black. Pamela must have run to the corner grocery that morning for the cream, Maxie realized, or had she known, as Maxie had, that their passionate reunion at the party was as inevitable as firecrackers on the Fourth of July?

"Have a bite?" Maxie invited, holding out the toasted English muffin she'd buttered and slathered with strawberry jam.

"You know I never eat breakfast." But Pamela bent to lick a spot of jam from the corner of Maxie's mouth. "Well—just a taste."

"Silly!" Maxie munched her muffin contentedly. It was like falling in love all over again. Their three-week separation had done both of them a world of good, she thought. They had each matured, gotten a new perspective on life, learned to see the other person's point of view. Why, the new air-conditioning unit was proof of that, if nothing else was!

Last night their words had overlapped and intertwined even as their bodies had, as they both confessed their unabated passion for each other in incoherent snatches. "We've got a connection, Maxie," Pamela had panted, shedding her white shirt, "that just won't be broken!" As she spoke, the junior executive was pressing all the old buttons with the sure touch of an expert piano tuner working on a favorite concert grand. And nearly naked Maxie had to agree: "You're the girl for me, Pam," she choked out. "I can't stop myself from coming back for more!" The newly appointed magazine assistant had thought then of how salmon swim upstream to mate, thrusting themselves out of the water, leaping over obstacles, higher, and higher—

"Cold?" Pamela asked with tender concern as Maxie shivered a little in delicious remembrance.

"No, it's perfect here," said Maxie. "I still can't believe you finally broke down and got air-conditioning!"

"It wasn't so expensive after all," said Pamela, naming a sum that sounded extravagant to Maxie. "That included installation," she added, laughing at Maxie's shocked expression. "Why, Maxie, I believe you've finally learned the value of a dollar!"

Her remark reminded Maxie of the last time she'd been in this apartment, and the bill she'd torn in half. She wondered if Pam was thinking of it too. But Pam continued more seriously, "And you've proved you know how to work hard as well. Lois told me all about your stint as a Recreational Aide. I even went by one day last week, looking for you. When they told me you weren't working there anymore, I—well, I just assumed you'd quit." Pamela dropped her head in shame. "It wasn't until I saw Lois the other day that she told me how you got booted out for the boss's niece. Then I realized I'd misjudged you yet again."

The words were as sweet as the jam on Maxie's muffin. "We have lots to catch up on," she murmured. "I want to hear everything you've been doing and tell you everything I've been doing! Every single thing!"

"It's a darned shame the Parks and Rec department did

that to you," Pamela continued hotly. "Did you at least file a complaint? You really should!"

"There's no need," said Maxie hastily. "I've got the *Polish* job." The true reason for her sudden departure from the Summer Recreation Program for Disadvantaged Youth was *not* one of the things she wanted to tell Pamela, as it turned out.

The mention of *Polish* distracted her ambitious girl-friend. "Maxie, I'm so proud of you." Pamela's voice practically throbbed with emotion. "Working at *Polish*! One of the top magazines in the city! Why, it's the pinnacle of almost anyone's publishing ambitions!"

Maxie waved her hand dismissively, all the while lapping up the praise as a kitten laps up cream. "I was mostly hired for my social connections, you know. Hal Hapgood seemed to think it would make up for my deficient typing skills!"

"Who cares how you got in the door?" said her practical girlfriend. "What matters is, you're in! And you'll be writing copy in no time, I bet. Look at your *Step Stool* piece!"

Maxie squirmed slightly. Stella had rewritten her gay little story so thoroughly she'd barely recognized it when it finally appeared in print. "I'm not so sure of that." She tried to laugh off Pamela's misguided praise. "Hal Hapgood said I'd have to turn my hand to anything that came along. And, really, that kind of appeals—"

"Once he sees your talent, he'll change his mind," Pamela insisted. "Now that you've finally found your focus, you'll move up faster than an express elevator!"

Had she found her focus? Was her career finally fixed and moving ahead like a train on a track? Maxie threw a pillow playfully at Pamela. "Oh, you—you'll have me running the magazine in a month!" She was tempted to point out that only a few weeks ago Pamela had been pushing her toward Grunemans' packing room, but she stopped herself. She had resolved not to fight with Pamela anymore.

They drifted to the kitchen, talking of Grunemans' upcoming summer sale, Janet's party and prospects, and the latest gossip about the gang. Maxie offered to do the dishes, eager to show off some of the new skills she'd been learning. "Doing dishes in a fully equipped kitchen is a cinch after the bathroom dish-washing techniques Phyllis has been showing me," she insisted over Pamela's protest.

"Have you ever heard of Amalgamated Enterprises?" she asked, her thoughts reverting to her job destiny as she soaped the china.

Pamela shook her head. "Why do you ask?"

"I met a woman who's a big muckety-muck there—Velma Lindqvist—and—"

Pamela had been tilting back in the kitchen chair, blowing smoke rings, but now she came upright with a thump. "Velma Lindqvist! I've heard of *her*. She's got her own personal salesgirl at Grunemans—she's always picking up something for the Children's Hospital Benefit, or the Poolside Picnics Fund-raiser. She came to Bay City a few months ago, bent on making a big splash in the society pages. Quite a looker, for a woman her age, too." Her eyes narrowed in sudden suspicion. "How did you happen to meet her?"

"A mutual friend." Maxie decided not to mention Elaine's name. And she'd better not ask if Pamela had picked up on any gossip on Velma's possible variance! "I applied for a job at Amalgamated Enterprises." That was the truth, she thought, scrubbing a skillet industriously, if not the whole truth.

Pamela relaxed. "Speaking of fund-raisers," she said, "why don't you come with me to the *Step Stool* meeting

Thursday? We're planning an ice-cream social to raise money for the next issue."

"Fine by me," Maxie agreed. "Unless I have to work late, of course." After all, she, too, now had a job that demanded her time.

"We can pick up Lois, and maybe get a bite to eat before-hand," Pamela planned.

"Lois?" Maxie wrung out the dishrag and hung it up. "I didn't realize you'd shanghaied her—I mean, that she'd gotten interested in *The Step Stool*."

"I took her to a meeting a week ago. Poor kid." Pamela sighed. "She needs distraction. She's getting thin from brooding over Netta."

Maxie felt a pang of guilt. She'd been so preoccupied with her own problems, she hadn't paid much attention to the young office manager. Now she realized that Lois had been down in the dumps for weeks. Even her Auto-mated Office class hadn't cheered her.

"She's been eating her heart out since the last letter." Pamela shook her head. "Sometimes I wonder if . . . well, if Netta's developed another interest!"

"No!" Maxie leaned against the sink. "You mean one of the other voting rights volunteers?" She considered the idea, and shook her head vigorously. "Netta may share a political passion with her fellow workers, but she's not fickle, like me." She faltered and continued quickly, "I mean, like I used to be. Netta and Lois are solid, I'd swear to it. It's just the strain of the separation."

"I hope you're right." Pamela stubbed out her ciga-rette.

"I'm sure if Netta knew how Lois was suffering, she'd leave those Negroes to fend for themselves and head home like a shot," Maxie declared.

"Of course, I have all the respect in the world for

Netta and her convictions," said Pamela, following her own train of thought.

"Yes, of course," agreed Maxie. She was thinking how awkward it would be for Dolly and Stella if Netta did return to the Magdalena Arms unexpectedly.

"This country needs people of conviction; I've always said that," Pamela declared.

"Yes," said Maxie, wondering who Pamela was arguing with. She wanted to ask Pam if she thought Dolly and Stella might be more than business partners, but that would have meant explaining their "Around the World, Through the Seasons" photo project, and Pamela had never approved of Dolly's art-photo sideline. Maxie sighed. She admired Pamela's moral certainty, but it certainly interfered with gossip.

"Oh!" she said as she remembered the juiciest tidbit of all. "I forgot to tell you, I found out all about Kitty Coughlin, and I was right—she's not a psychology student at all! She's a supposed 'sociologist' and she's doing a book on Bay City deviants!" Maxie described to the astounded Pamela her impromptu tailing of her fifth-floor neighbor and how it had led her to Sociological Survey Editions.

"The book is going to be called *The Coral Reef: Bay City's Deviant Community*," Maxie told Pamela triumphantly. "The cover line is 'Floating just below the surface, ready to wreck an unwitting society!' "

Pamela frowned. "Lois mentioned Kitty once or twice," she said. "But I had no idea there was anything suspect about her. You'd better steer clear of that sleazologist."

"Maybe if we all talked to her," Maxie argued, "we could get her to change her book's tune." She'd always preferred meddling to a hands-off attitude.

Pamela shook her head decisively. "More likely you'd find some twisted version of yourselves in her book. Not that you'd ever read it, of course."

Maxie thought that while she certainly wouldn't approve of such a book, it might make interesting reading.

"Mrs. DeWitt must be turning senile, putting someone like that on the fifth floor," Pamela continued heatedly. "Is nothing sacred these days? First Francine's and now this!"

"Mrs. D. does her best," Maxie excused, thinking of the aging landlady's patience with her penniless tenant. "As for Francine's, I've been thinking we should try to convince Mrs. Flicka to pay up." Maxie warmed to the subject, which had been on her mind after the nervous evening she'd spent at her old hangout. "After all, Francine's only objection is the exorbitant prices the new mob is charging. She's like Mrs. DeWitt—she doesn't take inflation into account, and she thinks you can still buy a sergeant for twenty dollars a week. Honestly!"

"How do you know all this?" Pamela asked, frowning.

"Oh—someone at Janet's party was talking about it." Maxie didn't want to tell Pamela about the visits she'd made to the Knock Knock Lounge, sniffing around for information.

"I would never encourage anyone to pay protection money." Pamela was stern.

"Then we should find out who's behind the shakedown," Maxie suggested. "I got quite a bit of practice tailing Kitty—"

"Who are you going to tail?" Pamela's skepticism was apparent.

"Well, I—I know a girl who saw a cop taking a payoff. And she can identify the—the person who did the paying off. Now, say we followed this person and they led us to the mob boss. Then—"

"Then what?" Pamela prompted.

"Well, at least we'd know!" Maxie persisted. Wasn't

knowledge power? They'd figure out the next step once they knew.

Pamela was shaking her head again. "Your friend sounds rash and impulsive. She's bound to get into trouble if she tries to play PI." Her voice took on that familiar lecturing tone. "The homophile movement has spent years fighting the pervasive myth that variant women are inevitably drawn to crime. It is the duty of every Sapphic sister to be *extra* law-abiding."

Pamela seemed to have forgotten that Maxie had herself dozed through similar sermons on the subject. "The last thing any of us wants is to see some misguided girl spattered across the headlines in some sordid underworld affair." Pam continued, becoming more impassioned, "Your Mamie McArdle was awfully fond of that sort of thing. Gosh, I'm glad you're not working for her anymore!"

Maxie wanted to rise to her old mentor's defense, but held her peace. She and Pamela had never seen eye to eye on Mamie.

"Now," said Pamela, changing the subject, "what should we do today?"

Maxie considered. Her idea that she and Pamela go to the Knock Knock and try to tail Lon in tandem was clearly out.

"We could go shopping," Pamela suggested. "There's a chafing dish out there with my name on it."

"It's too hot," Maxie decided. "Why, you could keep casseroles warm on your windowsill. Let's just stay inside and enjoy your air-conditioning. I can read your back issues of *Polish* in preparation for my new job."

Pamela looked at her sideways. "You know, the air-conditioning is only in the bedroom."

"Then I guess we'll have to spend the day in bed,"

Maxie said, with a suggestive smile. It *was* warm in the kitchen—or did her sudden flushed feeling emanate from the anticipatory heat spreading through her body?

*We may disagree on almost everything,* Maxie thought as she led the way to the air-conditioned room, *but we're certainly united when it comes to desire!*

# Chapter 17
## Magazine Assistant

It was wonderful how everything had worked out. That was Maxie's refrain the next few weeks. There she was, reporting to her glamorous new job on the seventeenth floor of the Schuyler Building, and going home each night to the girlfriend of her dreams. Her financial worries were a distant memory, and even her cigarettes were safe from Phyllis's relentless budgeting.

How little she had thought, back in May, when she limped home to the Magdalena Arms with $2.38 in her pocketbook, that she was destined for a glamorous career in publishing!

There was never a dull moment at *Polish*. Maxie spent her days carrying out a dizzying array of tasks: fact-checking Vivian Mercer-Mayer's social schedule, carrying dummies from the art department to Hal and back again, cajoling an overdue writer into sending *something*, and hunting for hours through the files to find out when *Polish* had last featured a certain shade of citron.

Maxie loved every minute of it, although she needed three cups of coffee to really wake up in the morning. Brewing coffee in the office kitchen was one of the first things she'd learned, and she was proud of her new skill. Both she and Hal were coffee fiends.

The second assistant was learning about more than making coffee from her dynamo of a boss, who was on the phone coaxing some society doyenne to let her country estate be photographed while he simultaneously approved layouts or wrote a "Sincerely Yours" editorial on youth fads ("Your editor is persuaded that the 'Fab Four' are no fly-by-night sensation, and that their screaming fans will multiply, not fade away as some have predicted"). Under Hal's instruction, Maxie was learning to proof and edit; she wrote photo captions, and Hal had even entrusted Larry Lathrop's column, "Larry's Advice to the Lovelorn," to his new employee.

Maxie enjoyed ghostwriting crooner Larry Lathrop's replies to the mailbag of questions that arrived each week. She'd looked forward to working with the handsome lounge singer, but he was far too busy to read the column that bore his name—his publicist took care of it. Maxie felt quite cosmopolitan, whenever she called Hollywood about last-minute edits.

"Just take out the bit about how Larry loves to take phone calls from pretty girls. We're selling Larry as a traditional man when it comes to boy-girl stuff."

"'Larry likes to do the dialing himself'?" Maxie suggested, scribbling rapidly.

"That's the ticket, honey," the public relations man approved.

Hal told Maxie she would likely meet the famous crooner when he visited later that month. "But don't expect a lot of input into the column," he told her. "It's not brains he's famous for, but that profile." His eyes grew dreamy. "And what a profile!"

Publicists played a big role in the magazine world, Maxie discovered. At the *Sentinel* Mamie had sometimes passed on tickets to the grand opera or the fights, but at *Polish* Maxie and the other office girls divvied up not only tickets to the theater but the latest books, liquor, perfume, stockings, lipstick, and even, once, a gold watch with a patented clasp.

"Of course, you need to be careful," Pamela instructed over lunch one day. "Never promise a publicist anything! But the presents are a definite perk."

"I remember one Christmas getting a big bag of nuts from the Nut Growers Exchange," put in Lois with a reminiscent look. "They lasted until Easter!"

The three working girls, whose offices were not far from one another, sometimes shared a tuna sandwich and shoptalk on their lunch hour.

She was part of a larger scheme now, Maxie thought. A cog in the smoothly operating machine of buying, selling, and advertising that had made America what it was. Was this how Great-grandpa Mainwaring had felt when he swung his ax in the virgin woods of Loon Lake? Of course, Great-grandpa hadn't been a cog, but something more important: a gear, or vital spring, Maxie thought.

Still, she'd been missing something all those years she'd played while her friends worked. She finally felt she really belonged on the fifth floor. She, too, had stories of office politics, angry bosses, and horrendous mistakes almost made and avoided at the last minute. She too had suffered, eating nothing but applesauce, polishing her shoes herself, and even visiting a pawnshop.

Did other girls also have a Lon-like interlude they kept secret?

Her mind snapped back to the present as Pamela stood up, brushing the crumbs from her skirt. "Back to the grind! See you tonight, Maxie." She looked both ways, and laid her fingers on her lips to signify a kiss.

Maxie mimicked the gesture, which had become routine. "So long." She waved to Lois, and her two friends hurried away, already deep in a discussion of fall's new colors.

Maxie sopped up the last bit of caviar from the tiny tin she'd lifted from a promotional basket sent by a new Russian restaurant. She was always a little slower than her two friends to leave the summer sun of Schuyler Plaza and return to the office, no matter how many times Pamela pointed out the importance of promptness.

In the lobby of her building Maxie picked up the *Sentinel*'s afternoon edition and glanced at the headlines. MYSTERIOUS DOCKSIDE DEATH! The words jumped out at her from the front page. She read the story as the elevator rose. There'd been a rash of injuries on the docks, reported the *Sentinel*, culminating in this latest incident when Lukas Olafsson, thirty-three, was crushed by an improperly secured load. "As the winch swung the netted boxes from the pier to the ship, the net somehow came undone, and the recently elected shop steward was buried in a pile of packaged powdered milk."

Powdered milk again! It was a reminder that under Bay City's high-society surface, its dark underbelly still seethed with crime and corruption. Maxie realized with a start that she was mentally quoting from an old Mamie McArdle column. Sometimes she missed Mamie!

Why not ask Hal about covering the story? She tossed her hat and handbag on her desk, and picked up her notebook and pencil. Tucking the paper under her arm, she passed Lucille, who ignored her as usual and went on with her furious typing. Lucille resented being saddled with all the typing, and made it clear she considered Hal's second assistant a washout. Maxie tapped on Hal's door. At his distant, "Enter," she slipped in.

"Yes, yes, Inga, I'll make sure it gets straightened out. Yes. You can count on me. See you at the symphony." Hal hung up the phone and announced, "There's been another brouhaha over the Bay City Beautification Benefit—Mrs. Houck is out as chairwoman and Mrs. Hanson is back in."

Maxie tried not to roll her eyes. The dummy for the "Here and There" party page was thick with pasted-over changes. If she were Hal, she'd cut the whole lot of feuding ladies, but her boss secretly relished this sort of society catfight.

"I'll make the change." Maxie scrawled on her steno pad, *H.H. out, H.H. in.*

"Hazel isn't completely out," cautioned Hal. "She still needs to be listed as a committee member."

Maxie crossed out *out* and wrote *comm.* "Hal, I had an idea," she began.

"Are we set for the visit to the polo field tomorrow?" Hal interrupted anxiously. "This may be our last chance to photograph Horacio Enrique Suárez!"

"Yes, Hal, I talked to the club manager," Maxie told him patiently. "He's a close family friend, and he said it would be fine. The photographer should arrive at three. And yes," she forestalled his next question, "I told him you'd be there too, and were hoping to chat with Señor Suárez."

Hal had been obsessed with the polo-playing Argentinian playboy ever since he'd landed in Bay City. Hoping she'd reassured him sufficiently that he'd have his moment with the man the press was calling "the pocket Apollo," Maxie said, "I was wondering, what would you think about a piece on Bay City's underworld activity?" She handed him the paper. As he skimmed the story, the fledgling second assistant continued eagerly, "I'm sure this is connected to the mob shakeup. I've got some inside information, and I'd be willing to work overtime, if—"

Hal wrinkled his nose. "Powdered milk? Remember, Maxie, my dear, our readers are the crème de la crème!"

"I know, but what about that John Donne poem about how each man's death affects me?" Maxie argued. "These dockworkers are part of Bay City too!"

Hal pushed the paper back at her with a dismissive gesture. "Unless there's a society angle, our readers will remain unaffected." His eyes brightened. "Is there one? 'Ex-deb Embroiled in Underworld Power Struggle,' something like that?"

"No, nothing like that." Maxie picked up the paper and exited the office, disappointed. She didn't want to *be* the story, she wanted to tell it!

"Hal's the best boss in the world," she told Phyllis that night. "But he's so determined to keep anything sordid out of *Polish*!"

Phyllis looked up from the *Sentinel*'s story. "There's no mystery here," she declared. "Those dockworkers are in my district. The local is voting for a new president, and the mob is doing some heavy-handed campaigning for the corrupt candidate!" She brightened. "I think I'll ask Miss Ware's advice on how to handle this."

As if the mere mention of Miss Ware had taken care of the corrupt union, she asked Maxie, "Dinner out with Pamela?"

"At the Blue Danube," said Maxie, picking up her hair spray. Noticing Phyllis's lonely look, she suggested impulsively, "Why don't you join us? My treat!" Maxie knew Phyllis missed their companionable evenings practicing radiator recipes. They had dwindled away, once Pamela and Maxie were an item again.

Phyllis protested, "I'm sure you'd rather be alone."

"Don't be silly." Maxie discounted her objection. "Pamela just phoned to say she's invited Lois—the more the merrier!"

Maxie could afford to be generous. It wasn't only that she was up-to-date on her rent, had repaid Lois's loan, and cleared her debt at Luigi's. When Maxie finally called Grunemans about her overdue account, she discovered it had been taken care of—and the story was the same at Countess Elfi's and the Tip-Top Tailor Shop. Maxie wondered once or twice if Pamela was her benefactress, but it seemed unlikely her girlfriend would choose to be anonymous. More likely she'd make it an occasion for advice on staying out of debt!

It was easy to be frugal, with money in her pocket, Maxie thought that night, ordering a salad instead of the steak. Gone was the fatalistic feeling that since she was destitute anyway, she might as well spend a dollar as a dime. It was only when Pamela criticized—or at any rate, suggested—that Maxie should put the price of her new sailor-striped sweater in her savings account, that the ex-deb still got the yen to take all the spare cash in her purse and go on a spending spree.

But so far she hadn't. And she hadn't quarreled with Pamela either. Not even when the ambitious girl suggested for the twenty-third time that Maxie use her evenings and lunch hours to practice typing until she could match Lucille's speed.

Two and a half weeks, and no sharp words had been exchanged. It was some kind of record, Maxie reflected. It demonstrated just what two girls in love could accomplish if they both tried their darndest!

Maxie had even been attending *Step Stool* meetings regularly. She'd grown interested in spite of herself, now that she was in the publishing business. After years of mocking the newsletter for its self-importance, she now took a more constructive attitude. In fact, she had a few ideas up her sleeve that would stir up the staid *Step Stool-*ers, when she outlined them at the next meeting.

Cheering up Lois was another shared activity, Maxie thought, as she looked across the table at her forlorn friend. The recent disappearance of three civil rights workers in Mississippi had turned the office manager's worry over Netta into panic. It had taken Maxie and Pam's joint efforts to distract the distraught girl.

Lois was speaking now, with bright determination.

"I've decided to take the bull by the horns. I'm going to stop sitting around worrying—I'll just head on down to Mississippi and help Netta with her voter drive!"

Pamela dropped her fork with a clatter. "Are you sure that's wise?" she cried. "What about your job?"

"I have two weeks' vacation. I'll use that for my trip."

"I think that's a noble idea," Phyllis told the lovelorn office manager warmly. Maxie echoed her sentiment, although she couldn't help feeling a little sorry for Lois, whose summer vacation would be spent dodging the Klan and going door to door like a civic-minded Avon Lady. Impulsively she offered, "Take my burnt-orange linen when you go. It's bound to be sweltering in Mississippi."

Maxie thought of the Mississippi heat again when Pamela let them into her apartment and switched on the air-conditioning. "What a way to spend your summer vacation!"

"I don't think it's safe," Pamela fretted. "Netta has some experience with unsavory types, but Lois is too trusting by far!"

Pamela had always had a protective streak a mile wide when it came to the younger girl who hailed from her hometown.

"Lois is all grown up now," she reminded Pamela. Her

girlfriend went off to brush her teeth with a worried furrow between her eyebrows.

Maxie wasn't sleepy. She sat on the couch and lit a cigarette. Pamela used to be protective, possessive even, of her. Maxie remembered the thrill she'd felt when Pam told a good-looking girl at Francine's who'd asked Maxie to dance, "She's with me!" It had been so different from Mingy Patterson and her ilk, who pretended in the morning that the previous night's experimentation had never happened.

But then the possessiveness that charmed her had begun to chafe. It was a good thing the idea of Maxie moving in was still a touchy topic, because Maxie wasn't sure she wanted live with her beloved. If she did, Pamela would know everything Maxie did—and there was so much the ex-deb did of which Pamela wouldn't approve! The evenings she went out instead of practicing her typing, the visits to the Knock Knock Lounge—*which were completely innocent,* Maxie argued with her conscience. It wasn't like she was looking for Lon. She was just keeping her ear to the ground to pick up any underworld rumblings.

And she'd miss the gang at the Arms. The fun she had helping with Dolly and Stella's photo shoot; getting the inside dope on the Dockside from Phyllis. And someone had to keep an eye on Kitty!

"Are you coming to bed?" Pamela called. Maxie stubbed out her cigarette and packed her wandering thoughts away. But when she slipped into bed and switched off the light, she had to ask, "What if we stole Kitty's manuscript and told her we wouldn't give it back without final approval on copy?"

"Stealing is against the law," Pamela said drowsily. "I've got an early day tomorrow, and you've already been late once this week. Forget about Kitty Coughlin."

Maxie sighed as her law-abiding girlfriend turned over. She dreaded the alarm clock every morning. The job was perfect, of course, but it would be even more perfect if she didn't have to get up before ten.

She had a wonderful job, she reminded herself. A wonderful girlfriend, a wonderful life. In fact, it was all so wonderful, Maxie was a little bored.

The problem was, leaping up at the alarm, gulping her first cup of coffee, and running for the bus had lost its novelty, she decided the next day. Composing Larry Lathrop's pretended answers to the silly questions foolish women asked (*My husband wants me to stay home, but if I keep working we could afford a new car. . . .* ) seemed a little dull. If only Hal had given her the go-ahead on her mob investigation, Maxie thought, pouring herself a third cup of coffee.

Suddenly she stopped mid-sip. Why wait for Hal's go-ahead? She'd work on the investigation on her own time, and dazzle her boss with the result. Even Pamela couldn't criticize her project if it was carried out in the name of career advancement! She'd been pestering Maxie to use her lunch hour to improve her office skills. Investigating the mob would be much more interesting!

That noon, Maxie left Lucille typing like a demon and headed for Pete's pawnshop. She'd engage the owner in casual conversation, convince him she was a close friend of Lon's, and see what she could squeeze out of him.

Her spirits lifted as she approached the bar where she and Lon had gone. She relished the idea of pitting her wits against the shifty pawnbroker. On the off chance that the bar was a regular stop for the butch girl, Maxie pushed open the door and peered in. The back booth was empty—there was no Lon lounging against the worn leatherette.

Her mind was so full of Lon and her plan that she paid little attention to the veiled woman exiting the pawnshop. It was only after the woman climbed into an Olds and drove away that Maxie belatedly recognized her. Even if the ex-deb had never been a very dutiful daughter, no veil could disguise her own mother!

# Chapter 18

## Uplift with Pamela

Maxie slipped quietly into the crowded *Step Stool* office. Louise was speaking.

". . . so we have a shortfall of a hundred and thirty-nine dollars, which is better than last month," the serious *Step Stool* editor said. "In fact, we might have been in the black if the old Electromatic hadn't conked out."

Maxie spotted Pamela and Lois on the other side of the room. Lois returned Maxie's wave, but all of Pamela's attention was trained on Louise.

"Let's hear your ideas," their leader continued. "How can we make up the difference?"

Maxie decided not to bother squeezing through the crowd to join her girlfriend. She'd missed most of the meeting, and it would end soon anyway. She worked her way to the back of the crowd and found a seat on the corner of Stella's desk. "Hi," whispered the features editor.

Martie Schub had been recognized and was standing up. "We could easily make up that amount, and more, by raising our rates," she said argumentatively.

"But our subscribers—"

"Point of order!" Martie said. "Let me finish . . ."

Maxie's thoughts drifted away, like a leaf in a current. It wasn't just that she'd heard the well-worn arguments, pro and con, about raising *The Step Stool*'s subscription rates many times before. She was still preoccupied with the puzzle of what had brought her society-minded mother to Pete's pawnshop!

She'd pressed Pete to tell her about his recent customer. But the pawnbroker had played dumb. Even when Maxie spotted her mother's butterfly brooch in the glass cabinet, Pete simply shrugged his shoulders and said lots of ladies needed to raise a little cash.

Of course it was laughable, the idea that Mabel Mainwaring needed money! And if she did, Maxie thought practically, she'd do much better hocking the Mainwaring diamonds.

Yet hadn't Mamie suggested back in May that the Mainwaring family was short on funds, and that was the real reason Maxie had lost her allowance?

*Ridiculous!* the heiress had told herself as she left the pawnshop, having completely forgotten the original purpose of her visit.

Back in the office, she'd persuaded Hal to take her along on the polo-field photo shoot that afternoon—knowing full well this special favor would only add to Lucille's grudge against the second assistant. But Maxie had to find her father, and see what he knew about her mother's odd behavior.

Dad had been easy to find, standing on the edge of the field watching the polo team practice. "How's my little alfafa sprout?" he said absently, when his daughter greeted him. Maxie wondered if he was aware of her banishment. Her father had always preferred ponies to people.

Behind her, Hal and the photographer were discussing

the best angle to capture Horacio Enrique's appeal. "I want him to be a centaur," Maxie heard Hal saying excitedly. "Something out of Greek mythology!"

"How's Mumsy, Daddy?" Maxie asked her father.

"Fine, pumpkin," her father murmured. His eyes followed Horacio Enrique as he galloped past on a sweat-streaked pony.

Maxie tried again. "I know she was a little upset by that misunderstanding we had in May." She chose her words carefully. "Has she been acting at all . . . odd, lately?"

Maxie's father shook his finger playfully in Maxie's face. "I know what you're up to, muffin!"

"You do?"

"You think you can get your allowance back if you convince some judge that Mother's as mad as Aunt Alta. Really, kitten, did you expect me to play along?"

That had been all she could get out of the Mainwaring patriarch. Maybe everything *was* hunky-dory at home, but would her father notice if it wasn't? With him it was ponies, ponies, ponies. *He knows his horses' names by heart, but can he even remember mine?* his daughter asked herself bitterly.

With an effort, Maxie tuned back to the meeting. The *Step Stool*ers were still debating the subscription rates. "Six dollars may not seem like much to some people here." June's voice brimmed with resentment. "And all I can say is that if that's the case, you're to be congratulated! But some of us aren't so fortunate, and an increase of even two dollars would be a real hardship!"

Maxie had been thinking about cost all afternoon—the cost of the Mainwaring way of living, which she'd never questioned before. She penciled some estimates in the back of her budget book. Why, the polo ponies alone meant the expense of stabling, feed, trainers, grooms, equipment—and that didn't even take into account the amount her father gambled! The idea that the Mainwaring fortune was threatened seemed less unthinkable.

But how could it be saved by pawning a butterfly brooch?

"Maxie!" Stella whispered, pulling the distracted girl back to the present. "Maxie, you're up!"

Maxie had forgotten all about getting herself on the agenda for this meeting. But now Louise was looking at her quizzically. "Maxie, you wanted to present something?"

"Yes." Maxie stood up and collected herself. She'd planned this presentation and had even brought props. She wasn't going to let Mumsy's strange behavior discombobulate her!

"I've been kicking around some thoughts about *The Step Stool,* and I'd like to share them with you," she began. "Of course, we all agree that *The Step Stool* is a superlative example of homophile reporting." Maxie didn't point out that it was the only example. "But that doesn't mean it can't be improved, does it?" She looked around hopefully, and then plowed on, despite the unencouraging expression on Louise's face. "I think *The Step Stool* could use an update—something to bring it into the modern age. We could start with the name—"

"You want to rename *The Step Stool?*" Louise bristled.

Maxie stuck to her guns. "Doesn't the name *Step Stool* strike any of you as, well, rather unambitious? I mean," Maxie hurried on, "If we really want to 'help reach a higher place,' wouldn't a stepladder make more sense?"

"Or one of those funny things the fellows in the supermarket use to get goods from the high-up shelves," suggested June helpfully.

"My idea is we leave behind those homely associations with hardware stores altogether. I give you," Maxie paused dramatically, ". . . *Ascend!*"

She held up the newsletter cover mock-up she'd put together in *Polish*'s art department, with some help from a
friendly illustrator. There was a gratifying murmur.

"Or maybe, *Ascension!*" It was June again, still trying
to be helpful.

"Another idea I had was *Vista.*" Maxie ignored June.
"But whatever our choice, I think the name change
would let our readers know that our ambitions are growing, that we're not mired in the past—"

"I think it's a super idea!" The vote of confidence came
from Stella.

"I don't," said Louise flatly. "It would confuse our
readers. And I happen to like the old name!"

"Maxie's right, we need to be more ambitious in achiev-
ing our goals!" This came from a new recruit named Valerie, who burned with revoutionary zeal. "The time for
appeasement is over!"

A dozen voices were raised in response. "Be practical!"
shouted Donnie over the hubbub. "A change like that
would be costly—purchasing new stationery and what-
not—and we're still trying to balance our budget!"

"Point of order!" proclaimed Martie. "I second the
motion to change the newsletter's name—"

"It wasn't an official motion!"

"—and add the amendment that we take this opportunity to also raise the rates!"

"Move to table the discussion until next month!"
Louise was clearly at the end of her tether.

"Second!" chorused Donnie and Pamela. *Well!* thought
Maxie resentfully. *Not a word about* Ascend, *but you're
ready enough to second Louise!*

"Better luck next time," sympathized Stella, as Louise
closed the meeting and the girls began chattering and
helping themselves to the tin of butter cookies and supply

of soft drinks. Maxie's eyes were on Pamela, who was working her way through the crowd. "Thanks for speaking up for me," she couldn't help saying sarcastically, as Pamela leaned over to kiss her cheek.

Pamela pulled back. "You've been in publishing for how long and already you're an expert?" She paused, the way she did whenever she was restraining sharp words. "There are practical problems that have to be considered," she said in the patient voice that made Maxie's blood boil.

"I'm well aware of the practical problems," Maxie said between gritted teeth. "I just don't think they're as insurmountable as you do."

"I'm not saying the idea doesn't have possibilities." The business girl chose her words carefully. "But what with the shortfall and the upcoming ice-cream social, do we really want to spend time on cosmetic changes, like the newsletter's name?"

It was lucky that Louise called to the veteran *Step Stool*er just then, or Maxie might have boiled over!

"The old-timers are kind of overcautious." Stella had overheard the whole exchange. "We'll just have to wait until we've got enough adventurous types, like Val, to outvote them. Then *Vista,* here we come!"

Maxie looked at Pam, in a self-important confab with Louise and Donnie, and wondered how she'd ever summon the patience for such a long-term plan. "I'd almost rather start my own magazine," she muttered.

Stella laughed, and Maxie relaxed a little. Valerie came over and handed the deflated girl a cookie and a Coke. "I'm so glad you spoke tonight," she said in her earnest way. "Change is blowing in the wind, while those three"— she nodded disdainfully at the triumvirate—"are writing persnickety articles about pants!"

Maxie knew she should defend Pam, but she basked in

the political girl's approval. Pam hadn't even thought to bring her a beverage!

"If you do start your magazine, I'll write for you," Stella proposed, after Valerie went for more cookies.

"I'd hire you in a second—you've got a way with words," Maxie told her, thinking of how the features editor had transformed her article.

"Do you really think so?" Stella looked suddenly shy. "I've always aspired to be an author—photography is just a hobby."

"Have you written anything?" Maxie asked absent-mindedly. "I mean, besides for *The Step Stool?*" Pamela and Louise were chuckling over something on the other side of the room.

"I've finished my first novel," Stella confided. "I don't know if you'd be interested in reading it. . . ."

"I'd love to," Maxie said automatically, her eyes on her girlfriend.

"Really?" Stella looked ecstatic. "I've been wanting to ask you—you have so much experience, what with working for Mamie and now *Polish.* Are you sure?" She pulled out her desk drawer and took out a thick brown-paper-wrapped package. "It's all ready to send out, but I didn't know where to send it!"

"I'd be happy to help you." It was nice to be treated as an expert, instead of an ignoramus. At least Stella appreciated her!

The magazine assistant took the package and departed for the Arms. She needed a night off from Pam—not even her girlfriend's air-conditioning would cool her temper tonight!

The Arms seemed smaller and dingier to Maxie after so many nights at Pam's place, and the heat was oppressive as she mounted the stairs. The assistant grew even more irritated at her exasperating girlfriend, for choosing such a hot night to be so provoking!

The distant tapping of a typewriter told Maxie that Kitty was hard at work again. As she reached the fifth-floor corridor she could hear the loud rattle and bang of the carriage return. Maxie tightened her lips. Really! Enough was enough!

She knocked imperiously on room 502 and, without waiting for an answer, flung open the door. Kitty was seated at the desk, clad only in a filmy white nightgown. Stripped of her Peter Pan collar, the nearly transparent material revealing the mature woman underneath, her college-girl pretense seemed more farcical than ever.

"Are you going to be typing all night?" Maxie demanded as Kitty jumped and turned toward her.

"I'm awfully sorry," the pseudo-student apologized. "I have a paper due on stimulus-response in lab mice—"

"Save the applesauce!" Maxie interrupted. "I've eaten it until I'm sick of it. You're not enrolled in school, and you're not typing any paper!"

Kitty recoiled, covering her typewriter protectively as Maxie continued, "I've known your real game for weeks—digging up salacious stories to titillate the ignorant public, when what's really needed is an honest account of gay life!"

"Have you told anyone else?" Kitty gasped.

"Not yet." Maxie seated herself on Kitty's bed and lit a cigarette in a leisurely fashion, while the unmasked girl swiveled nervously to face her. "What's your motivation, Kitty? You don't seem the type to write this sleazy stuff."

"We all have to live." Kitty defended herself. "You should know that."

"So you're just in it for the money? I'm willing to wager something else drew you to this topic—something deep inside you that you can't deny!"

The rise and fall of Kitty's barely concealed breasts quickened as Maxie sent her a smoldering glance. Moonlight filtering through the window made the sleaze writer's skin glow with a pearly luminosity. "I'm just a social scientist," the scantily clad girl gulped. "I'm merely here to observe and report."

The room was heavy with heat and repressed desire, and Maxie knew she'd struck a nerve. "I can help you out or I can hinder you," she declared, deciding to leverage the mixture of lust and alarm emanating from the conflicted writer. "If you play ball and include some upstanding, well-balanced lesbian ladies in your book, all well and good. But if you limit your observations to alcoholics and frustrated housewives, I'll put the lid on your so-called research!"

"Are you threatening me?" Kitty asked. "This kind of intimidation is against the law, you know!"

"Call it a trade." Maxie was suddenly tired of toying with her repressed neighbor. She rose. "And if you're still typing after midnight, I'm complaining to Mrs. DeWitt!"

She closed the door behind her, and to her relief, the tippy-tapping did not resume. She unlocked 505 and switched on the light. There was a piece of paper on the floor, and Maxie picked it up. It was a message from Dolly, scrawled on Magdalena Arms stationery.

*9:30 p.m. Her majesty your mother called—*
*demands your presence at Loon Lake Fourth*
*of July weekend. Call her tomorrow.*

## Chapter 19
## Loon Lake

Maxie was packing for Loon Lake. Hal hadn't wanted to give her the time off, but Maxie had soothed him with the promise of society gossip, assuring him, "All sorts of powerful people are going to be there—you wouldn't want me to miss it!"

In truth, it was Maxie who couldn't miss this opportunity to ask her mother a few casual questions about pawnshops and butterfly brooches.

Maxie went to the fifth-floor washroom to gather her toothbrush and toiletries. Kitty was there, washing out her underwear. The second assistant had thought the unmasked sleazeologist would avoid her, but Kitty looked up and brightened.

"I've been thinking about your suggestions for my—project." She lowered her voice when she said "project." "Why don't I interview you? You're an excellent example of a well-adjusted deviant."

Maxie was taken aback, both by the unexpected approach and the flattering characterization.

"I'd want to know especially about your relationship with your mother," Kitty continued earnestly. "Whatever you may think, I truly want to get to the root of deviancy!"

"Maybe," Maxie temporized. She might have added that she was just as curious about her mother as Kitty was. "I'll think about it over the weekend."

Lois was in Maxie's room when she returned, putting a package on the busy girl's bureau. "Your sun lotion," she said.

"Thanks loads, Lois." Maxie tucked the tube into her toiletries bag.

Lois sat on the bed, sighing, "You're lucky to get away this weekend. The temperature is supposed to climb to the nineties!"

"I know," said Maxie. She was glad to get out of the city, not just to escape the heat wave, but to get some perspective on herself and Pamela. She picked up Stella's manuscript, still in its wrapping, and wedged it in her bag.

"At least it's not too humid." Lois tried to look on the bright side. "Netta says her little town is like a swamp!"

"Goodness, Lois," Maxie couldn't help saying, "that's no kind of place for a vacation!"

"The important thing is that we'll be together," Lois said loyally.

Maxie thought about Lois's devotion as she settled herself on the Loon Lake–bound bus. Lois would be a better candidate than Maxie for Kitty's study, the ex-deb admitted. She was the most well-balanced member of the fifth-floor gang.

*On the other hand, I've improved quite a bit,* the magazine girl thought, watching the familiar landmarks flash by. It was odd seeing them from the bus instead of the family Oldsmobile, but they hadn't changed. There was the farm, which meant they'd left the city behind; there was the neon-lit roadhouse that had fascinated Maxie as a child; there was the turnoff to Lake Ulm, where they'd always stopped for lunch.

Yes, she'd definitely changed for the better, Maxie decided, remembering the bored and sullen child she'd been, the restless teenager, the debutante with a passion for danger. Sure, she'd quit one job, lost another, and was currently in Hal's bad books, but she'd managed to make it on her own for more than a month!

She even enjoyed munching the leftover roast beef, saved from a *Polish* lunch meeting, instead of eating a restaurant meal her parents had paid for. *Better a stale sandwich by myself than a turkey club, with Mumsy as company!*

Of course, she still liked luxury, she thought, dusting off her "uncrushable" seersucker shift and climbing in the Olds Mumsy had sent to meet her at the bus station in Illiniwek. It was pleasant to lean back in the air-conditioned car while the chauffeur stowed her overnight case in the trunk. To know that when she arrived at the cabin, Sigrid would press her party dress; that her meals would be made and her dishes washed. She could sleep as late as she liked without missing breakfast!

The car turned in between the rustic gateposts that, according to Mainwaring family lore, Great-grandfather had hewed himself from two hefty pine trees. Maxie privately suspected that the pine baron, busy running his logging camps, had hired it done. The log cabin where he and Great-grandma once lived had been expanded and improved over the years so that the founder of the Mainwaring fortune would hardly have recognized it. Loon Lake Lodge, it was called now.

The car stopped by the stone terrace. Maxie got out and stood a moment, sniffing the pine-scented air and peering down at the sparkling blue of the lake. She could see figures sunning themselves on the swim raft, and she wondered who the other guests were. Mumsy had said it would be an "intimate" weekend.

The subject of her thoughts emerged from the house, wearing a plaid shirt tucked into a pair of neatly pressed slacks.

"Finally!" said Mrs. Mainwaring. "The rest of the guests arrived ages ago. They're swimming now, but you'd better go shower and change. The Lunds will be here shortly."

"The Lunds!" Maxie didn't know what irritated her more, her mother's assumption that she could arrange Maxie's schedule, or the thought of sitting across from the disapproving DAP dowager at dinner. "Why on earth did you invite them?"

Her mother bristled. "Why shouldn't I invite them? They're old family friends!"

It was as if Maxie and her mother had seen each other only yesterday, instead of mid-May. They'd picked up the nagging and grumbling precisely where they'd left off.

*I'm independent now,* Maxie reminded herself. She seated herself in an Adirondack chair. "Sure, why shouldn't you?" she echoed. "But I think I'll need a cocktail if I'm going to sit through dinner with Inga. How about rustling up a martini, Mumsy, dear?" Her mother opened her mouth, but Maxie forestalled her. "Or had I better hitchhike into town and catch the bus back to Bay City where I can do as I like?"

Her mother hesitated, torn between the desire to tell Maxie off and something stronger that stopped her. Maxie knew suddenly that Mumsy wanted something from her. But what?

"I'll have Oscar mix your drink," she choked out, and retreated into the house.

And she didn't even remind me to comb my hair! Maxie marveled. Now, of course, she wanted to freshen up. She went to her old room, where Sigrid was unpacking her overnight case. "Welcome home, Miss Maxie," she said politely. "Would you like me to draw your bath?"

Maxie told her not to bother, and after Sigrid had left, she splashed some water on her face and changed into a raspberry-colored polished cotton. She was combing her hair when there was a tap on the door. It was Oscar, bearing a martini on a tray. Maxie sipped the drink, wondering again what her mother wanted so badly.

It couldn't have anything to do with money. As Maxie wandered to the Lodge's living room, carrying her cocktail, she could see that the expensive machinery of the Mainwaring household was moving as smoothly as ever. Now that Maxie had developed the habit of calculating costs, she was staggered as she added up the amount that would be spent for this casual country weekend. She could start a dozen *Vista*s for that price!

Only her parents were in the big, screened-in room, and Oscar, who was arranging appetizers under the totem pole at the far end. "Hi, cookie," her father said as he turned a page in *Bit and Spur*. Maxie's mother was sipping Scotch.

*She never used to drink,* thought Maxie. *What gives?*

"Who else is here?" she asked, helping herself to a deviled egg.

"A mix of old friends and new," Mumsy answered evasively. "I thought you'd enjoy seeing Sookie Carmichael, and—"

Before her mother could finish her list, the guests themselves arrived. Sookie embraced her boarding school chum with squeals of girlish enthusiasm. Maxie swallowed her egg as Sookie turned to the square-jawed, slightly bucktoothed young man who'd followed her in. "Maxie, meet Ted—Ted Driscoll. Ted, Maxie Mainwaring."

"I've heard so much about you," Maxie said, shaking the young man's hand, wondering what he knew about her and Elaine. Was this another of her mother's attempts to get Maxie engaged? Her daughter felt almost disappointed.

Then her attention was caught by a head of platinum hair, and her astonished gaze traveled down to meet a pair of serene brown eyes. Below the gold-embroidered summer shift, the legs were as lovely as ever. Maxie scarcely noticed her mother taking her arm and bringing her forward. "Velma, I want you to meet my daughter,"

"Maxie, what a delight to see you again." The attractive blonde took Maxie's hand warmly in both her own. An invisible, radiant energy seemed to leap from her and envelop Maxie, making the younger girl feel turbocharged.

"You've met?" Maxie's mother sounded incredulous at the idea that the dynamic businesswoman who was making her mark on Bay City society was acquainted with her disgraced daughter.

Velma let go of Maxie and turned to Mrs. Mainwaring. "Oh yes." She shook her finger at Mumsy in mock reproof. "And had I known in time that your talented daughter was looking for work, I'd have snapped her up before Hal Hapgood got hold of her!"

So she *had* gotten the phone message, Maxie thought, pleased. Velma turned to greet Mr. Mainwaring, and Maxie's mother pulled her aside. "I won't have you working for Amalgamated Enterprises," she ordered Maxie. "It's defeminizing!"

Maxie shook off her mother's grip. "Relax, Mumsy, I'm happy at *Polish*. But why shouldn't I work at Amalgamated if I want to?" She looked appreciatively at Velma. "It hasn't hurt her!"

It was strange that the two women had become close. Maxie looked from one to the other as she absently ate

Anna's herring balls. They hadn't much in common. Or had they? Maxie sensed a certain steely quality in the attractive executive that Mumsy shared. And they were both keen on DAP politics, as if it mattered who was elected for what office! Velma's variance, which set Maxie's geiger counter clicking, simply didn't register with Mumsy. Unlike Maxie, Velma was careful to hide her tendencies.

*It might be fun to make her unveil herself,* Maxie mused. Then she turned from temptation to Ted, who'd been seated next to her.

"How is Elaine?" Maxie asked after Ted's fickle ex-fiancée mischievously.

Ted's brows drew together. "The engagement is off."

"I'm sorry, I didn't realize," Maxie fibbed.

"Everyone thinks it's just a spat," Ted told her bitterly. "Even my family! Of course, they've been pushing us together since we were in kindergarten."

*So it had been a merger as much as a marriage,* Maxie thought. But all she said was, "I wouldn't think it would be a hardship. Elaine's quite attractive."

Ted lowered his voice. "She's a very sick girl," he confided. "How could I marry someone who can't keep her hands off my own—" He stopped abruptly.

Maxie wondered who, precisely, the heartless hussy had handled. She couldn't help feeling sorry for Ted, even as she defended her former flirtation: "Elaine *is* sort of selfish, but she's healthy as a horse!"

Ted shrugged. "Dad will have to find some other way to shore up the dry-cleaning business. What he doesn't realize," Ted continued earnestly, "is that dry cleaning is a thing of the past—the money in the future is going to be in Laundromats!"

"I think you're right," Maxie agreed. "Especially with the new drip-dry fabrics."

"Exactly," said Ted. "I finally persuaded Dad to sell off a few of our lowest performers, and once the deal with Amalgamated Enterprises is done—"

"You mean Velma"—Maxie gestured with a forkful of *kyckling pölsa*—"is the buyer?"

"She's negotiating the deal," said Ted. "And she drives a tough bargain!"

Maxie pictured Velma, those beautiful legs crossed in a smoke-filled room of hard-faced businessmen. She found the image stimulating.

". . . and then I'll open Sudso! That's what I'm going to call 'em—Sudsos. I plan to have a whole chain of them!"

While Ted droned on about Sudso, Maxie listened with half an ear. Her eyes were on Velma across the table, laughing politely at one of Mr. Lund's jokes. Even ambitious Pamela paled beside the powerful businesswoman!

"You're an awfully sympathetic sort of girl," Ted said as they left the dining room.

"I have more in common with Elaine than you think," Maxie advised. "You'd better stick to Sookie!"

Late that night, Maxie was in her room, gazing out at the moon, which peeped through a filigree of pine branches. She was thinking of her long-gone youth, when she saw the glow of an orange ember on the terrace. Velma's shapely form emerged from the shadows as she, too, paused to look up at the moon.

Maxie raised her hand to the handle of the sliding screen door. Only thin mesh separated her from the blond beauty. She had merely to slide open the door and she could join the older woman for a cigarette—and perhaps more. Every nerve in her body urged her on, but was she attracted or merely intrigued? Was this chemistry or curiosity?

*And what about Pamela?* Maxie remembered the pledge she'd made the night of Janet's party. She let her hand slip from the door, but she watched the orange dot wax and wane until finally it fell to the ground and winked out.

With a sigh, Maxie turned away. She pulled Stella's manuscript out of her bag and unwrapped it. Climbing into bed, she propped herself on the pillows and began to read.


## IF LOVE IS THE ANSWER, WHAT IS THE QUESTION?

### *a novel by Stella McSweeney*

Sally opened the door to the Homophile Handbooks office and slipped inside, her heart pounding. She'd never thought she'd have the courage to join this intrepid organization, frowned upon by "normal" society. . . .


Why, it's a roman à clef, Maxie realized, reading with mounting interest. It was all about *The Step Stool,* its staff, and volunteers. They'd certainly been a busy bunch of girls! "Sally" must be Stella, while "stern-jawed Lydia," the secret object of Sally/Stella's affections, was obviously Louise. Maxie wondered if Stella still carried a torch for the managing editor.

But no, after "Sally" was disappointed by "Lydia," she proceeded to cut a swath through the rest of the staff. *Stella has quite a knack for the racy stuff!* Maxie thought admiringly, as she read how "Sally" and "Edna" were trapped together in an overheated elevator and forced to strip to avoid heatstroke.

In a sudden gesture, Edna tore open Sally's blouse, panting, "Our lives are at stake," as her eyes dwelt on Sally's lacy C-cups, which heaved up and down in an effort to obtain enough oxygen.

Was Stella really a C-cup, or was that poetic license? Maxie snuggled down in her pillows and read with satisfaction the steamy denouement between Edna and Sally.

But it was the next chapter that really got her attention. "Patricia," a "lanky redhead and faithful volunteer who worked at the perfume counter in a large department store," appeared on the scene. Pamela would not appreciate the demotion, Maxie mused, her eyes skimming ahead for more mentions of "Patricia."

Suddenly a sentence leaped out at her: *For there were Jane and Patricia, entwined in a tight embrace!*

What? Maxie backed up. "Sally" was pursuing "spunky little Jane," who must be June. Now Sally/Stella, while visiting the office late at night to return a borrowed typewriter, had surprised Jane/June in a tryst with the "lanky redhead." Maxie read rapidly: "Sally stood stock still, unable to look away" as things heated up between Jane/June and Patricia/Pamela. Snatches of text burned themselves into Maxie's brain: *Jane tugged off Patricia's navy skirt. . . . Patricia moaned as Jane pushed her against the cracked plaster wall. . . . Their moans turned to howls of ecstatic release.*

Maxie put down the pages and stared at the pine-paneled wall with unseeing eyes. This was fiction, she told herself. Not a private detective's report.

On the other hand, the novel's account of "Minnie" and "Lydia's" brief but torrid affair was an exact descripton of what had happened between Martie and Louise, down to the scene where Minnie/Martie threw

Lydia/Louise's clothes out the window and into the street. Wasn't it highly probable that Pamela and June had had some sort of fling?

And Maxie knew for a fact that Pamela could make a lot of noise when she was expressing her pleasure!

It must have happened that Christmas Maxie'd been forced to go to Acapulco with her family. They'd had a terrible fight just before Maxie left—had they broken up? Maxie couldn't remember.

Maxie felt pulled every which way by all sorts of emotions, like a tourist who can't decide what to do first. She was shocked at the discovery; angry at Pamela for taking her in with that loyal girlfriend line; and she certainly regretted restraining herself tonight with Velma!

Mostly, she was terribly curious. What else had her devious girlfriend been up to?

Maxie picked up Stella's novel and began to read where she'd left off.

# Chapter 20
## Fireworks

Maxie was still asleep the next morning, when Sigrid entered carrying her breakfast tray. Her "Good morning, miss" woke the tired girl, who'd been up until the wee hours poring over Stella's novel. Heavy-eyed, she struggled into a sitting position, as Sigrid put down the tray and opened the curtains. She'd scarcely finished creaming her coffee when her mother came in.

"We're having a dinner-dance to watch the fireworks this evening," she began. "You'll greet the guests with me at five. I've arranged for our house guests to tour the lake in the pleasure boat, and I think it would be nice if you went with them and showed them the sights. . . ."

Mabel Mainwaring continued unfolding the day's agenda while Maxie ate her fruit cup, paying only token attention. Then:

"I suppose you've been wondering why I've decided to forgive you and pay off your accounts," her mother began. Maxie looked up in surprise. She hadn't even suspected her mother. "I'm prepared to go on paying them, and restore some of your allowance," her mother continued crisply.

Maxie gaped. "Why the sudden change of heart?"

"I won't have our family affairs exposed to the public!" Maxie's mother flared. At first, Maxie thought her mother meant Mamie McArdle's column, but the Mainwaring matron was continuing angrily, "Hiring that shyster lawyer to suggest that Aunt Alta is insane! Have you no sense of shame?"

"Aunt Alta *is* nuts," Maxie objected. "And Janet's no shyster!"

"Someone stole the trust papers from your father's den," Mumsy accused. "Who else would be responsible for such an underhanded trick?"

"That was me," Maxie informed her.

"You!" Mumsy stared at her, outraged. "After the money we've spent raising you—"

Mumsy launched into her usual lament about Maxie's bad behavior, and her daughter decided it was time to turn the tables.

"Listen, I'll call Janet off if it means I can collect my allowance," she interrupted. "But if you want to avoid scandal, why are you visiting Lake Street pawnshops? It's not the sort of appearance you want mentioned in 'Here and There.'"

Maxie's mother put her hand to her throat. The blood drained from her face. "Who's spreading such lies? What utter nonsense! I never did such a thing in my life!" She stood up and practically ran from the room. "I have a house party to host!"

Even if Maxie hadn't already been positive she'd seen her mother at the pawnshop, Mumsy's hasty retreat would have convinced her. Whatever it was her mother had been doing, she wanted it kept very, very private— that much was clear.

Today Maxie was leaning toward an illicit affair. Maybe it was just the soap-opera story she'd been following in *If Love Is The Answer, What Is The Question?*, but if Pamela could go from faithful to faithless, why not Mumsy? After all, Daddy was practically married to his ponies. It would explain a lot—the Scotch and her apparent distraction—the way she'd given a little jump when the phone rang last night during dinner. She hadn't even relaxed when the call turned out to be for Velma.

And speaking of Velma . . . Maxie threw back the covers and went to take her shower. She'd been Pamela's patsy the other night, reining in her impulses out of misguided loyalty. She was going to correct that situation today!

Unfortunately for Maxie, Ted Driscoll stuck to her like glue all afternoon. He nattered on about Sudso through the tour of Loon Lake and was still at it during the afternoon swim. Sookie was the one to give Velma diving tips, and the ex-deb had to watch her prep school friend put her hands all over the attractive executive, while Ted, who could talk and tread water at the same time, explained the term "loss leader."

Her chance came after dinner, when the guests drifted out to the terrace to watch the Fourth of July fireworks, Maxie made her way to Velma's side: "Want a better view? I know just the spot."

"How nice of you." Velma followed her from the terrace. Their feet crunched softly on the pine needles covering the forest floor as Maxie led her through the woods to a point of land where their view of the lake was unobstructed.

"Lovely," approved Velma. "Like having the best box at the opera." As if on cue, there was a loud crack and whistle, and a shower of sparks lit up the sky.

"I was admiring your diving form this afternoon," Maxie told her. "You could have competed, I'll bet."

"Oh no." Velma discounted the praise. "I've never been much for sports."

Maxie thought she had never seen anyone lovelier than Velma, as a blue skyrocket screamed overhead and added frosty highlights to her platinum hair and aqua shadows to the moss-green chiffon that blended with the forest. She reached for Velma's hand, in the grip of a desire so powerful she could hardly stand.

"Not even the indoor kind?"

The unearthly radiance in the sky seemed to magnetize them, drawing them together. Their lips fused, as if welded together by a superheated energy source. Their bodies moved as one unit, like negative and positive electrons paired in a sensual sub-atomic dance. Velma's tongue touched hers, setting off a shower of glowing particles inside Maxie's head. The younger girl gathered a fistful of green chiffon skirt in her hand, exposing the shapely legs that had first caught her eye.

"Maxie," breathed Velma huskily, "I don't think this is a good idea."

"Of course it is." Maxie ignored the pro forma protest. But the hand that had been caressing her breast, exciting her to the point of pain, was now pushing her gently away.

"What gives?" Maxie gasped, as Velma detached herself and lit a cigarette. It was as if the blond businesswoman had stopped a nuclear reaction at the moment of fusion.

"It would be rude," Velma said regretfully. "A breach of etiquette to engage in an activity my hostess disapproves of while enjoying her hospitality!"

"What she doesn't know won't hurt her!" Maxie begged. She couldn't believe that a woman who radiated wantonness the way Velma had would put some fuddy-duddy social stricture before satisfaction.

"And besides." Velma glanced at her watch as if calculating how much time she had until her next appointment. "I'd like to offer you a job at Amalgamated Enterprises, in the new dry-cleaner division. We have a policy against office romances."

As another burst of light lit the air, all Maxie could think was that her private fireworks had fizzled. Her trysts had often been interrupted or curtailed by circumstances out of her control, but Maxie Mainwaring had never been out-and-out rejected! "Well, thanks for the offer," she lashed out in rage and hurt. "But I'd sooner work at Sudso!"

She thrashed her way back through the woods, not caring whether Velma followed. In fact, she made a point of ignoring the Amalgamated executive the rest of the evening, flirting with Nancy Nyhus, who reminded her a little of Lon, if Lon were to wear a dress. Mumsy retired early, with a bad headache, leaving the coast clear—and increasing Maxie's fury at Velma's excessive caution. But even opening Nancy's eyes to her true nature was an insufficient sop to the ex-deb's injured pride.

On the bus the next day, Maxie decided sourly that reading Stella's book had been the only productive part of the weekend. Listlessly she unfolded the *Loon Lake Gazette,* preparing to shade her face while she snoozed. Then she spotted the picture on the front page, and suddenly she was wide awake.

VACATIONING MAN DROWNED ran the headline. Below was a photograph of a lantern-jawed man with a prominent Adam's apple. It was the police officer Maxie had last seen in the alley behind Francine's, taking a payoff from Lon.

# Chapter 21
## Raid!

By the time the bus pulled into Central Station, Maxie had practically memorized the story. Franklin "Frankie" Schuster had been discovered floating next to his own pier a few hours after the end of the fireworks display. "The tragedy began," the *Loon Lake Gazette* reported, "when Mrs. Schuster noticed the bratwurst smoking on the grill outside their summer cottage. Knowing her husband would never leave the bratwurst to burn, she became alarmed."

A half-drunk bottle of beer on the pier led to an investigation of the lake. Schuster had "apparently slipped off the pier, perhaps distracted by the fireworks." He was "past help" when he was pulled out—newspaper-speak for deader than a doornail, thought Maxie. But the part she read and reread was Mrs. Schuster's assertion that "Frankie" was a strong swimmer, who would never drown in the shallows of Loon Lake. The sheriff's office blamed an underwater piling for the "unfortunate accident," pointing to the "contusion on Schuster's head."

The article ended with a brief note that Mr. Schuster was a police officer in Bay City and that he and his wife had been coming to Loon Lake for twelve years, and had just recently purchased their own lakeside cottage.

An accident, they called it, and yet Maxie couldn't help suspecting something more sinister. Maybe it was knowing the all-American swimmer had probably paid for his cottage with bribes and kickbacks; maybe it was the odd proximity to the Mainwaring cabin—half an hour by road, but only a five-minute paddle. Maybe it was the way the dots connected: the cop to Lon, Lon to the pawnshop, the pawnshop to Mabel Mainwaring. And what about the previous evening—was a headache the real reason Mumsy had retired so early?

Maxie rubbed her forehead in an effort to clear her thoughts. She supposed the average daughter wouldn't leap to the conclusion that her mother had committed murder. But Mumsy wasn't your standard-issue mother! Maxie could easily picture her in one of the Mainwaring canoes, floating silently up to the Schuster pier and bludgeoning the policeman with a paddle.

Yet what possible motive could the Mainwaring matriarch have for such a deed? Maybe Maxie was making a mountain out of a molehill.

On the other hand, the girls at Francine's had plenty of reason to resent Officer Schuster! Had one of them had the opportunity this past weekend to vent her anger?

Maxie had a date with Pam for dinner, but rather than going straight home to change, she yielded to an impulse to stop by Francine's and see if news of the crooked cop's death had reached the familiar haunt. Besides, she still wasn't sure what she wanted to say to Pamela about her girlfriend's past pecadillos.

To Maxie's surprise, Dolly and Stella were at a table, having a beer. The latter greeted her gaily. "How was the glorious Fourth? I see you got some sun!"

*I got more than that,* Maxie thought, but all she said was, "It was swell."

Dolly signaled the waitress as Maxie set down her overnight case and hitched up a chair. "Stel and I are celebrating," she told Maxie. "We finished the last of the photos."

"Now all we have to do is make up the sample," Stella added.

"And then sell it," Dolly finished.

"I wonder how long it will be before we see any money," Stella sighed.

"If you want money, sell your novel," Maxie told the amateur photographer as she scanned the bar. "With a few changes you could probably make a pile."

Stella looked positively starstruck. "You really think it's good?"

"It kept me turning the pages. If you like"—she warmed up, forgetting the reason for her visit to Francine's—"I'll call Mamie and get possible publishers from her. She's been writing under a pseudonym for years." It was the perfect excuse to make up with her old mentor.

"I can make any changes you think it needs!" said the aspiring author. "Could you, maybe, go over the manuscript with me, Maxie?"

"If only I was talented as you two," mourned Dolly. "As an actress, I'm yesterday's hash."

Maxie was about to say something to reassure her old friend when she felt a funny prickling on the back of her neck, as if she were being watched. The air stirred, and suddenly a low voice murmured in her ear, "Better scram, college girl. Betty Blue is on her way."

"Lon!" Maxie whirled around. It was a shock to see Lon at Francine's, but there she was, in a T-shirt and jeans, looking around uneasily—and she didn't look like she was joking. Maxie turned to her friends, who were eyeing the beautiful butch with interest. "Girls, we've got to go—the police are on their way!"

"Let's warn the others!" said Dolly. Suiting action to word, she cupped her hands around her mouth and shouted in a voice that carried to the corners of the room, "Cheese it! The cops!"

Francine's clients were always on the qui vive, and the alarm was instantaneous. The girls leaped up like over-bred racehorses at the sound of the starter's gun. There was a clatter of chairs being shoved back, the smash of glasses tumbling from tables, a melee worse than a rugby scrum as more and more women joined the fray, clogging the narrow flight of steps in their attempt to escape.

"Your friend started a stampede." Lon pulled Maxie away from the frenzy. Her touch started off a potent re-action in Maxie, like the fizzing of bicarbonate in a glass of water.

"We'll take the back way." Maxie picked up her over-night case, and she and Lon went behind the bar, through a tiny kitchen, and up a short flight of wooden steps to the alley. In the sudden quiet, they looked at each other.

It was hot and still, and yet Maxie shivered in her un-crushable seersucker traveling dress. This was where she'd seen Lon pay the dead policeman to harass Francine's. Yet tonight the laconic girl had warned Maxie of the raid. Was she switching sides or did she have some darker purpose?

"You were away this weekend." Lon broke the silence.

"Did you stop by for a visit?" Maxie asked. But she wasn't in the mood for their usual exchange of caustic quips. She took out the *Loon Lake Gazette*.

"News about a friend of yours." She handed Lon the story, watching the other girl's reaction closely. There was no mistaking the puzzlement, followed by shock, and then speculation. Maxie wished she could read Lon's thoughts.

"You need to be careful." Lon was dead serious. "You *and* your sorority sisters."

"How can I convince you I've never been to college?" Maxie burst out in exasperation. "Careful of what? Of who?"

"Of this." Lon handed the picture of the drowned man back to Maxie. "Of everyone."

"Can't you be a tiny bit more specific?" the ex-deb begged. "Who's the new power in town who's upsetting the applecart? You don't have to name names, just give me a hint. Maybe some initials. Does the last name end in 'son'?"

"You're not even close," said Lon. "And yet you're so much closer than you realize."

And with that, the enigmatic butch melted away into the night.

*Not this time!* thought Maxie, following her.

# Chapter 22
## Tail Job

Lon had only melted as far as 47th. She was walking down the street with an easy athletic stride. At the corner of 47th and Osage she flagged a cab. Maxie sprinted to the corner and waved frantically. Luck was with her. An empty cab swerved to the curb.

"Follow that cab!" she said, jumping in. It felt nice to be cabbing again—to feel the familiar jerk as the taxi took off, to slide on the worn seat as the cab swerved wildly from lane to lane. *Bus drivers are so staid in comparison,* she thought.

As the cab rocketed toward a red light, Maxie opened her overnight case, thanking her lucky stars she hadn't taken the time to unpack. Off came the seersucker shirtwaist with its too visible red and white stripes, and on went a pair of jeans and a navy sweater. Glancing out the window as she changed her flats for canvas boat shoes, she saw the docks flying by. Ahead were the neon lights of Pingst Street.

*So we're going to the Knock Knock,* Maxie thought. But Lon's cab stopped short of the Lounge, pulling up in front of an establishment called the Café de Paris. Maxie hesitated when Lon got out and strolled inside. Lon's cab stayed put, engine running. Maxie glanced at the meter uneasily and sat tight.

Five minutes later, Lon was out again, walking down the street while the cab trailed her. *Making collections, like a newspaper boy with a route,* Maxie decided, as Lon went into the Gilded Cage.

"You gonna sit here all night, lady?" the cab driver grumbled.

"Maybe." Maxie threw him a fin to keep him quiet. Thank heavens she'd cashed her paycheck before leaving for Loon Lake. She dug out her budget book from her purse, and noted the expenditure.

"Your fellow two-timing you?" asked the driver, his curiosity mixed with sympathy.

"That's right," said Maxie. It still surprised her how easily Lon passed. To Maxie Lon's distinctively female appeal was only too apparent. Were a pair of pants and a short haircut all it took to fool the "normal" members of society? *Are they normal, or just slow-witted?* the jaded girl couldn't help wondering.

Lon was coming out of the Gilded Cage, only to be buttonholed by a fellow in a slick suit, who kept her there, jabbering away. Even the underworld had its Ted Driscolls, Maxie supposed. Finally she was free and headed for the Knock Knock, her pace quickening.

"Pull up, across the street there," Maxie instructed. Lon's stay inside the seedy bar was longer than her other two stops. *Enough time to drink a beer and kiss a few girls,* Maxie thought jealously. When Lon finally emerged, she was smoking a cigarette, and paused to take a last drag before leaning down to toss something inside the cab window. "I think I'll walk." Maxie could hear the words plainly from across the street. The cab pulled away, and Lon strolled in the direction of Little Bohemia.

Maxie looked at the amount on the meter and ground

her teeth. "Here you go." She handed her driver her last ten and tipped him from the change.

"Sometimes it's better not to know," he said as he pulled away.

Maxie followed Lon, staying across the street and a little behind the other girl. The sweater was too warm for the summer night, but in it Maxie disappeared into the darkness. She worried about her overnight case, an expensive leather affair in powder blue. Darting into a corner grocery store, she wangled a paper bag from the puzzled proprietor and placed the overnight case inside. Perfect. Now she was just another beatnik girl, going home with her groceries.

Maxie hurried to catch up with the glimmer that was Lon's white T-shirt a block and a half ahead now. Dodging into doorways, letting Lon's lead lengthen or closing the gap, the ex-deb followed her quarry to a broken-down residential hotel. Lon pushed open the lobby door. Above, a vertical neon sign read SENECA HOTEL. The A flickered erratically.

Maxie watched from across the street and was rewarded when a light on the eighth floor winked on a few minutes later.

A hollow feeling reminded the girl detective that lunch had been a long time ago. She spotted a dinette a few doors down. Taking a table by the window, she ordered eggs and coffee. The little square of light on the eighth floor glowed like a beacon.

Lon was too tight-lipped to tell her who was running the show. But Maxie had a hunch the beautiful butch might lead her to the major players in this underworld shakeup, if Maxie just stayed on her tail. And hadn't Miss Watkins said to follow her hunches?

This was no longer just about a story, Maxie thought, putting eggs in her mouth as she watched the window.

This was about the girls at Francine's and the kids at the Summer Recreational Program. It was maybe about Mumsy.

Pushing her plate away, Maxie lit a cigarette, keeping her eyes pinned on Lon's window. Maybe she should become a private dick. Or was the proper term "private jane"? *Maxie Mainwaring, Private Investigator.* The magazine assistant tried out the title mentally.

"More coffee?"

"Please." Maxie flashed the waitress a smile and eyed her appreciatively as she walked away, shapely legs showing beneath the wrinkled white uniform. A good-looking girl for a dumpy dinette. When she looked back at the hotel, she couldn't remember which window was Lon's. Darn! She'd just keep an eye on the entrance.

She glanced at the waitress, now leaning back against a refrigerated case filled with rotating slices of cream pie. In the glow of the display case, she reminded Maxie a little of Elaine. She had the same dark hair and fragile, baby-deer quality. Maxie had told her mother Elaine wasn't her type, but was that true? What was her type?

Maxie peered through the smudged glass of the dinette window. A figure had emerged from the Seneca's entrance. But the shapeless person shuffling along was too short to be Lon.

She went for rangy redheads and soignée blondes, girls who were buxom and girls who were boyish. Maxie went for all kinds of girls.

Now, Pamela had a definite type. She liked petite brunettes with spunk, like Maxie, Lois—and now June. Her obvious yen for Lois had made Maxie jealous when the budding secretary had arrived at the Arms all those years ago. But Lois had gone for no-nonsense Netta, and Maxie's momentary anxiety had brought her and Pam closer together.

Would she and Pamela reach a better understanding after Maxie told her girlfriend she knew about June?

The ex-deb's mind wandered, as she stared at the entrance to the old hotel, chin on hand. What made a girl limit herself to a hair color or a personality type? What made her limit herself to one girl? For years, Maxie had thought Pamela was it, even as she flirted outrageously with so many others. But if she truly loved Pamela, why had she kissed Elaine and pursued Velma? How could she be attracted to both bad-girl Lon and the hardworking sportswear buyer?

The dinette was closing. Maxie gathered her goods, and, with a last glance at the pretty waitress, moved to an apartment doorway a few doors down. She danced from foot to foot, jittery from coffee and wishing she had more cigarettes. She stared up at the Seneca Hotel, wondering what Lon was doing, and if she was alone.

She'd figured the coffee would keep her up for a week, but a few hours later she was fighting drowsiness. The sweater had stopped being hot—Maxie felt almost cozy, curled in her doorway. Between two and four A.M. there was a spurt of activity that kept her alert—tenants stumbled up the steps and wove through the lobby; guests departed. Then the streets were still again—more still and silent than Maxie had ever seen Bay City.

She yawned, and struggled to keep her drooping eyes open. *I'll think of something stimulating.* Kissing Velma on the point. Kissing Elaine in the powder room. Kissing Lon in the bar near the pawnshop. Lying naked with Pamela in her deliciously cool air-conditioned bedroom. Pamela certainly had an advantage over the rest that way, Maxie thought sleepily. *Is she the one, or is it her air-conditioning?*

Dawn found Maxie dozing in her doorway. The slam

of a car door jerked her awake from a dream of Stella photographing a roomful of girls, all lined up against the wall, their heads turned in profile as if for a mugshot. Maxie wiped a dribble of drool from the corner of her mouth and climbed stiffly to her feet, hoping the dinette had reopened.

At eight forty A.M. she called the office. "Where on earth are you?" demanded Lucille, as if she were an hour late instead of ten minutes. "The work is piled up on your desk! You have a Lovelorn column due today!"

Darn, she'd meant to work on it over the weekend, but she'd spent all her spare time reading Stella's stuff. "I've been held up," Maxie improvised, "family emergency. Tell Hal I'll get there as soon as I can."

"Mr. Hapgood isn't going to be happy," Lucille warned before she hung up. Maxie hardly heard her. Lon was coming out of the Seneca Hotel. She looked more boyish than ever in gray slacks and a navy-blue windbreaker. In one hand she carried a canvas bag.

At last, some action! And Maxie would bet Loon Lake Lodge that Lon was taking the week's payoffs to the big boss!

Lon boarded the bus, and Maxie breathed a sigh of relief—last night's taxi had made a big dent in her pocketbook. Yet a little later she wished Lon *had* grabbed a taxi. Following Lon last night had been easy as pie compared to today, during the morning rush hour. The mob girl unexpectedly jumped off the bus at Herring Drive, and ran across the street to climb aboard the Linden Lane Express, with Maxie chasing breathlessly behind.

*This is silly,* Maxie thought as she squeezed aboard. Now we're heading back the way we just came. She looked at Lon, over the sunglasses she'd slipped on. To Maxie's astonishment, Lon pulled out a compact! She peered into it, turning it slowly from side to side.

*She thinks she's being followed,* Maxie thought. *Has she spotted me?*

She didn't have time to speculate. Lon was on the move again, swinging off the bus, bag in hand, almost before it came to a halt. With Maxie still on her tail, she plunged into Central Station.

Later, Maxie realized how well Lon had timed it. A trainload of hurrying commuters had just disembarked from the Muskrat Local. They came at Maxie like a wave, and the amateur detective was swept away while Lon disappeared in the sea of suits. *She even dressed for camouflage,* Maxie realized, searching the navy-suited crowd. For a split second she thought she saw Lon's blond head, bobbing toward the public restrooms. But when she dashed into the ladies, there was no Lon. The men's room yielded nothing, except red-faced businessmen.

Unwilling to admit she'd lost her quarry, Maxie circled the vast hall, trying to catch the scent. As she worked her way through the oncoming crowd, Maxie realized she wasn't alone. There were other figures, also going against the morning tide. Shadow shapes, who seemed to vanish when she turned to look at them. The follower was herself being followed!

But by whom? Maxie left the terminal and paused at the corner to admire some shoes in a store window. In the reflection, a woman slowed and then strolled past. When Maxie moved on, a man turned away from a newstand.

*Two of them,* Maxie thought. *Time to turn the tables.*

She headed for Grunemans, not bothering to take any more clandestine peeks at her pursuers. She hurried through the strolling shoppers, as if she'd suddenly remembered an engagement. She wanted her pursuers hot on her heels.

She burst into Grunemans, flew up the escalator, and was almost running by the time she reached Ladies' Lingerie. Snatching up a panty girdle, she darted toward the dressing rooms. She ignored the cubicle doors lining the little corridor and opened the one at the end marked PRI-VATE. She and Pamela had once shared a coffee break in this employee cloakroom, with its shelves of pantyhose overstock. Now she peered out the crack.

She didn't have long to wait. A few seconds later, a woman's head poked cautiously around the corner. The girl had covered her dark hair with a silk scarf and her intense eyes with sunglasses. But under the Mata Hari getup Maxie recognized Kitty Coughlin. She felt a wave of annoyance. All this rigamarole only to net a snooping sociologist!

She flung open the door. "Boo!" she said sarcastically.

Her fifth-floor neighbor jumped a foot and whirled around. A wicked-looking gun leaped into her hand. She pointed it at Maxie.

## Chapter 23

## The G-Woman

"In!" Kitty waved her weapon at an empty dressing room, and Maxie obediently backed in. Had she pushed the repressed girl too far? But no—that wasn't the wild-eyed look of a girl who'd gone over the edge, but the cold calculation of a killer.

"You dirty crook!" Maxie said hotly. "You don't dare kill me in Grunemans department store! One shot and you'll be surrounded by salesgirls!"

Kitty's eyes widened. "Don't be ridiculous," she said shortly. She slipped the gun into a shoulder holster concealed by her periwinkle cardigan. "This isn't a hit—I'm with the FBI."

There was a tap at the door. "Are you finding everything all right?" chirped the salesgirl. Maxie opened the door and thrust out the panty girdle. "I need this down a size." When she'd gotten rid of the intruder, she turned back to Kitty.

"First you're a psych student, then a sociologist, now a G-woman. Seems to me like you're heading for an identity crisis, Kitty! What's behind the multiple masquerade?"

The federal agent seated herself on the triangular bench built into one corner of the cubicle. "My name is Kathy

O'Connell," she told Maxie crisply. "I've been undercover for the Bureau since May, as part of Operation Smorgasbord. How do you know Yolanda Laney, aka Lon?"

"I don't really. I just keep running into her around town," Maxie admitted. "What's Operation Smorgasbord?"

"It's a probe into mob activity here in Bay City. Why were you following Lon this morning?"

"I wasn't following her." Maxie decided to deny everything.

"My partner and I saw you transfer buses when she did. And you followed her into the terminal."

"Why were you following her?" Maxie asked.

"I'll ask the questions!" the agent said sharply. "Where were you last night? Why didn't you return to the Arms?"

Maxie rolled her eyes. "Really, Kitty! You've lived next door to me long enough to know that there's nothing unusual about me staying out all night!"

Kitty, or rather Kathy, blushed. "Please cooperate, Maxie. This is government business."

"I will if you tell me what's going on, and why you have two false identities instead of one!"

Kathy unbent a trifle. "It's a technique I invented called the double blind," she explained with a touch of pride. "If someone got suspicious of the student story, I had the sociologist to fall back on."

It was clever, Maxie admitted. It had worked on her. "But why are you interested in the Magdalena Arms? There are no mobsters there—just a bunch of hardworking career girls!"

"We're interested in Francine's," Kathy told her. "There's a new mob in town, taking over the extortion rackets. Everywhere else the transition has been smooth—no one on Pingst Street has made a peep. But they hit a rough patch with Francine Flicka. She even went to the police—"

"The police are in their pay!" Maxie cried. "Look at this—" She brought out her battered copy of the *Loon Lake Gazette*. "I saw this officer accepting a payoff after raiding Francine's, with my own eyes."

"Did you see who made the payoff?" Kathy questioned.

"I—it was dark in the alley," said Maxie weakly. She wasn't ready to finger Lon until she found out what the attractive butch was up to.

Kathy's intense green eyes bored into the guilty girl. "The mob is a cancer, feeding off healthy American society," she said forcefully. "And we're going to cut it out, even if it means taking normal cells with it!" Fire flashed in her eyes.

*Does she mean me?* Maxie wondered. *Am I a normal cell?*

"We've been tracking the gangs of Bay City for quite a while. People believe there will always be criminals to cater to society's illicit vices, but they don't realize how deeply entrenched the mob is in every strata of Bay City life. It started with the great Scandinavian immigration of the last century. Sure, most of the immigrants were ordinary folk, looking for a better life, a place to practice their traditional crafts making simple furniture and cheerful, brightly colored textiles. But criminal elements came over as well. The Larsens, the Olssens, the Swensons— Bay City's top three crime families all got their start back then."

Maxie listened, fascinated. This was not the kind of history the Daughters of the American Pioneers highlighted in their living picture pageants!

"The Larsens quickly dominated gambling." The G-woman ticked the three families off on her fingers. "The Olssens made money manufacturing *glögg* in illegal stills in the North Woods. The Swensons were specialists

in the shakedown—collecting protection money from ignorant immigrants and selling them 'services' they were
actually entitled to. After the war they extended their activities to the docks, offering 'protection' from their own
thieves! But they've grown weak since Bill 'the Big Swede'
Swenson died. The hit on his son Sven is just one sign
someone new is taking over the Swenson family's opera-
tions—the question is, who?"

The crime fighter ran a hand through her hair in frustration. "It was hard enough getting a handle on the current clans with their secretive ways and the confusing
alternate spellings—Olsen, Olson, Olsson, and even Olsin!"
She illustrated by spelling the names on the dressing-
room mirror with her lipstick. "But whoever the new
boss in town is, he's protected himself so well we don't
even know his name. We've been on the case for months
without getting a lead. We don't even know if he's Swe-
dish, or Norwegian, or something else entirely!"

Maxie wondered if criminology might be her true calling. Hadn't Miss Watkins mentioned that as a possible
penchant? She could listen to Kathy explain the intrica-
cies of Bay City's underworld all day.

"But you still haven't said why you were following me
this morning," she recalled. "After all"—she smiled—
"I'm not connected to any of these crime families."

"Actually you are," Kathy told her tersely. "Mainwaring is an anglicization of Mänvaarik, isn't it?"

"Well, sure," said Maxie. "We've never hidden our Finnish roots! But that doesn't mean we're criminals. You said
yourself that the majority of immigrants were honest."

"Your great-grandfather, Markus Mänvaarik, had ties
to both the Olssens and the Larsens," Kathy told her.
"Gambling was popular among the logging crews, and
the rumor is he got a kickback from the games of Gurka
that were played in his camps. And he actively protected

the production of illegal *glögg*. In fact, he purchased the land around Loon Lake with money borrowed from the Olssens."

"Those were frontier days," protested Maxie. "He probably needed the *glögg* to pacify the Indians or something. You can't hold Great-grandpa to modern-day standards."

"We have to look at all the angles," Kathy retorted. Inadvertently her eyes flickered over Maxie's figure, and she busied herself, wiping the lipstick writing off the mirror.

Maxie pounced on the G-woman's weak spot.

"Student, sociologist, or agent, I'm still wondering: Which side of the Sapphic fence do you fall on?"

"I'm at Francine's strictly on business," Kathy said stiffly.

"Is it all business and no play?" Maxie murmured. "You know, you're like an onion. I keep peeling away layers, but I'm not sure I've gotten to the core." She watched the flush that rose from Kathy's Peter Pan collar and stained her scarlet.

"Onions can sting," the G-woman warned through trembling lips.

"Peeling this one hasn't made me cry," purred Maxie. She reached forward and fingered the handle of the gun under Kathy's armpit. "Would you really have used this on me?"

Kathy flinched and grabbed Maxie's hand. "That's government property. I know all about you and your madcap ways, Maxie Mainwaring—I've read your file. But this time, you're playing with fire!"

"I'm a Campfire Girl from way back," Maxie assured her. "I know how to stoke the flames and put them out."

Kathy's breath was coming in short bursts and her eyes were shooting sparks.

*I really shouldn't,* Maxie thought, as she'd thought a

hundred times before, leaning toward Kathy, whose lips were already parted in anticipation. But the stormy eyes and willing lips bespoke a conflict Maxie simply had to help resolve.

She was so close the G-woman's warm breath fanned Maxie's face, and still the courageous crime fighter didn't shrink away. Maxie's lips brushed Kathy's and . . .

"I have your panty girdle," the salesgirl said as she knocked. Kathy jerked away. "I brought a couple sizes so you'd be sure of finding the right one."

Maxie bit her lips in frustration. Damn Grunemans and their personal service policy! "Just leave it on the doorknob," she called.

Kathy was on her feet before the salesgirl's footsteps had trailed away. "I'll leave first," she told Maxie. "You follow after a few minutes. It's better if we're not seen together."

"You've done this before, haven't you?" Maxie couldn't resist taunting.

"Keep what I've told you to yourself," Kathy ordered, ignoring Maxie's jab. "Or I'll have you taken into cusody for your own protection."

"You sure know how to turn on the charm," muttered Maxie. After Kathy was gone, she sat thinking.

*If they're so interested in Lon,* she wondered, *why do they have a file on me?*

# Chapter 24

## Lounge Lizard Lothario

After a refreshing facial at Countess Elfi's and another cup of coffee, Maxie headed to the magazine's offices, feeling virtuous. Her sleepless night and heart-stopping morning certainly entitled her to a sick day, but her Lovelorn column *was* due, and Maxie was putting *Polish* first.

She felt a little guilty for not telling her gang-busting neighbor everything she knew, but then Kitty/Kathy hadn't been completely candid either. First there was that file; and then, the more Maxie thought about it, the more she realized Kathy wouldn't have had much time to investigate Francine's, the way she'd kept popping up wherever Maxie went that summer. Why had the crime fighter lingered in the lounge, watching Maxie and Dolly play Ping-Pong, while this new mob took over Swenson's extortion rackets? Did Kathy really think Great-grandpa Mainwaring's mob connections had somehow been handed down to Maxie's generation?

"Hal's furious!" Lucille told Maxie the minute she spotted the tardy girl. "He said he wanted to see you as soon as you came in!" Her fellow assistant hovered nervously as Maxie tried to smooth the wrinkles out of the uncrush-

able seersucker, whose wrinkle-free reputation was unde-
served.

"Well, look what the cat dragged in!" was Hal's acid
greeting when she entered his office, still swatting at her
skirt ineffectually.

"I'm sorry, Hal—"

"You're skating on very thin ice, young lady. *Polish* is
not a debutante dance you can waltz in and out of de-
pending on your mood. I won't tolerate any more ab-
sences or tardiness! One second after eight thirty A.M.,
and you're out!

Maxie winced. She'd hoped Hal hadn't noticed what a
hard time she'd had adjusting to the early hours. She
racked her fatigue-fogged brain for an excuse that would
appease her wrathful boss, but came up empty. "It won't
happen again," was the best she could do.

"Cross your heart and hope to die?" Maxie flinched at
her boss's unsuspected sarcastic side. "Start with a pot of
coffee. Then I want to look at your latest Lovelorn column. Larry Lathrop got in last night, and he'll be here
any minute."

"Larry Lathrop—here?" Maxie squeaked. "I thought
he wasn't coming until next week!" She had picked a few
letters to feature, but she hadn't even roughed out a response!

"I guess he forgot to call you and consult." Maxie
winced again. "Do me a favor and don't go all bobby-
soxer. Try to make a better impression on him than you
have on me."

Maxie returned to her desk and pulled out the Lovelorn folder. *The answers never take very long,* she told
herself. The only problem was her typing. Maybe Lucille
would help her out. She looked across the room hopefully, but the competent assistant was thin-lipped with
disapproval.

"People have been calling you all morning," She picked up a sheaf of message slips. "Stella McSweeney—personal. Pamela Prendergast—no message. Doris Watkins—urgent." She dropped them on Maxie's desk with a sniff. "Just in case you forgot, I'm Mr. Hapgood's assistant, not yours!"

Maybe Larry wouldn't mind reading her handwriting, Maxie thought. Oops! She jumped up from her desk. Coffee! She'd almost forgotten, and she needed it more than Hal.

She dashed to the little kitchen and set the coffee brewing, heaping in extra grounds for additional oomph. Sneaking into an empty office, where Lucille wouldn't overhear her making personal calls, Maxie dialed Pamela.

"Where have you been?" Pamela burst out. "We had a date last night! I've been worried sick!"

Maxie framed last night's adventure in a way her career-minded girlfriend could comprehend. "I had a lead on a story for *Polish,*" she explained. "Literally!"

"Couldn't you have at least called?"

"Pamela, I can't explain right now—I'm up to my ankles in hot water here at work, and if someone hears me making private calls, I'll be sunk. 'Bye!"

She glanced at one of the questions she had picked. *My husband is gone all day, and I feel so isolated and alone in our house with just a one-year-old who can't even speak the English language. I know I ought to be happy, but I'm not. What can I do to change my attitude?*

*Hobbies can help,* Maxie began. Why had she stuck in one of the depressed housewife letters this week? They were always hard.

She put her pencil down and dialed Miss Watkins.

"Maxie—I'm terribly sorry to disturb you at work"—Miss Watkins sounded breathless with excitement—"but

Mrs. Spindle-Janska is here on a flying visit and she wants to speak to you—may I put her on?"

"I guess so." Maxie scribbled, *Friends—clubs—join a church group.*

"Maxie Mainwaring, at last! This is Mrs. Spindle-Janska." A rich mezzo-soprano voice filled her ears, and at once Maxie felt calmer. It was a voice that promised to heal old wounds, soothe away minor irritations, and open up broader vistas. "Permit me to skip the polite preliminaries. I know from studying your PPA that such niceties are not necessary with you. Tell me, have you been experiencing difficulty arriving at your office at the appointed hour?"

"Why, yes!" Maxie was flabbergasted at the career guru's prescience.

"Midnight for some is noon for others," Mrs. Spindle-Janska remarked. Her voice alone made Maxie feel so much better she didn't even try to guess what the intuitive woman meant.

"Truth to tell, I'm in trouble about it today," Maxie admitted.

"Ah." Even the monosyllable was expressive, redolent of wisdom. "I want very much to meet you, Maxie. Until that time, remember this: Some birds nest in trees, while others cling to the sides of cliffs, and still others seek out decaying logs on the forest floor. Do we condemn some and praise others?"

"I guess not," said Maxie. "I know more about bugs than birds."

"How interesting." Mrs. Spindle-Janska's melodious voice faded away and was replaced by Miss Watkins, who wanted to schedule an appointment for that very afternoon.

"I'm afraid that's impossible," began Maxie, feeling more harried than ever. An ominous, sizzling sound pen-

etrated her consciousness. "Miss Watkins, I have to go—
the coffee's overflowing!"

Hanging up the phone, Maxie rushed to the kitchen. In
her eagerness for extra energy she'd added too much coffee. The grounds had overflowed into the pot. She peered
at the sludge in despair. If she could filter it somehow—

Lucille found her five minutes later, trying to strain the
coffee through a dishcloth. "This is no time for chemistry
experiments," she hissed. "Larry Lathrop is here, and
Hal wants his coffee!"

Snatching the pot from Maxie, she poured a cup and
added cream and sugar.

"No, don't—" Maxie tried to warn her, but Lucille
yanked her along and they arrived at the outer office an
instant before Larry and Hal entered, laughing heartily.

Maxie gazed at the famous profile. Even Technicolor
had never done the crooner's deep tan justice. Larry
Lathrop's skin had the patina of an old suitcase. Automatically she extended a hand as Hal introduced her to
the teen idol. Larry took it, and the next thing Maxie
knew, she was cuddled uncomfortably in the crook of the
crooner's arm.

"So you're the little girl who makes me look so smart!"
He turned to Hal. "And she's gorgeous too! Hal, you old
son of a gun, how do you get any work done with all
these distracting females around?"

"We're the ones doing all the work," said Maxie, wrig-
gling out of Larry's embrace. She had to keep Hal away
from the cup of coffee Lucille was holding!

Larry laughed again. "Well, I'm here to learn how it's
done. Where can we roll up our sleeves and get down to
business?"

"You can use the conference room, Larry," said Hal.
"Maxie will show you the latest column." Maxie watched
helplessly as Lucille handed him the horrible brew.

Maxie led Larry to the conference room, wondering what form Hal's wrath would take. "I hope you can read my handwriting, Mr. Lathrop," she said, putting the Lovelorn file on the table.

"Call me Larry," said the leathery-skinned crooner. "No need to be in such a hurry—let's get acquainted first."

Just as Larry attempted to embrace the exhausted assistant, Maxie heard the distant cry of rage that meant Hal had tasted the tainted coffee. Perhaps it was the sudden sound that lent extra energy to her rebuff of the singer's amorous overture. In any event, Maxie's firm push turned into a powerful punch that sent the star reeling. "I'm not that kind of girl," she started to say primly, then changed it to, "You're dripping blood all over your shirt!"

Larry whipped out a handkerchief and held it to his gushing nose. "I think you broke it, you boob!" he howled.

Hal appeared in the door, glowering, with a white-faced Lucille right behind him. At the sight of the injured teen idol, he, too, turned pale.

"You—broke—Larry Lathrop's—nose?" Hal looked from Larry to Maxie, his horror at the destruction of Larry's classic profile writ large on his face. He pointed a finger at the door. "Out!"

# Chapter 25
## Breakup!

Maxie left the *Polish* building scarcely an hour after she'd arrived, carrying a cardboard box of odds and ends from her desk in addition to her overnight case. She really should have gone back to the Arms and to bed, Maxie reflected as she waved down a cab. Her effort to be a model employee hadn't been rewarded!

Maxie leaned against the seat with a sigh. Was it lack of sleep that made her feel so indifferent to her lost livelihood? Or did this odd sense of relief mean that magazine publishing wasn't her field? She had enjoyed being Hal's assistant, but it took so much time, and she had so many other interests she wanted to pursue! Besides, she preferred not to be pawed. If that was part of working at *Polish,* someone else was welcome to it!

She looked out the window as the office buildings of downtown Bay City flashed by. Where would she work next? Maxie realized all at once that it wasn't the indifference of exhaustion but a certain self-confidence that kept her from taking this latest job loss so hard. She knew now she could support herself. There were plenty more jobs out there for her to land and lose.

She heard again Mrs. Spindle-Janska's soothing, hypnotic voice that said without words that there was no need to worry. Phantasms of jobs beckoned the tired girl in infinite variety. Maybe Kathy could find her a position in law enforcement, once she straightened out the business about her FBI file. Or why not public relations? It was unfortunate Larry Lathrop wouldn't hire her, because Maxie knew just how to spin that broken nose. Or why not use her family connections and manage the milk production at Sunshine Dairy? She certainly preferred giving orders to taking them. She could find and fire that thug who'd threatened her!

*I'm getting loopy with lack of sleep,* Maxie decided as her thoughts meandered to the art of milking cows and whether it would be a valuable skill to have. She overtipped the driver, hoisted her belongings, and headed toward the elevator, which had finally been fixed.

"Have you seen Kath—Kitty?" she asked her downstairs neighbor Kay, who was coming out of the lounge.

"She went out a little while ago," Kay reported. "Said she was going to the library."

*Library, ha!* thought Maxie as she pressed the button for the elevator.

The fifth floor was deserted, and Maxie shed her thoroughly crushed seersucker shirtwaist and ran herself a bath. It was nice to be home in the middle of the afternoon and have the shared bathroom to herself.

*A night job would be nice,* she thought, as she wiped the steam off the mirror and combed her hair. *A schedule that lets me sleep in.*

Back in her room, Maxie lay down and closed her eyes. It was almost worth it, the long night, the coffee disaster, breaking Larry's nose and losing her job, for the ineffable sense of well-being that stole over her as she finally relaxed and put her cares aside. The late afternoon sun slanted in the windows, and drowsiness crept over her like a big eiderdown being gently pulled up and tucked under her chin. Maxie slept.

She had no idea how much time had passed when her eyes opened. Someone was sobbing somewhere, heart-rending sobs. There was a jumbled buzz of voices—comforting, remonstrative—but the sobbing kept on. Maxie sat up in bed. Footsteps hurried by outside her door. She threw off her covers and got up. When she opened the door, she saw Dolly and Janet huddled in Lois's doorway across the hall.

"What's going on?" she asked anxiously. "Did something happen to Netta?"

"She sent Lois a telegram telling her not to come," Janet turned to report. "Netta says she's found someone new!"

Maxie reeled back in shock. "Not Netta!"

Lois and Netta had been the model of domesticity for five years, and Netta herself had always been so upright and honorable that Maxie had sometimes found her uncomfortable company. There must be some mistake.

Maxie crossed the hall. Inside the room Lois was sitting on the side of her bed, shoulders bowed and shaking. Phyllis sat next to her, patting her hand, and Pamela was kneeling at her feet. "There, there," said Phyllis helplessly, while Pamela begged, "Don't take on so!"

"I was just—checking off—my—trip-to-do list!" sobbed Lois.

"Netta's no good!" Pamela looked like she wanted to wring the absent school-teacher's neck.

"Don't say that!" contradicted Lois. Maxie could have told the misguided sportswear buyer that it was too soon to start excoriating the ex.

"No one who would leave you in the lurch like this is worth your tears!"

Maxie made her way through the crowd. "Lois, I'm awfully sorry!"

She nudged Phyllis, who surrendered her place with an expression of relief. Maxie sat down. "What happened? What did Netta say?" She looked over Lois's shoulder at Dolly in the doorway and mouthed, *whiskey*. Dolly nodded and disappeared.

"Just this," sobbed Lois, handing Maxie a crumpled piece of paper. Maxie smoothed out the telegram.

VACATION OFF STOP NO REASON TO COME STOP THERE'S SOMEONE ELSE STOP SINCERELY SORRY STOP NETTA

"She doesn't offer much of an explanation, does she?" Maxie took the tumbler from Dolly and urged Lois to take a sip. The office manager's sobs turned to sputters.

Phyllis pointed out, "Maybe Netta didn't have the money to pay for a longer message. She did say 'sincerely,' though—and that's not strictly necessary."

"This is not the time to pinch pennies!" Maxie declared. She turned back to her snuffling friend. "Lois, you have to call Netta and make her explain this cryptic message!"

"I don't have a number for her!" Lois wailed.

"When has the lack of a phone number stopped you?" Maxie scolded, giving Lois a gentle shake. "If your boss, Mrs. Pierson, wanted to talk to Netta, you'd find a way!"

"I could call the Progressive School Alliance," Lois said in a watery voice. "Or I'd try the training center they stopped at on the way south." She wiped her eyes. "If all else fails, I have a friend at the phone company. . . ." She stood up. "Maybe this is all a misunderstanding!"

"Don't forget to make it person-to-person," Phyllis reminded the jilted girl as she hurried downstairs to the phone.

"That should keep her distracted for a little while," Maxie said.

"Good work, Maxie," Janet approved.

"I'm afraid she's fooling herself with the idea that this is all a misunderstanding," Pamela said soberly. "She's in for some sorrow."

Maxie yawned. "We'll help her through it."

Pamela seemed to really see her girlfriend for the first time. "What are you doing in your nightgown?"

"I was taking a nap," Maxie hedged. She crossed the hall and climbed back into bed. Pamela followed her. Maxie wished she would go away and let her sleep. She just wasn't in the mood for Pamela's comments on her latest job woes or her girlfriend's patented mix of sympathy and scolding.

"You changed into your nightgown to take a nap?" persisted Pamela.

Maxie decided she might as well get it over with. "The truth is, I was fired—"

"Oh, Maxie!" Pamela's mournful tone turned Maxie's name into a dirge.

Maxie held up a hand. "It wasn't my fault! Larry Lathrop made a pass at me, and I punched him in the nose." She couldn't help giggling as she remembered Larry's shock.

"Oh, Maxie!" Pamela repeated, this time with indignation. "That tone-deaf lech! I wish he had two noses, so I could break the other one!"

Maxie made a clean breast of it, while Pamela was feeling wrathful on her behalf. "Hal wasn't happy with my attendance record. I didn't realize he'd be keeping track like some schoolteacher! What difference does it make, anyway, so long as you get your work done?"

Maxie remembered her unfinished Lovelorn column. *Well, I would have finished it, if I hadn't been thrown out,* she told herself.

"Of course it isn't fair you were fired—but this does prove my point about punctuality!" Pamela was struggling to keep her disapproval out of her voice, Maxie could tell. The ex-magazine assistant lay back in bed.

"And then there was the coffee," she continued, suddenly not caring what Pamela thought. "I was trying to strain it when Lucille came in—" Laughter bubbled up again as she remembered the expression on Lucille's face.

"Can't you be serious?" Pamela demanded. "Unemployment is no joke!"

"Well, crying into my pillow's hardly going to help," objected Maxie. Pamela was pursuing her own train of thought.

"What you never seem to understand is that a girl in business has to be perfection plus if she wants to get ahead. Otherwise they pass you over for promotion. Look at Lois—"

"You look at Lois," interrupted Maxie rudely. She didn't want to be perfection plus, and she was tired of pussyfooting around Pamela to avoid offending her persnickety girlfriend. In fact, she was itching for a fight! She sat up in bed. "Or would you rather look at June?"

Pamela drew back. "What's that supposed to mean?"

Maxie quoted from Stella's roman à clef. 'The affair between the lanky redhead and the pert brunette started in December, and burned with the warmth of a Christmas candle.' That would be you and June last year, wouldn't it?"

Pamela colored. "I suppose Stella has been gossiping. Listen, I'm sorry. It was Christmas, and you were in Acapulco. Weren't we broken up, anyway?"

The cavalier attitude made Maxie even madder. "Gee,

now I feel all better!" she said sarcastically. "Can't you even pretend to feel regret? At least I made an effort to sound sincere in similar circumstances!"

"You want credit for *sounding* sincere?" Pamela was incredulous. "You've been playing at love for so long you don't even know what it means to be serious!"

"I can't believe *you* are criticizing *me,* when *you're* the one who's in the wrong!" sputtered Maxie. "You can't keep pretending to be a paragon of perfection when I know all about your heavy petting with Louise and your pass at Sally, I mean Stella!"

And then the two girls were going at each other, tooth and nail. The restraints were down; the efforts to make allowances were over. Pamela and Maxie unleashed all the pent-up resentments, grudges, and petty irritations of the past weeks in a torrent of insults.

Pamela told Maxie she was and would always be a lazy rich girl with lax morals, and illustrated with a cutting comment about the careless way she washed dishes. Maxie called Pamela a narrow-minded party pooper who didn't know how to have fun and hogged all the covers. Pamela said she was sick of hearing Maxie chatter about a new career every week, and that she'd been right in the first place—Maxie had no stick-to-it-iveness. Maxie said spending so much time with Pamela had made her feel as stifled as if she'd been buried alive. Pamela snorted that "stifled" was a good one, since she'd known all along that Maxie had only renewed the relationship because Pamela's apartment had air-conditioning—which proved her point that Maxie was unethical, amoral, and probably unstable.

"You've ruined my nap, but you aren't going to ruin my life!" Maxie shouted. "I won't let myself be limited by your provincial principles! We're through!"

"That goes double!" Pamela retorted. "I don't know why I've put up with your temper and tantrums all this time! I should have given you the heave-ho years ago!"

"It wouldn't have been soon enough. . . ." The words echoed in the empty room. Pamela had slammed out. In the sudden stillness Maxie could hear her own pulse pounding in her ears, like surf beating the shore. She unclenched her fists, wishing the blowout had taken place at Pamela's. Then *she* could have had the last word before storming out!

She certainly wasn't sleepy anymore. Maxie shed her nightgown and pulled on a pair of scarlet slacks and an off-the-shoulder, ruffled blouse. She felt as reckless as a sailor landing on shore. The ties that bound her to Pamela were broken, and other girls were fair game!

She picked up her purse and flung open the door. Janet, Dolly, and Phyllis all jumped. Maxie realized that they must have heard every word. Neither she nor Pamela had bothered to lower their voices.

"Pamela seemed in an awful hurry when she left," Janet began diplomatically.

"We're through." As she repeated the words she'd hurled at Pamela in anger, Maxie realized they were true. She felt a little dizzy at the idea. "This time for real."

"Are you sure?" asked Phyllis. "You've been together so long—and broken up so often—"

"We were like oil and vinegar," said Maxie. "We tried to emulsify ourselves into some kind of salad dressing, but we never really mixed. And now we both know it."

Her friends were silent. There was nothing more to be said.

But as she was hurrying down the stairs Janet caught up with her. "Just a moment, Maxie."

Maxie turned impatiently. "What?" She didn't want any advice just then about not doing anything impulsive.

"I want to talk to you—about the Nyberg Trust."

Maxie slowed down. "Oh, you don't have to worry about that anymore," she assured Janet as they descended the stairs together. "Your plan worked. Mumsy got the windup about Great-aunt Alta's illness being exposed, and she's going to give me my allowance again. You can drop the legal stuff."

"I think she might have got the windup about more than Aunt Alta," Janet told the heiress. "I've heard some alarming rumors that your trust's portfolio has been shifted from bonds to riskier investments. I don't like it— I can't help wondering what your mother is up to!"

Maxie's first instinct was to dismiss Janet's worries, but with all she'd learned lately it seemed plausible that her mother might be wreaking havoc with the trust port-folio for some nefarious purpose. On the other hand, she needed that allowance just now.

"Can you try to find out a little more, on the q.t.?" she suggested. "You know, not serving subpoenas or calling for points of order, or whatever it is you usually do?"

"I'll try," Janet promised dubiously.

Lois was hanging up the phone as Janet and Maxie de-scended the last flight of stairs. "Any luck?" asked Maxie.

"I put in a person-to-person call," said Lois forlornly. "The operator will ring me as soon as she reaches Netta." She put her hand on Maxie's arm. "I saw Pamela leave in a terrible huff—have you two quarreled again?"

"We're kaput. Over. Finished. Beyond resuscitation. Now stop," she said as Lois's brown eyes filled with tears. "Don't shed any tears over *that* romance, Lo. It was never true love, and lately, even the chemistry's started to fizzle."

"You're wrong, Maxie, you and Pamela are so right for each other!" Lois started to sob. She was the only one left who still believed that the off switch on Pamela and Maxie's romance might be flipped back to on. "The chemistry is still there!

"Maybe," Maxie conceded. "But there are lots more elements on the periodic table, and it's time for me to try some new combinations!"

# Chapter 26

# An Old Friend

Maxie entered the Knock Knock eagerly, looking for Lon. The bar was busy, in spite of it being a Monday, but she didn't see the blond butch. The bartender gave Maxie a nod of recognition, and Maxie slid on a barstool and ordered a beer. "Lon been by?" She made the inquiry casual.

As the bartender shook her head, one of the barflies said, "Lon's pretty popular. Every cutie-pie who walks in wants to know where she is." The woman leered at Maxie. "I'm right here, sweetheart—how about giving me a chance?"

"No, thank you," said Maxie politely but firmly.

"Go ahead, give her a tumble." Maxie turned at the new voice. It belonged to a striking-looking girl, staring into a tumbler of whiskey, at a table by herself. She was buxom and tall, her height increased by her beehive. "It's no use waiting for Lon," she said, still addressing her drink, "college girl!" On the last two words she looked up sharply, her black eyes glinting with spite as she stared at Maxie.

"I've never been to college," Maxie said. A little thrill went through her. Had Lon spoken of her to this strange girl? It was nice to think she'd been on Lon's mind. She swiveled around to fully face her jealous rival. "And I don't need to wait for Lon. I know where she lives."

The girl jumped to her feet, and her chair tumbled over behind her. "That's a lie," she spat. "Nobody knows where Lon lives!"

The barfly put a restraining hand on Maxie's arm. "You don't want to tangle with Tanya," she whispered. "Not when she's this tight!"

Maxie felt a little excited at the prospect of one of the Knock Knock's famous barroom brawls. "I think I can take her." She stared steadily at the black-haired vixen. "I've already wiped the floor once today with someone who crossed me."

Without warning, Tanya leaped at her, red-painted fingernails ready to claw Maxie's face. But Maxie slid off the stool and flung it in front of her. Tanya's torso met the obstacle and she folded over it, gasping "Ooof!" With a curse, she recovered and kicked it aside.

The two girls circled each other, as an audience gathered. "See, this is why the Knock Knock doesn't need a TV," Maxie heard one customer tell another.

Tanya lunged again and Maxie sidestepped. Then the ex-deb feinted right. As Tanya dodged, Maxie landed her left, a blow that caught the tousled temptress in the ribs. Tanya gasped again, and before she could recover, Maxie coiled her hand in Tanya's towering beehive and twirled her rapidly. At the last minute, Maxie let go, and momentum carried Tanya into a collision with the bar. Tanya staggered and fell, clutching her upper arm.

"You brute!" The leering barfly who had offered Maxie a drink glared at her before helping Tanya up tenderly. "Pick on someone your own size!"

The bartender clapped her hands. "Okay, ladies, show's over!"

Tanya's new friend supported her out of the bar, and the crowd dispersed. All except a plump woman in a crisp new pair of ill-fitting dungarees.

"Maxie Mainwaring, as I live and breathe!" she exclaimed with unfeigned pleasure. "Tell me—confidentially and off the record—where did you learn to handle yourself in a fight?"

"Mamie!" Maxie hugged her old mentor. "It's good to see you! But what are *you* doing *here?*"

"Ever since you abandoned me, I've had to do my own legwork." In unspoken agreement Maxie and her old boss sat down at the table Tanya had vacated. Mamie sighed in relief. "And I'm not as fit as you. Truthfully, Maxie, I never dreamed you had such a wicked left!" She reached out and felt Maxie's upper arm. "What muscle!"

"I learned a few things from playground scraps," Maxie said modestly, thinking of her disadvantaged youths. She noticed the gleam in Mamie's eye and warned her, "Now, Mamie, I don't want to see any items in tomorrow's column on two-fisted debutantes."

"Maxie, really." Mamie tried to look hurt.

"I'm serious, Mamie—I'll sue. I can produce half-a-dozen witnesses who will be happy to say I spent this evening at the Magdalena Arms, playing Ping-Pong."

Mamie couldn't help herself, Maxie knew. Let fall a piece of gossip, and she would snatch it up the way a dog does a scrap of meat. You couldn't blame the animal for following its instincts, but you didn't leave it alone in the kitchen.

Mamie's face fell. "Maxie, give me something," the columnist begged. "I've been on my feet all evening and I've got bubkes for tomorrow."

"Well . . ." An idea dawned in Maxie's head. "I do have something hot. But it'll cost you."

"Feed me a taste."

"We're talking about Larry Lathrop."

Mamie brightened. "Is he in town? Larry's always good for gossip. What is it—pregnant bobby-soxer? Did he bean someone with a bottle again? Even just an engagement—"

Maxie rubbed her thumb and forefinger together, and Mamie took the hint and put a ten-dollar bill on the table.

"It's not something he did, it's what happened to him," she explained as she picked up the money. "That famous profile of his is in the past. Larry poked his nose into the wrong place and it got busted." She held up the ten. "Another one of these gets you the details."

A delighted smile spread over Mamie's face. "When, where, and who?" she asked, getting out her wallet.

Maxie filled her in, leaving the offices of *Polish* unnamed, and describing herself as "an ordinary office worker who was horrified by Larry's uninvited advances."

"You always did get the good stuff," said Mamie scribbling rapidly. "How about coming back to work for me? At a raise in salary, of course!"

Maxie was tempted, but she temporized, "Let's keep this strictly on a per-item basis, huh? At least for now. I've got some other things cooking."

"Fair enough." Mamie put her notebook away. "I'll always pay top dollar for any juicy tip you have. And here's a tip from me to you, for free: If you can get a picture of Larry with his bandaged nose, *Idol Gossip* will pay you more than you'd make from me in a month."

"Thanks, Mamie!" Maxie knew it hadn't been a mistake making up with the savvy journalist. She remembered to ask her old boss about possible publishers for Stella.

"Try Mount Olympus Editions; tell George I sent you. Do the characters suffer enough? George is a stickler for suffering. He thinks it'll keep the censors off his back. I had to bury a couple of my girls in an avalanche at the end of *Boarding School Hussies*."

Maxie wondered how Stella would feel about putting the girls at Homophile Handbooks through similar trials. As far as Maxie could remember, aside from some jealousy and heartache, Sally and her friends had emerged at the end of the book pretty unscathed.

"I'm off." Mamie heaved herself to her feet. "A few more stops on Pingst Street, and then home to beddy-bye."

"You never did tell me what brought you to the Knock Knock," Maxie remembered.

"The mob shakeup. There's a rumor circulating I wanted to check."

"I thought your editor put the kibosh on crime stories."

"But scandal always sells," Mamie reminded her. "Rumor has it that the underworld's newest kingpin is a queenpin—and nothing's more scandalous than a girl with a gun!"

Maxie pondered this last tidbit after Mamie left. Lon *must* be mixed up in the new gang. But why had she come to Francine's to warn the ex-deb the other night, if her employers were trying to force Francine Flicka to fork over protection money?

*Does she have a soft spot for me?*

There was a little stir in the air, like a ripple in a still pond when a fish sucks a waterbug under. The hairs on the back of Maxie's neck lifted, and she turned, knowing exactly what she'd see: Lon, standing at the bar, and surveying the place as if she owned it. Lon looked over as Maxie looked up, and their gazes met and locked. The force of Maxie's desire bludgeoned her like a police baton. Lon moved toward her, sauntering in what seemed to the bewitched ex-deb to be slow motion. She slid into the seat across from Maxie.

"I've been looking for you," Lon said.

"I've been looking for you," breathed Maxie.

Lon looked at her some more. "Now we've found each other, what do we do?" Her blue gaze was like the neon in Francine's sign, promising fun, troubles forgotten, new friends. It was hard for Maxie to breathe.

"Find someplace private," she said boldly.

# Chapter 27

## Lon

L on unlocked the door and opened it. Reaching in, she switched on the light, then stood aside, waving Maxie in first with a mocking half bow. Maxie looked around the small room, lit by the bare bulb. Was this how mobsters lived? In anonymous rooms with stained ceilings? There was a sink in the corner, a bed, and a bureau. Instead of a closet there was an old armoire.

Lon hadn't wanted to come here. When Maxie suggested they go to Lon's place, she told the ex-deb point blank that she didn't like people to know where she lived. She liked it less when Maxie told her she already knew, and proved it.

"Did you just move in?" asked Maxie. There was nothing that marked the room as Lon's except a couple of books on the floor and a single postcard stuck in the frame of the bureau mirror.

"I travel light," said Lon. She shut the door behind them and moved toward Maxie purposefully, switching off the dim bulb. "You've seen enough."

Instinctively Maxie backed up until her heel hit the baseboard. With the lights off, the room was alive with green and violet shadows from the Seneca's neon sign.

Lon's eyes were pools of darkness, and a chartreuse streak on her cheek gave her the allure of a portrait by Matisse. Was the mob girl going to murder her, or make out? Madcap Maxie found the uncertainty exciting.

She slipped sideways, eluding Lon's grasp. The two circled each other like gladiators, looking for a weak spot in each other's defenses. As Maxie edged along the armoire, Lon pounced and pushed her up against the wall between the old wardrobe and the bureau. "There isn't anywhere to run," she said, before pulling the aroused girl against her. Her lips located Maxie's most vulnerable spots, and Maxie found herself trapped and tormented by Lon's talented tongue. When the thrill-seeking ex-deb could bear it no longer, she wrenched down the hand that Lon had pinned against the wall, and used it to twist Lon's arm behind the startled girl. She whirled her around until Lon was wedged against the bureau. Now the tables were turned, and Maxie took her time, making the other girl writhe and squirm with helpless pleasure.

The tiny room became a battlefield, each girl aiming for ascendancy in this sensual contest.

"How do you know where I live?" Lon whispered, between punishing kisses.

"How did you know I was out of town?" countered Maxie, squeezing Lon's muscular buttocks until the other girl groaned in reluctant delight.

Their clothes were early casualties. Maxie lost her scarlet pants somewhere between the bureau and the bed. Her ruffled blouse disappeared as they tumbled onto the narrow matress. The two girls grappled in growing excitement, their naked bodies slick with the sweat of ecstatic exertion.

"These sheets—did they come with the room?" Maxie gasped. The fine linen she felt with her fingertips didn't belong in the seedy hotel any more than Lon did.

"I live in a dump, but I live like a king," Lon boasted, trapping Maxie between her legs. Maxie felt the full length of Lon pressed against her, a surfeit of sensation that made her head swim.

The battle was over—or was it just beginning? Every inch of Maxie's skin was tingling with a pleasure so intense she couldn't take it. Then Lon's seeking hand reached between the unemployed girl's legs, and Maxie bit her lip so hard it almost bled. It was if every breaker in her private fuse box had been thrown with one flip of Lon's wrist. Maxie felt almost electrocuted with pleasure, and even Lon was trembling as the same current coursed through her.

It was a scientific law that when one person became a conduit for a live current, anyone touching the victim became part of the chain. Maxie's Girl Scout handbook advised would-be rescuers to knock the victim loose, not latch onto him. But who could knock Maxie and Lon off this current, before it incinerated them with unbearable ecstasy? The two girls shuddered, locked in their electric embrace, until the jolt finally found ground eight stories below.

After a long moment, when the breath was still knocking in Maxie's lungs, Lon reached down beside the bed and dug out a cigarette. The orange tip flared in the neon-lit dimness. Lon handed it to Maxie, who took a deep drag.

"Have you ever been in love?" Maxie asked, handing the cigarette back to Lon.

"I'm in love right now." Maxie could make out her lazy, satisfied smile.

"Silly!" The ex-deb swatted the mob girl playfully. "I'm serious."

Lon looked up at the stained ceiling reflectively. "I thought I was once. Sometimes I still think so."

"You're with someone?" Maxie hoped it wasn't that

beehive-topped Tanya. She was so limp that if Tanya burst in right now she wouldn't be able to lift a finger to fight her.

"Aren't you?" Lon looked at her. "That Pat, or Priscilla, or Pam?"

"She's not in the picture anymore." Maxie took another drag on their shared cigarette. "And I'm not sure I ever loved her. Maybe I just liked her, and the rest was chemical combustion."

"Isn't that what love is?"

Now it was Maxie's turn to roll on her back and stare at the ceiling. If that was love, she'd been in love an awful lot. She dismissed the philosphical questions for more concrete queries.

"How do you know about Pam anyway?"

"How do you know where I live?" countered Lon.

"But that's the only thing I know. Sure, I've speculated, but you seem to have a detailed dossier on me. Even the score a little."

Lon thought for a moment. "I'm a college dropout," she said finally.

"What?" Maxie shrieked. "After all the guff you've been giving me!"

Lon laughed. "Now tell me some of your speculations," she challenged.

"Well . . . you're working for the mob."

"That's not speculation, that's observation!" Lon jeered.

"The new mob in town. You seem like you're just an errand girl, but I've got a hunch you're running errands for the boss—the Queenpin herself!" Maxie tried to make out Lon's expression.

"Queenpin? What do you mean 'queenpin'?" Lon said too quickly. "The mob is strictly men-only—real old-country stuff."

"Then how did you get involved?" challenged Maxie.

Lon looked at her suspiciously. "I don't need to read about myself in the *Sentinel*."

"Call it career research," Maxie assured her. "Job placement has been on my mind all summer."

"Well, I was flunking French," Lon began. She told the familiar story in a few terse sentences: the uncomprehending parents; the decision to stay on her own in the city; the job handing out towels at the local YMCA, which barely paid the bills. "One Christmas when the gym was closed, I had to survive for three days on a single can of soup."

"Did you consume it cold?" Maxie interrupted.

"No," said Lon, puzzled. "I had a hot plate."

Then there had been the fateful encounter. Where and with whom, Lon wouldn't say, but "A while ago, I met someone who took a shine to me. They said their outfit could use me, and they sort of took me under their wing and showed me the ropes. I was like their—their protégé."

*They was a she, and she was Lon's love,* Maxie guessed. But all she said was, "Surely you could have found something else—why, you've got more schooling than I have."

"Tell me where I can find another job where I don't have to wear a dress!" Lon shot back. "And where I can sleep till noon, and that pays pretty well to boot!"

Maxie could understand Lon's allergy to early hours. She had the same ailment herself. Still—"But you're working for hardened criminals," she argued. "Extortionists at least, maybe murderers!" She thought of the cop and wondered again who had caused his death.

Lon shrugged. "They only kill each other. And the way I look at it, there will always be people who want to gamble, indulge in forbidden substances, or invest in crooked enterprises. If the mob didn't provide opportunities, someone else would."

Lon was practically repeating what Kathy had called a common myth.

"So you're saying if the people want their vices, let them have them." Maxie rephrased Lon's spurious argument.

"Aren't *we* vicious, in the eyes of society?" Lon argued back "This scene"—she gestured at the rumpled bed and their nudity—"isn't going to win any prizes from the DAP!"

"Well, but the mob is hardly the champion of variant vices!" Maxie pointed out. "Shaking down poor old Mrs. Flicka!"

Lon sat up. "I don't like that either. But why does she have to be so stubborn? Insulting, too—calling the boys who tried to explain the new street tax 'barbarous Finns.' Then that whole business of a sergeant only costing fifteen bucks a week in 1946."

Maxie struggled to keep her expression impassive. So the new mob was Finnish! She now knew something that even the Bureau didn't.

"Anyway, I plan to move on soon." Lon pulled on her T-shirt. "That's why I've stayed on at the Seneca. I'm piling up a nest egg, and come fall, I'm setting sail for new horizons!"

"What are you going to do?"

"Buy a boat." She looked at Maxie shyly. "I've always had a yen to do deep-sea diving, like that French fellow. Sail around collecting specimens from the bottom of the ocean!" She sighed. "That's my idea of heaven."

When Lon left to visit the bathroom down the hall, Maxie threw back the covers. She had no time to ponder Lon's plans—this unexpected yearning for the distant deep sea. She was more concerned with Lon's current career path.

She switched on the light. Next to the bed were a pack of cigarettes and Lon's gold lighter, lying on top of an untidy pile of books. Maxie looked at the titles: *The Silent World, Boy Beneath the Sea, The Open Sea: Its Natural History.* Lon was evidently serious about her secret ambition.

Maxie moved to the bureau. She plucked the postcard from the mirror frame. *Greetings from the Hebrides,* was printed across an aerial view of some green islands. On the other side was a cryptic message in hasty handwriting: *We're two for four. Not time to celebrate yet. Wish you and the gang were here. Chick.*

A code? What gang did this Chick mean? Maxie put the card back and busied herself with the bureau drawers, sliding them out and in, looking through tidy piles of snowy white T-shirts, rolls of socks in all shades, pressed pants, and dress shirts fresh from the laundry. Lon had told the truth: Everything was top quality, luxurious even. On an impulse, Maxie went over to the sink and picked up the soap. Expensive castille, of course.

In the handkerchief drawer, Maxie found a cigar box hidden under the crisp white linen and fancy silk pocket squares. She thought it would contain money, but when she lifted the lid, she found makeup. She stared at the tube of lipstick, the face powder, and mascara. There was jewelry too—a few earrings, bracelets, a ring. She picked up the gold band and peered at the faint engraving. *To SY from LW Pray Love, Remember.* This couldn't be Lon's. Why was it here? Her puzzlement grew.

Between the bureau and the wall, Lon had wedged the canvas bag she'd carried the other day. Maxie pulled it out and unzipped it. Empty. She put it back and opened the armoire. Coats, jackets, and pressed pants, in a rainbow of colors. Maxie shoved the clothes along the pole like a bargain-hunting shopper. Between a pair of gray flannels and a dark red rayon shirt, there was a flash of pink. She pushed the clothes farther apart, revealing a pink dress in dotted swiss with a matching bolero jacket, obviously expensive. They'd been hung from a hanger on a hook at the back of the armoire.

The doorknob rattled, and Maxie shut the armoire and leaped back into the bed. There was no time to turn off the light. She snatched up *The Silent World* and pretended to be absorbed in it. Her heart was pounding.

The only explanation possible was that the pink suit belonged to Lon's special someone. A change of clothes for a faceless female, who visited Lon often enough to leave an extra outfit. The only thing Maxie didn't know for sure was whether this "someone" Lon thought she might still love was also the "they" who had introduced Lon to the mob; and whether the rumored Queenpin made up the third member of this unholy trinity, three shadowy figures in one person.

"You seem perturbed," said Lon, sliding into the bed. "Penny for your thoughts."

"I was thinking about true love, and true callings," fibbed Maxie.

"I thought you were regretting being in bed with a vicious mobster," Lon mocked her. "Looking for an excuse to leave."

Maxie put the book down and turned on her side. "Are you vicious?" She twirled a lock of Lon's hair into a point. She could picture the beautiful blond butch in underwater garb, kind of like Kirk Douglas in *Twenty Thousand Leagues Under the Sea*. She felt a pang of jealousy. Lon had a clear career goal, while Maxie was still all at sea.

"Pretty vicious," Lon said seriously.

"Prove it," said Maxie, reaching for the other girl.

# Chapter 28
## A Busy Day

It was nice to be with a girl who slept in, Maxie thought the next morning. Pam was always popping up, even on Saturdays, as if early hours were a virtue. Lon looked so peaceful, with the late morning sun casting a golden glow on that smooth face, so innocent in sleep.

*Thanks for a lovely evening,* the ex-deb wrote on a piece of paper torn from her old reporter's notebook. *I had a wonderful time.* She hestiated a moment over the signature, her pen hovering, then decided to keep it casual. *See you around, Maxie.*

That was another benefit of a late sleeper, she thought, as she quietly closed the door behind her. No awkward conversations—no questions about where she was going and what she was doing and would they get together again?

On an impulse, she walked to the end of the corridor and peered out the window to the street below. She could see the dinette—the reverse of the view she'd had the night before last, when she'd been watching the Seneca, instead of enjoying Lon's company inside it.

The dinette reminded her it was past breakfast, almost lunch in fact. But just as she reached the little restaurant, she stopped short. The man she'd met at Sociological Survey Editions was sitting in the window, polishing his plate with a piece of toast.

Maxie backed away, hoping he hadn't seen her. That was no publisher—that was Kathy's partner, almost certainly staking out Lon.

If he'd spotted Maxie, it would only confirm Kathy's worst suspicions, Maxie thought as she hurried off. The G-woman would never believe that the ex-deb's night at the Seneca Hotel had been a pickup, pure and simple!

She has nothing on me, Maxie reminded herself as she breakfasted in Little Bohemia. Just the old business about Great-granddad and the *glögg*. Maxie frowned over her second cup of coffee. Of course, it was an odd coincidence, the new mob being Finnish, just like the Mainwarings. But that's all it was—a coincidence.

Like the coincidence of seeing her mother in the same pawnshop frequented by mob girl Lon. Or the coincidence of that crooked cop meeting death by drowning just down the Loon Lake shoreline from the Mainwaring Lodge.

Maxie put all three coincidences out of her mind. She had a busy day ahead, and the first order of business was to capitalize on Mamie's advice from last night. For that she needed a photographer. She dialed Stella at the photo supply store where the aspiring author worked mornings.

"Can you get your camera and meet me downtown?" she queried. "I've got a little scheme that could bring us both some cash, if you're game."

Stella was willing, and a couple hours later the two girls entered the Knickerbocker Hotel. Each was dressed in her daytime best, and carried a large bouquet of flowers.

"Are you sure he's here?" Stella muttered nervously as they headed for the elevator.

"Positive." Maxie was as cool as a cucumber. "Seven," she told the elevator operator, as she and Stella stepped in.

She knew from the preparations at *Polish* for the popular crooner's arrival that Larry Lathrop always stayed at the Knickerbocker under an assumed name when he visited Bay City, in order to evade his hysterical hordes of teenaged fans. Maxie had called that morning and confirmed that "George Wade," Larry's preferred alias, had not yet checked out of suite 712.

The ex–magazine assistant wondered if Pamela was right, and she was lacking in the ethics department. Few girls with Maxie's upbringing would take to prowling hotel corridors and negotiating with sleazy gossip rags with Maxie's eagerness. But she had no time for soul-searching now. She knocked on the door to suite 712.

"Don't forget to lift up your bouquet," Stella whispered. A deep voice grumbled, "Who is it?"

"Delivery for Mr. Wade." Maxie tried to imitate the maid they'd encountered while they waited for the hotel hallway to be empty.

"Leave it outside the door," instructed Larry.

"I need you to sign, sir." Maxie stood aside and lifted the bouquet when she heard the door being unlocked. It opened a crack. When Larry saw only Stella with her flowers, he opened the door wider. "Where do I sign?" he said shortly.

Maxie's bouquet emitted flashes of light and loud pops, while Stella's bunch of flowers clicked continuously. "What the hell—" Larry raised his fist, then thought better of it and beat a retreat into his room, locking the door behind him. The two girls ran down the hall to the stairwell. They climbed to the eighth floor, where Maxie discarded the flowers and spent flashbulbs on a room service cart. Stella tucked the camera into a large handbag.

"Remember, if anyone asks, we're part of the Beautification Planning Committee," the ex-deb instructed Stella.

"Is there such a thing?" asked the nervous photographer.

"Of course," said Maxie. "It's meeting in the Rose Room."

But no one stopped them as they strolled through the lobby and made for the street. There they paused, laughing with pent-up excitement.

"How long until I have something to show the editors at *Idol Gossip?*" Maxie demanded.

"The end of the afternoon," promised Stella. "Want to be my darkroom assistant?"

"I'm always game for a new job," Maxie quipped.

In the little closet that served as *The Step Stool's* darkroom, Maxie stood shoulder to shoulder with Stella in the pitch black, feeling the photographer's arm move as she loaded the developing tank with the film. The novice paparazzo followed Stella's instructions—handing her chemicals and the thermometer, setting the timer. Stella had Maxie turn the film while she mixed the hypo. Then Maxie watched as Stella ran cold water through the top of the tank for a final rinse.

"In a few minutes we'll be able to see if we got anything," the camera bug told her eager apprentice after she poured in the hypo. "How much did Mamie say *Idol Gossip* would pay?" She whistled when Maxie named the figure.

"How do you feel about a sixty-forty split?" the ex-deb proposed. "Your camera, my contacts—an extra ten percent for me on account of I'm the one who broke Larry's nose?"

"Fair enough," agreed Stella. She opened the tank and emptied the hypo. After rinsing the film, she unrolled the reel and peered at the tiny frames. "Looks like we've got it! See?"

Maxie studied the dark smudges. "I don't see anything."

"It takes practice. See Larry raising his fist in this one? You'll see once I make the contact sheet. But the film has to dry first."

"This isn't the career for me," Maxie complained as Stella hung the film in a little cupboard. "Waiting around was never my forte."

Stella leaned back against the counter next to the enlarger. "What *are* you going to do?"

Maxie was writing down the cost of the film and flowers in her budget book, trying to decide how to classify them. Finally she wrote *Independent Enterprise* in the "for" column where she usually put "food," "rent," or "sundries." She put the budget book back in her purse.

"I've got another date with Miss Watkins next week." It felt like Maxie was practically going steady with the career counselor, she'd been seeing so much of her this summer. "If nothing comes through, I can live on the income from the picture sale—Mumsy said she'd give me an allowance again, but I'd rather be independent. Oh!" Another idea occurred to her. "I got Mamie's contact at Mount Olympus Books—if I sell *If Love Is the Answer* to them, how would you feel about me taking an agent's percentage?" A dream drifted through the unemployed girl's mind, of swinging from deal to deal like a monkey in the jungle, and putting off forever the realities of a regular workday.

"Not really!" Stella's jaw dropped. "You mean—you found time to talk to Miss McArdle after everything else that's happened? I wasn't even sure you'd want to after—well, after you lost your girlfriend as well as your job."

So the grapevine between the Arms and *The Step Stool* was operational. Maxie wondered how long it would take for the buzz about her tussle with Tanya and subsequent exit with Lon to migrate from the Knock Knock back to the Arms.

No rumor had reached Stella, evidently. "I can't help feeling sort of responsible," she confessed. "I realized later my book must have suggested some possibilities that had probably never occurred to you before. Of course it's complete fiction," she added quickly. "Even if I was sometimes inspired by actual events."

"Don't blame your book," Maxie told her kindly. "It was a catalyst maybe, but not the cause."

Stella looked at her closely. "You don't seem too broken up about the breakup."

"I feel like a horse let loose from the barn," Maxie confessed.

"And here I was, ready to offer you a shoulder to cry on!"

Maxie laughed. "What with all that's been happening I've been too distracted to think about losing my steady!"

"Well, if you ever need more distraction . . ." Stella laid her hand on Maxie's, and looked at the girl through her lashes. "Truth to tell," she murmured, "I never thought you and Pamela were terribly well suited."

Her meaning was unmistakable. "That's a friendly offer," Maxie flirted back automatically. She remembered the unanswered C-cup question, and felt tempted to recreate one of the racy scenes from Stella's novel. If only she wasn't worn out from her night with Lon! But would she have skipped last night with Lon for this afternoon with Stella? It was a riddle without a solution.

*Pace yourself, Maxine,* she commanded her libidinous side. Was this what Miss Watkins meant, when she warned about impulse control?

"I've always liked you, Maxie," Stella told her frankly. "From the day you came into the *Step Stool* offices and left us the lemon drops."

"I'm surprised they didn't sour you on me," Maxie murmured. She remembered how Sally, the heroine of *If*

*Love Is the Answer,* had made up her mind at the end of the novel that "there was no sense in being shy when you saw a girl who set off sparks in your stomach."

Stella laughed. "I don't like things that are too sweet." She glanced at the clock. "How shall we pass the time, while we wait for the film to dry?"

Certainly a little heavy petting wouldn't hurt, Maxie decided judiciously. She'd always been partial to the talented features editor. Now, as they necked in the dim darkroom, her attitude of vague goodwill sharpened into a definite appreciation for Stella's many fine qualities.

At the end of the afternoon, as promised, Maxie was hurrying to the offices of *Idol Gossip* with the contact prints in her purse. The photos had turned out perfectly— Maxie especially liked the one of Larry raising his fist, unshaven and wild-eyed, his mouth twisted in anger below the startling white of his bandaged nose. He looked more like a dissolute prizefighter than the dream angel of the popular song. She wondered if the editor of *Idol Gossip* would go for that one.

He preferred the one of Larry still in shock, with his mouth hanging open. "Half to seal the deal, half on delivery of the negative," he said as he wrote out the check. "A pleasure doing business with you, young lady."

"How much if I throw in an article?" Maxie was struck by a sudden inspiration. "Something like, 'My Date with Larry Left Me a Sadder and Wiser Girl'?"

"We pay more for pictures," the editor said, "but I can give you twenty-five dollars. Keep it under seven hundred and fifty words and bring it with the negative." And Maxie was on the elevator back to the lobby before the ink on the check was dry.

Entering the amount under "income," Maxie looked at her budget book with satisfaction. She'd made as much since last night as she had her whole time as an Recreational Aide!

At the Arms, Maxie went looking for company. In the lounge there was a party of pinochle players and Kathy, brooding in a corner over her textbooks. Why the charade? Maxie couldn't help wondering. Wouldn't the crime fighter's time be better spent catching crooks rather than polishing her performance as a psych student?

Kathy had her own question. "Run into Lon, lately?" she asked sarcastically.

So Maxie *had* been spotted that morning. "Maybe," said the ex-deb, sitting down opposite the undercover girl. "Are you interested professionally—or for personal reasons?" She enjoyed the flush that flooded the G-woman's face.

"It's always professional with me," said the tense girl tightly. "I'm interested in capturing criminals and advancing my career—period."

"Such dedication." Maxie sighed in mock envy. "You remind me of Pamela. You'll be head of the branch office or whatever you call it, just as sure as Pamela's going to be running Grunemans one day."

Kathy ignored Maxie's teasing. "Listen," she said earnestly. "You know the difference between right and wrong, however much you pretend not to care. Give me the dope on Lon and square yourself with Uncle Sam!"

"You mean—be an informer?"

"We call them two-oh-nines," said Kathy. She took out a manila folder. "I have a form right here."

"Telling tales on my friends isn't my cup of tea," Maxie said, discovering that she did have a few ethics after all. "But I'll give you a tip for free—two, in fact. The new mob is Finnish and the big boss is female!"

The telephone rang, allowing her to escape before

Kathy had a chance to ask any awkward questions. She exited the lounge and picked up the receiver.

"Maxie, my dear, it's Velma, do you have a moment?" The smooth voice of the high-powered businesswoman flowed over the wire like well-beaten cake batter. "A little bird told me you were free again, and I just had to call and make my pitch."

For an astonished instant Maxie thought Velma had heard about her fight with Pamela, but her mother's protégé was continuing: "The job I told you about at Amalgamated Enterprises is still open. It would be a marvelous opportunity, and I assure you, I'll appreciate you more than Hal Hapgood has!" Her laugh told Maxie she'd somehow gotten the inside scoop on the ex-deb's abrupt departure from the pages of *Polish*.

"Well—" Maxie couldn't even pretend to be tempted by the dull business of dry cleaning. "The answer's still no. I've got some other wieners on the grill, as the saying goes."

"Really? Jobs like this don't grow on trees." Velma's voice sharpened slightly. Maxie could have sworn the magnate was miffed. "We've dozens of applicants. It was only my personal friendship for your family that made me call."

"I appreciate the thought, but the answer is no," Maxie repeated patiently. "You'll have to give one of those other applicants a break." What game was Velma playing, giving Maxie the hard sell on this job after her very definite rejection of Maxie's other talents at Loon Lake?

"I'm sorry to hear that." Velma's voice was smooth and sweet again. "I wish you best of luck with your new endeavors." She hung up.

Maxie headed upstairs to get started on the Lathrop tell-all. She was working too hard to even think about a job!

## Chapter 29

## The Mysterious Phone Call

Maxie was in her favorite place—in her bed at the Arms, propped up on pillows with a cup of coffee and a cinnamon roll on a tray next to her.

Despite her leisurely appearance, the unemployed girl was hard at work. Blue pencil in one hand, she was studying Stella's manuscript. When she'd told Stella yesterday about Mamie's advice to inject a little suffering into the lives of the Homophile Handbooks girls, the budding author had looked stricken.

"You want me to kill one of them?" she gulped, her fingers frozen on the blouse she was rebuttoning.

"Or maybe just maim?" suggested Maxie. "Perhaps you could commit someone to a sanatorium."

Stella had declared she could never decide which of her fictional characters to destroy and had begged Maxie to make the hard choice.

Now the former editorial assistant frowned thoughtfully as she turned the pages of *If Love Is the Answer*. Who could go—and how? What if Stella rewrote it so Jane was run over by a bus in chapter 32? But then what would motivate Minnie to make out with the new volunteer?

Maxie circled Patricia's name and wrote *drugs?* in the margin. There was a tap on the door. "Come in," called Maxie.

It was Dolly, still in her pajamas. "Breaking up agrees with you," she observed as she collapsed into one of Maxie's slipper chairs. "Who'd you bribe to bring you breakfast?"

"No one!" Maxie bragged. "I bought the bun last night at the bakery before it closed—you get half off then. And I picked up this cunning little coffee percolator at the secondhand shop!" She was pleased to demonstrate her independence to Dolly.

"It's too bad you can't share a little of this *joie de vivre* in Splitsville with Lois. She could use it!" Dolly remarked.

Maxie had already heard how hard Lois was taking Netta's defection. The efficient office manager was devastated by the abrupt end to her romance. The call to Netta had finally gone through, but there'd been no misunderstanding. "She was up almost all night afterward," Phyllis reported, "wondering what she'd done wrong."

Now Dolly told Maxie, "Pamela collected her from work the other night and made her take a sleeping pill to get some rest."

"I wish there was something I could do for her." Maxie's heart went out to the suffering girl. *At least I can warn her not to go into the office short on sleep,* she decided.

"Time heals everything, or so they say," Dolly sighed. "What with Lois spending her time at Pamela's home for heartbroken girls, Netta gone, maybe for good, and you off frolicking who knows where, the fifth floor feels like a ghost town," she complained. "After Phyllis goes to work, it's just me and that kooky Kitty. Remember the good times we used to have, when the whole gang was here? Nowadays I can't even rustle up a game of Ping-Pong." She looked at Maxie hopefully. "How about it?"

Maxie shook her head. "I have to finish these edits." She didn't add that she was avoiding Kitty/Kathy, who would almost certainly be in the lounge. The brooding way she gazed at Maxie made the ex-deb uneasy. "I miss the old days too," she told Dolly. "But on the other hand, I can see why the girls move out. Running down five flights of stairs because there's only one phone! It's outrageous!"

"Mrs. DeWitt's old-fashioned." Dolly defended their landlady loyally. "She just doesn't realize Bell Telephone has superseded Western Union!"

A voice floated up the stairwell. "Maxie! Telephone!"

"See what I mean?" Maxie swung out of bed, thrusting her feet into her slippers and pulling on her dressing gown in one coordinated movement. She ran lightly down the stairs, feeling cheerful and energetic in spite of her complaints.

Picking up the receiver, she caroled, "He*llo!*"

"Maxie Mainwaring?" A man's voice, raspy and uneducated. "Mainwaring" came out "Mainwarin'."

"Yes?"

"You Mabel Mainwaring's daughter?"

"Who is this?"

"Never mind who." The man gave a sinister laugh. "I've got something you want. Only I need some, like, reward money."

"I haven't lost anything," Maxie said, growing more and more puzzled.

"Aren't you maybe missing a paddle?" suggested the man.

"Please speak plainly." Maxie was growing impatient. "Are you trying to say I'm up a creek without a paddle?

Is this some sort of prank?" Kids, she concluded in disgust. That fake raspy laugh should have tipped her off.

But before she could hang up, the raspy voice became anxious. "No, no, that ain't my meaning at all. I got a real paddle—bloodstains on one end and fingerprints on the other. Your ma's fingerprints!"

Maxie froze. Even though she'd pictured her mother murdering the crooked cop, it was a shock to find her theory was correct.

"How much do you want for this used paddle?" she asked tersely.

"Five thousand."

"Five thousand! I can't raise that kind of money, and I'm not even sure I want to."

"How about twennyfi'hundred?" the voice offered.

"One thousand, and that's my limit," countered Maxie.

"Pier thirteen, ten o'clock tonight. Bring the dough in small bills, and come alone." There was a click and the line went dead.

Maxie replaced the receiver, and sat a moment, thinking. What to make of this startling phone call? Doubts set in. Had she been too quick to believe her mother was a murderer? Was this a shakedown or a setup? Why was this fellow contacting her and not her mother, if he had the incriminating oar? And that raspy voice—why had it sounded so familiar?

She snapped her fingers. The dairy thug at Eleanor Roosevelt! Of course! How on earth did he connect with the crooked cop? Or her mother, for that matter?

These were murky waters indeed. And there was only one way to find out more. Show up tonight at Pier 13.

Mrs. DeWitt drifted through the hall, reciting one of her favorite poems:

*"Alone stood brave Horatius*
*But constant still in mind,*
*Thrice thirty thousand foes before*
*And the broad flood behind."*

Horatius managed to hold off a whole army of Etrus-
cans, Maxie thought, as she slowly climbed back upstairs.
Surely she could face down a few Bay City miscreants!

# Chapter 30

## Accident!

It felt odd to be getting ready for a date with a black-mailer—or maybe a killer—amid the gay hustle and bustle of the fifth floor. The gang was going out to dinner—Dolly had organized it as a kind of cheer-up-Lois excursion. "So she'll know she still has plenty of pals, even if she's lost that special someone," Dolly explained.

Maxie had found out about it when she returned from an afternoon of hectic preparation for her mysterious meeting. She'd gotten a good price for her pearls and garnet set, at the jeweller recommended by Dolly. "All the chorus girls sell to him," Dolly had explained to Maxie. "They turn the presents they get from stage-door johnnies into cash. Only poor people go to pawnbrokers!"

After Maxie had raised the blackmail money, she'd done some shopping. Finally she'd visited Pier 13 to get the lay of the land. The pier was piled with crates bearing the Sunshine Dairy label.

Preoccupied with crime, she'd returned to find party preparations. Everyone was coming, even Kitty/Kathy. "I invited Pamela," Dolly told Maxie a little anxiously. "Be polite, okay?" Maxie promised. Lois, with her pallid face and red-rimmed eyes, was such a pathetic sight that the tenderhearted heiress vowed once again she'd find some way to help the hapless secretary heal her broken heart.

Pamela must have been warned as well. "I'm here for Lois, of course," she told Maxie stiffly when they met at Luigi's.

Maxie wanted to say, "Why do you think I'm here, the food?" But she answered "Of course!" Then she wished she'd said something equally patronizing, like how she believed in being civilized and that she bore Pamela no ill will even though Pamela . . . No, it was better she'd kept it brief.

Kathy had been watching Maxie like a cat. When she observed Maxie tuck her newly purchased canvas bag behind her chair, she muttered acidly, "Expecting to 'run into' your mobster friend?"

"I'm starting to think I'm a 'person of interest'—at least to you," Maxie murmured mischievously.

Kathy flushed on cue. "To the whole agency!" she snapped. Then stopped as if she'd said too much.

Maxie twirled her fork thoughtfully in her fettucine. She wished she knew as much as the Bureau seemed to think she did. This business was as tangled as her pasta. Lon, Sunshine Dairy, Mumsy, the pawnshop, and the corpse of the crooked cop—she still didn't understand how they connected.

"Summer is the slow season at Sather and Stirling," Lois said in answer to an inquiry about the office. "I'm sure I'll be back in shape, come fall." She attempted to smile, but the result was more of a grimace.

Maxie leaned forward impulsively. "Lois, you should take that vacation—after all, you already had it scheduled. And you need it now more than ever."

"But where would I go?" Lois's eyes filled with tears. "I have nothing p-p-planned."

Janet refilled the sobbing girl's wineglass and pushed it

toward her. "You could go anywhere. Use the money you were saving for the deposit."

At the reminder of her broken dreams, Lois's eyes overflowed again.

"Go to Loon Lake." Maxie came to the rescue. "It's empty now. Take a friend, or two! It'll make a new woman out of you."

The gang chimed in, urging Lois to take advantage of Maxie's offer.

"I didn't realize you were on such good terms with your mother," Kitty/Kathy said suspiciously.

Maxie got up. "Oh, Mumsy and I have reached an understanding," she said, stretching the truth only slightly. She'd lifted the spare key to the Lodge during her last visit.

"Are you leaving already?" Janet asked. "I wanted to talk to you, about that trust."

"I'll call you tomorrow," Maxie told her. She put her hands on the G-woman's shoulders and felt her start. "Kitty, tell Lois about the psychological stages of grief. Weren't you saying earlier there are four?"

That should keep the government girl pinned down long enough for Maxie to escape. She threw some bills on the table as Lois turned expectant, if watery, eyes on Kitty/Kathy. Outside the restaurant she hailed a cab. "The Knock Knock Lounge, on Pingst," she told the driver. A glance behind showed an empty street.

She'd reverted to her old habits—throwing money on the table and catching cabs. Except now, of course, she noted everything in her budget book. She hesitated in the "for" column as she noted the cab fare, and finally wrote *Independent Enterprises* again.

Inside the Knock Knock she went straight to the bathroom and changed into the clothes she'd carried in the canvas bag—jeans and a dark sweater. When she emerged, she stopped at the bar and ordered a whiskey. *A little liquid courage,* she told herself, tossing it back in one long gulp. "Seen Lon tonight?" she asked the bartender, coughing a little.

Della shook her curly gray head. "She'll probably be in later," she volunteered.

Maxie unzipped the canvas bag and pulled out a pair of flippers, wrapped in brown paper and tied with string. "Give her these when she comes in, will you?" If Maxie didn't return from Pier 13 she wanted the beautiful butch to have something to remember her by. Fleetingly, she thought of Stella, and regretted not getting a memento for her too. And really, why not Pamela as well? And Elaine, and Velma, and all her friends on the fifth floor.

*I'm getting morbid,* she chided herself as she slid off the stool and exited the bar. It was time for positive thinking. She would go to Pier 13, turn the tables on that dairy thug, find out what her mother was up to, and who the new mob boss was to boot! Under her breath she recited the line from Mrs. DeWitt's favorite poem: " 'Alone stood brave Horatius. . . .' "

She turned off Pingst Street, leaving the raucous, neon-lit district behind. The docks weren't far. Already she could smell the faintly fishy scent of the lake, and see the sleeping cranes, visible above the tops of buildings.

The gates in the chain-link fence were closed and locked at night, but someone had thoughtfully left the one to Pier 13 ajar. Maxie shivered in spite of her sweater, as she walked quickly toward the pier. The light posts were widely spaced, inadequate golden pools in this great black swamp. The lone girl stumbled on the uneven pavement and almost fell. She peered all around, searching the darkness and seeing nothing.

She had that queer, prickling feeling on the back of her

neck as she walked along the pier, which told her she wasn't alone. Hearing a rustling sound, she whirled around in time to see an enormous rat scuttle under the warehouse to her right. Ugh!

Maxie slid on the brass knuckles she'd purchased that afternoon and looked at her watch. It was two minutes after ten, and no sign of the raspy-voiced thug with the paddle. In the stillness she could hear the splash of water on the pilings below.

She'd just circle around to the other side of Pier 13's warehouse, a low building almost at the end of the pier. As she passed the side of the building facing the water, she saw the big crane that was used to load the lake boats.

There was no lake boat anchored at Pier 13, but the crane suddenly came to life with a grinding, mechanical noise. Something made Maxie look behind her. An enormous steel beam was swinging through the air, coming straight at her!

Instinctively Maxie dropped to the ground and covered her head with her hands. *Thank heavens for all those duck-and-cover drills!* she thought. She felt a whoosh of air on her hands and neck, so closely did the I beam pass over.

Already the gears were grinding into reverse. Maxie staggered to her feet. The steel beam was swinging next to the warehouse, cutting off her escape route. Now it began to move toward her again, gaining speed in its deadly assault.

Maxie ran toward the end of the pier, thinking wildly of Horatius plunging into the Tiber. She felt the beam behind her, coming closer. Then she dropped over the side of the pier, and the beam swung out into the empty air over the water.

There was no splash. Maxie crouched on the worn wooden ladder, peering up at the beam that spun slowly overhead. She was glad she'd taken the time to inspect the pier that afternoon!

Now she would wait, until her would-be killer got down from the cab of the crane and came over to the edge of the pier to see what had become of his prey.

*He'll get a big surprise!* Maxie thought grimly, fingering her brass knuckles.

The steel beam was swinging back. She could hear the mechanical whir as it disappeared from view. Then she heard something else—running footsteps—at least two sets. Cautiously poking her head up, Maxie saw the wavering beam of a flashlight, and two figures running along the warehouse. They were almost at the end of the pier. The beam began to move again.

"Behind you!" Maxie shouted. One of the figures flattened, the other was a fraction too slow. The beam caught him chest high, and flung him off the end of the pier, like a sack of powdered milk.

"Joe!" the figure on the ground screamed.

*That's Kathy's voice!* Maxie dove into the water and swam toward the sinking body. She heard muffled shots and hoped none of them were aimed at her. She reached the half-submerged figure, and was pleased she could remember the drowning swimmer hold the other Recreational Aide had taught her in May. Maxie towed the unconscious agent to the ladder, hoping she wasn't carrying a corpse.

"Kitty! Kathy! Help!" she gasped, clinging to the ladder with one arm, while the other encircled the G-man.

Kathy's face loomed overhead. "Have you got Joe?"

"Yes, but I can't lift him," Maxie managed. "The crane operator?"

"Got away. Wait."

A moment later, Kathy returned with a rope she'd fashioned into a kind of lasso. Bumping and scraping the waterlogged G-man, the two girls managed to haul him onto the pier.

While Kathy anxiously examined her limp partner, Maxie was overcome with a sense of deep disappointment. The evening had been a crushing failure—no new information, just an injured agent. Why couldn't the FBI stay out of her affairs?

# Chapter 31

# The Knock Knock's New Owner

It was nearly midnight when the two bedraggled girls climbed their weary way to the fifth floor. The ambulance had taken injured Agent Freitag to the hospital. After an almost endless conference with a covey of policemen, Kathy had told the exhausted ex-deb that they were finally free to go.

The fifth floor was silent except for the faint sound of Dolly snoring. Kathy went to the washroom, and Maxie squelched after her. The G-woman had been tight-lipped on the ride home, but Maxie wasn't going to sleep until she got some questions answered.

"Why were you and Joe following me?" she demanded as Kathy mechanically washed her hands and splashed her face. "And don't give me that bunk about hoping I'd lead you to Lon—you know where she lives!"

Kathy looked up, green eyes glittering. "Of course we weren't looking for Lon! It was you we were following— just as we've been following you all summer!"

"Me? But why?" Maxie stammered in astonishment.

"Drop the charade!" Kathy lashed out. "You knew we

were after you. You deliberately lured us out to the pier in order to drown us in another dockside 'accident.'"

"Kathy, no, it wasn't like that!" Maxie protested, but Kathy refused to be calmed.

"We have a file on you a foot long! You consort with all kinds of criminals, from mob girls like Lon to that unsavory Ramona, the dope peddler—yes, we know all about her. You needn't pretend these brass knuckles I found on you"—she shook the pair she'd taken from Maxie in the ex-deb's face—"were just something you picked up today. When we interviewed your former boss, Mamie McArdle, even she admitted that you often bragged about being able to procure witnesses to give false testimony with ease. You're a dyed-in-the-wool bad egg!"

Maxie understood now why the *Step Stool* gals were so concerned about Sapphics being associated with crime. She'd have to do some fast talking to convince Kathy that each incriminating item had an innocent explanation!

"Listen, Kathy, it was me that crazy crane driver was trying to kill!" Quickly Maxie poured out the story of the blackmailer's phone call, and her desire to find out what the man had on her mother.

"See, I even brought the money to purchase the paddle, in case the blackmail business was legit." Maxie pulled up her shirt to reveal the waterproof money belt she'd purchased that afternoon. Kathy just stared, still suspicious. "And you must have seen that the I beam was aimed at me—and why would I have pulled Joe from the water if I wanted him dead?" When Kathy still didn't respond, Maxie burst out angrily, "For heaven's sake, you've been following me all summer—have I ever done anything illegal?"

Kathy's thoughts behind her green eyes were unreadable. "You jaywalk when you're in a hurry," the G-woman said finally. "But aside from that, I haven't personally observed any criminal behavior." She added almost too low for Maxie to hear, "Except your lethal way with women."

Maxie sagged against the sink in relief. "So why all the suspicion?" she begged. "It can't be just that stint of reefer rolling!"

Kathy turned off the water, which had provided a gushing backdrop to their heated exchange. "Do you know whose name is on the title of the Knock Knock Lounge?"

"No," said Maxie more puzzled than ever. "Whose?"

"The deed was transferred this past May from one Selma Swenson, widow of Sven Swenson, to Mabel Mainwaring, who then transferred it to the Nyberg Trust, beneficiary Maxine Mainwaring."

The drip-drip of the leaky faucet sounded very loud in the tiled room. "But—but that's insane!" murmured Maxie after a moment of stunned silence. "Mumsy hasn't the slightest idea how to operate a ladies-only night-spot!"

"Being a front doesn't take any experience," Kathy commented. "Don't you see, Maxie? You and your mother are either patsies for the new mob, or you're working with them, hand in glove!"

Maxie started to say that Mumsy wasn't anyone's patsy, and then realized what that would mean. Instead, she protested, "I won't get my hands on that trust for ten years, and Mumsy would never risk her reputation! Why, if her DAP friends heard about this piece of property, they'd kick her off the board." She paced the tiled room. "There must be an innocent explanation. Why not pull Mumsy in for some old-fashioned questioning?" Even someone as tough as Mumsy would crack under an experienced interrogator, Maxie thought hopefully.

"I can't do that." The G-woman sank onto the wooden bench against the wall.

"Why not?"

"I'm not an actual agent!" Kathy put her face in her hands. "I'm just Joe's secretary!"

She poured out a shamefaced confession to the astounded ex-deb. The Director, she said, had never permitted women agents. Nonetheless, Kathy had entered the Bureau hoping to prove the exception. "My whole family's in the Bureau—my dad, my uncle, my cousins." Her speedy typing skills and analytic mind had ensured a rapid rise to Clerk Secretary III-A—the highest level most women achieved. But Kathy wasn't satisfied. "I persuaded Joe to let me work in the field—go undercover and infiltrate the Arms. He allowed it, on condition I continue my secretarial work." She looked apologetic. "I'm sorry I kept you up, typing his reports."

Exhausted with her late-night stints at the machine, the tireless girl nonetheless shadowed Maxie all over Bay City. "It was a relief you were such a late sleeper," she confessed.

"And this Knock Knock business—that's why you were so interested in my relationship with my mother!" the ex-deb realized.

"Psychology seemed the perfect ploy to quiz you about Mabel Mainwaring's activities and find out whether you were involved as well." The Bureau secretary shrugged. "I was sure your feud with your mother was phony, and you, with your criminal history, were the link to the mob!" She slumped against the wall. "Now I don't know what to think."

*Is this the last layer of the onion?* Maxie contemplated the complicated girl. Kitty/Kathy, student/sleazologist/ G-woman/secretary, seemed to have reached the end of her rope. She was shivering with fatigue. Her skirt was creased and stained and her sensible shoes were covered with mud and blood.

"There's no percentage in racking our brains right now, the state we're in," the ex-deb decided. "After a hot shower and a good night's sleep we'll see things more clearly."

She turned on the water in the shower stall and stripped off her soaked sweater. The G-secretary's shivering increased as she slowly unbuttoned her blouse, staring fixedly at Maxie all the while.

It took a moment for Maxie to realize that Kathy's eyes were focused on Maxie's brief brassiere and clinging dungarees. *She's not trembling with shock,* the experienced girl decided, *but pent-up passion!*

Swiftly Maxie shed the rest of her clothes, pretending not to notice anything amiss with the shaking secretary. "Nice and hot," Maxie announced as she tested the shower. "In you go; it will do you good." Grasping the staring girl, she pushed her into the stall. She pretended to ignore Kathy's start as she followed her in and pulled the curtain closed.

"Isn't that better?" The water had plastered Kathy's crisp curls to her head. Maxie efficiently removed the undercover agent's underwear, wondering if the drab garments were Bureau issue. She looked deeply into Kathy's lust-glazed eyes. "Isn't this what you've been wanting, all summer long?" She moved closer to Kathy, so that their torsos touched.

Kathy made an inarticulate sound, and clutched Maxie close. The ex-deb noticed with satisfaction that the G-girl's pallid skin was pinking up, warmed by both the hot water and the heat of desire. She was really quite an attractive girl, Maxie thought, peering through the clouds of steam. She didn't have Stella's lush figure, or Lon's movie-star good looks, but her compact, yet fit, frame and her fine-boned face had a certain appeal, especially when her green eyes rolled back in her head and her eyelids fluttered.

And besides, it was fun to be with a girl so tightly wound

that sucking a drop of water from her earlobe nearly sent her over the edge to ecstasy. A girl got a special sort of satisfaction from helping a naïve newcomer who'd reached the boiling point let off some steam. If Kathy was a kettle, she'd be whistling right now, Maxie decided, her own excitement growing as the undercover agent rained clumsy kisses on the ex-deb's face. Kathy was like a pea about to pop, like a chick pecking its way out of its shell, like a litter of kittens desperate to escape from the sack they'd been stuffed in for drowning—desperate to get clear of the canvas bag and live a little.

Wordlessly, she instructed the inexperienced girl on the finer points of French kissing. *That's where all this typing got you,* she thought hazily. *You had no time to pick up the really important skills in life!* It was too bad Kathy would be unable to appreciate the expertise that Maxie showed when Kathy finally boiled over, keeping her from those slips or bruises on the faucet that were so common in amateur attempts at shower sex. Someday, when Kathy had seen more of the world, she'd appreciate the skill with which Maxie managed to reduce her to a simmer and turn her back up to boil again.

A while later, a rejuvenated Kathy remarked, "That was refreshing!" as she toweled herself dry.

"You seem much more relaxed," replied Maxie. She opened the window wide. The washroom still billowed with clouds of steam.

Kathy wrapped her towel around her modestly. "I was thinking about tonight's attack," the indefatigable investigator announced. "If I reread last week's reports—"

"Not tonight," Maxie told her firmly. "You'll be able to think more clearly after a good rest. Besides," she added with a suggestive smile, "wouldn't you like a little company in bed?" She'd been so busy cooking for Kathy, she'd ignored her own appetite.

But Kathy only tucked her towel more tightly. "Really, Maxie," she said primly, "I've told you over and over that my interest in you and your Sapphic sisters is strictly on behalf of the government!"

Maxie's jaw dropped. She'd heard of lace-curtain lesbians, but this was the limit! "I suppose all that steam blinded you to what we just did in the shower?" she asked sarcastically.

"I appreciate your therapeutic massage." Kathy avoided Maxie's eyes. "But I think in the future we should keep our interviews on a more professional level. The Bureau frowns on close contact with suspects."

She hurried from the washroom, leaving Maxie fuming. That twisted sister needed a *real* psychiatrist to figure her out!

# Chapter 32
## A New Job

"Miss Watkins? It's Maxie. I just wanted to let you know, I have a new job!"

"Goodness, Maxie, you certainly don't let the grass grow under your feet. Where are you working now?"

"I'm at the Knock Knock Lounge," Maxie said proudly. "I'm the new busgirl!"

Just then Della called from the other end of the bar where she was wiping glasses. "Finish your call, Maxie, you've got lots to learn before it gets busy."

Maxie hung up on Miss Watkins's confused congratulations, promising that yes, she would still keep the appointment next week when Mrs. Spindle-Janska returned.

What she hadn't told Miss Watkins was that she had not one job but two. Ostensibly a mere busgirl, she was actually working for the FBI as an informer.

Or was it three? *I'm still working for myself,* Maxie thought. The busgirl intended to get more information from the Bureau than she gave. After all, she'd almost been murdered! And if the agents could mistake her for a criminal, who's to say they hadn't made the same mistake with Lon and Mumsy?

It had been easy to convince Kathy that a sudden love

of country had come over her since their shared shower—
and that a snitch at the Knock Knock would be a valuable addition to Operation Smorgasbord. Maxie had one
of her hunches that the Knock Knock—Lon's unofficial
headquarters and owned on paper by the Mainwarings—
was the key to the mystery.

Lon had been a harder sell. Maxie had pleaded desperate circumstances—her recent firing, her lost allowance,
and her longing for a job that would let her sleep late.

"I just don't see it," Lon said. "You want to work
*here?*"

"Why not? I think it'll be fun!" It was only when the
ex-deb threatened to write Lon's address on the Knock
Knock's bathroom wall that Lon agreed to "put in a
good word for you."

"Maybe you just don't want to see so much of me,"
Maxie suggested.

Lon evaded her look. "You know you're easy on the
eyes," she muttered as she hurried away.

Lon hadn't even thanked her for the flippers, Maxie
thought, disappointed. In fact, the mob girl seemed to be
avoiding Maxie!

The ex-deb's duties weren't difficult: restocking the refrigerator with bottles of beer and the shelves with liquor,
slicing limes and lemons, and scrubbing glasses in the little sink. "You'll bus the tables too," Della told Maxie.
"When it gets busy the girls will start throwing drink orders at you, so be ready to take 'em. Friday nights they'll
have you hopping!"

Maxie enjoyed the bustle and buzz of her new job, the
bits of overheard gossip, watching the never-ending drama
of who came in with whom and whether they left together. Della, the ex-deb discovered, was a regular Who's
Who of the twilight world. She knew everyone there was
to know, and enjoyed sharing her expertise. The only

time she clammed up was when Maxie asked her about the new mob in town.

"The less I know the better," she told Maxie shortly. "I don't want to get the business the way Francine did."

"What happened to Francine?" Maxie asked, alarmed.

Della looked over her shoulder nervously. "They killed her cats!" she hissed. "You better believe she's paying up now. But the big boss is still punishing her—got her place shut down on a health violation."

Maxie didn't know which horrified her more, that Francine's was shuttered or that her mother and Lon might be mixed up with a bunch of cat killers. Action seemed more urgent than ever, but all she could do was watch and wait.

And while she was waiting, Maxie was making money. She was pleasantly surprised, at the end of the first night, at how those nickels and dimes and quarter tips added up. And there was none of the nonsense about tax deductions she'd had at her other jobs. Everything at the Knock Knock was "under the table," Della told Maxie. Maxie had managed to sneak a look at the books, and, as far as she could tell, Stella's roman à clef had more relation to reality than the Knock Knock's accounting.

"I think they're using the joint as some sort of money-laundering operation," she reported to Kathy. They were in the lounge, deserted at two thirty A.M., and Maxie was making her nightly report.

"Who keeps the books?" Kathy questioned. "Is Lon involved? Maybe she'd flip if threatened with a tax beef." The aspiring agent furrowed her brow thoughtfully.

Maxie said hastily, "I'm not sure who does the books— I told you, Lon's just a baggirl, as far as I can tell. Why don't you put the pressure on Pete the pawnbroker? I hear he's some sort of fence for the Finns."

Kathy shook her head. "The mob's using Pete's pawnshop for a message center. We're going to plant a bug there, not close it up."

Maxie thought of her mother and the butterfly brooch with a sinking feeling. Her pawned jewelry must have been some kind of message to the mob!

If she hadn't been worried about her mother's criminal activities, Maxie would have thought that life was looking up. She slept in every day, and was paid to go to a gay bar every night, where her friends were always dropping by.

One day Dolly slid onto a stool, making her usual complaint: "I should be drinking at Le Cheval for these prices! When is Francine's going to reopen?" But she was too eager to share the latest gossip to keep it up. "Lois left for Loon Lake this morning," she reported. "And guess who went with her?"

"Who?" Maxie was wiping down the bar.

Dolly paused for dramatic effect. "Pamela!"

"So?" Maxie said, puzzled.

"Don't you get it?" Dolly exclaimed. "Can't you see where this is going?"

Maxie hooted. "You think they're going to come back a couple? Dolly, this soap opera you're on has gone to your head!" Dolly had picked up a bit part in a daytime drama, playing a visiting nurse.

The actress shrugged. "Don't say I didn't warn you."

"It's not that I'd mind, it's just unlikely," Maxie explained, sorting out her thoughts. "Lois is too devastated. She's not thinking of new love now. Besides, she and Pamela have already worked through that old high school crush. They're just good friends."

The busgirl went to pick up the empties. She didn't want to boast, but Maxie was also sure Pamela would be slow to move on as well. She and Maxie had shared a special something for so many years, after all. Wouldn't it be nice, Maxie thought, if she and the savvy merchan-

diser could learn to enjoy each other's company in a car-
nal way, without all the silly ideas—faithfulness, shared
values, a future together—that had tripped them up so
often?

Dolly had finished her drink. "Oh—I almost forgot.
Janet called *again*. She said to please call her back this
time."

"I will," promised Maxie. It was hard to remember to
call the young lawyer, when she never got to bed before
three A.M. and was up only after Janet was busy at her
new job. "I'll call her this evening," she said.

But something always seemed to happen that made
Maxie forget her promise. That night she was wiping
down the tables and wondering if maybe *this* was the
perfect job for her, when a dark-haired woman smiled at
her tentatively. It took Maxie a second to recognize the
tempestuous Tanya. Tonight, the tangled beehive had
been tamed and no longer towered above the vixen's vis-
age. "Won't you join me for a moment?" she asked
Maxie.

Maxie looked at Tanya's glass. The tigress was drinking beer. She shrugged and sat down.

"I'm awfully sorry about the other night," Tanya apologized. "I guess I'm still carrying a torch for Lon."

"That's okay." Maxie was relieved. "You're not alone,
you know."

"Lon's too popular for her own good." Tanya shook
her head. "And none of these dumb bunnies realize it's
hopeless." She leaned closer to Maxie. "You're a nice
kid, so I wanted to put you wise."

"Wise to what?" Maxie wasn't sure if she was asking
on behalf of the Bureau or herself.

"The other woman—the big femme in Lon's life."

"Who is she?" Maxie felt herself tense with excitement.

But Tanya shook her head. "I don't know. I only caught a glimpse of her once. Classy. But this I do know: When she says jump, the only question Lon asks is, 'How high?'"

Maxie tried pumping Mamie the next night when she sank down at the bar with her usual relieved sigh. "What's the word on the street about the big boss, the Queenpin? Anybody ever get a gander at her? I hear she's a looker!"

"Oh, Maxie, when are you going to stop chasing girls and settle down?" Mamie scolded. "Not with Pamela, of course—she was always a pill and you're well rid of her. But someone sweet, to keep house and mend your stockings. What about that nice little Lois? I always liked her."

"So you haven't heard anything?" Maxie was disappointed.

"Give me a Gibson, darling, and make it a double. No, no one would talk about the Queenpin. And now I'm so busy covering the DAP's annual election banquet, I haven't had time to sniff around. Your mother's pushing that Velma Lindqvist for the Bay City Beautification Committee. What's she getting in return, I wonder? Is she going to oust Inga as President?"

Maxie wanted to ask Mamie if she'd heard any rumors that Mumsy was in bed with the mob, but she stopped. *A dog that will fetch a bone will carry a bone,* she reminded herself. The memory of Mamie making incriminating comments about her ex-employee to the Bureau was still too recent, even if Mamie had apologized, saying, "That Agent Kathy hypnotized me with those intense eyes— she's a little peculiar, isn't she?"

Stella was the next one to carry a message from Janet. She'd stopped in to show the busgirl the published Larry Lathrop piece in *Idol Gossip.* "And here's the check!" She waved the slip of paper triumphantly.

"Stella, you did a wonderful rewrite on the tell-all."

Maxie was reading the pull quote, splashed across the picture of Larry: " 'The tearstained girl tried to hold the ends of her torn blouse together.' " She looked up. "Let's make it a fifty-fifty split!"

Stella waved away the praise modestly. "It was easy. I wish I could say the same about the revisions to my novel. I can't seem to make Patricia's dope addiction convincing! Maybe . . ." She hesitated, and looked at Maxie through lowered lashes. "Maybe if we worked on it together? You could stop by my place tonight, after the Knock Knock closes."

Maxie was conscious of Lon passing behind her and going into the little room she used as an office. She wondered if the beautiful butch had overheard Stella's unmistakable offer.

"Gee, Stella, I wish I could," Maxie told her honestly. "But I'm pretty tired by the time I get through here." She didn't want to tell the attractive writer that she had a date to meet Kathy. Stella was liable to misunderstand.

She'd used the same excuse to discourage Kathy the other night. But that time it wasn't just fatigue—she was steering clear of the unbalanced agent!

In truth, while the fires of passion still smoldered inside Maxie, her preoccupation with the underworld was distracting her. *I need to get to the bottom of this Queenpin business, pronto,* she thought as Stella's face fell. *And get on with living my life!*

The disappointed novelist delivered Janet's message as an afterthought. "Oh—I ran into your lawyer friend, and she's awfully anxious to talk to you. She said she's left you several messages." Stella brightened, as she concluded, "I guess you really are tired!"

Maxie vowed to call Janet the next day, even if she had to call her at work. But Janet beat her to it. It seemed to Maxie she had just laid her head on her pillow when someone was shaking her awake. She opened bleary eyes and peered at Phyllis, who leaned over her. "What time is it?" she croaked.

"It's seven thirty A.M.," Phyllis said apologetically. "I'm awfully sorry—but Janet insisted. She's on the line now, waiting to talk to you."

It took two tries for the groggy bar girl to insert her feet into her slippers and shrug on her dressing gown. Grumbling every step of the way, she descended the five flights to the first floor. *I'm firing Janet and hiring a lawyer who keeps reasonable hours,* she thought as she picked up the phone.

"Why haven't you returned my calls?" Janet demanded like a betrayed lover. Then, without giving Maxie a chance to explain, she said, "I need your authorization to ask for an injunction. Your parents are cleaning out your trust account, and if we don't take action quickly, there'll be nothing left when you're thirty-five!"

# Chapter 33
## The Switch

"What?" Maxie was awake now. "How? Why?"

"The Mainwaring finances are a mess." Janet spoke rapidly. "The Manse is mortgaged to the hilt and so are most of the other properties. Your father's been selling off shares in Sunshine Dairy to settle his gambling losses, and he's about to be kicked off the board."

Shocked, Maxie could only stutter, "But—but when I went to Loon Lake everything seemed the same as always—"

"They've been keeping up a front, heaven knows how, but it can't last much longer." Janet explained, in gruesome detail, the mistakes the senior Mainwarings had made, and the many ways in which they'd mismanaged their inheritance. "They should never have touched the principal," she said severely. "But your father and his polo ponies—I'm afraid he has a bit of a problem!"

Her mother probably hadn't helped, Maxie realized, what with her desperate desire to maintain social status at any cost. Was this what had gotten her mixed up with the mob? How much was she a victim, and how much a participant?

Janet was still pouring information into Maxie's ear:

that the Nyberg Trust had been invested in some sort of shell corporation—"the money's there on paper, but that corporation is your parents' piggy bank!"—and that she was prepared to go to court and make a case for mismanagement and freeze whatever assets were left.

"Hold off on that injunction a little longer." Maxie managed to interrupt the account of the Mainwarings' financial fiascos. "I know, I know," she said, holding the phone away from her ear as Janet squawked loudly. "But I must talk to Mumsy first!"

She knew where to find Mumsy that morning. The dowager would be preparing for the DAP's election banquet that evening by beautifying herself at Countess Elfi's.

Sure enough, when Maxie reached the salon on Linden Lane, she found Mumsy in the exercise room. Mabel Mainwaring was using the weight-reduction machine, the vibrating band jiggling away at her already trim waistline.

"Mumsy, I need to talk to you—privately." Maxie practically had to shout over the noise of the machine.

"I don't have time," the matron shouted back. "The banquet is tonight, and I'm beyond busy. Is this about your allowance? The check is in the mail."

"I've got bigger things than the allowance on my mind," Maxie shouted firmly. "It's about the Nyberg Trust."

Mrs. Mainwaring looked up uneasily at the name, and then around the room at the other vibrating dowagers.

"It's time for my steam," she said, switching off the weight reducer.

Maxie followed her mother into the small room and waited until the attendant had fastened the cover of the steam-bath machine and set the gauge.

"You don't owe me any allowance," she began. "My lawyer kept looking into the family finances, and she found out what you've been up to with the trust—robbing your own daughter!" Despite her best intentions, Maxie began to simmer with rage.

"Keep your voice down, young lady!" Mabel glared as steam curled out from the narrow opening around her neck. "I told you not to interfere with my management of family affairs! Is it too much to ask a little obedience from my only daughter?"

"Management?" Maxie laughed sarcastically. "Dad's gambling away the family fortune, and your solution is to get mixed up in the mob!"

A flicker of fear flashed over Mrs. Mainwaring's face. "You have no proof for these fantastical claims!"

"I have some, and the FBI has more! For God's sake, Mother, get out now, before you get thrown in jail or worse!"

"Don't threaten me, Maxine!" Her mother was pale, but stubborn. "I'm your mother and I know best!"

Maxie was tempted to turn up the temperature and try to steam some sense into Mumsy, but she knew her mother would sizzle like Joan of Arc at the stake before she admitted she was wrong. She made one more try. "That policeman at Loon Lake," she said quietly. "The truth is going to come out about his murder. If there *is* an oar floating around with your fingerprints on it . . ."

Mabel Mainwaring gave Maxie a freezing look. "I don't know what you're talking about!"

"I'm talking about you bludgeoning Officer Schuster with a paddle!"

"Only an unnatural girl would believe her mother was capable of murder! If you continue broadcasting these insane accusations, I'll have you committed!"

And Mabel closed her eyes and leaned back, the better to enjoy her steam.

She would never get the better of Mumsy, Maxie concluded, cast down, as she exited Countess Elfi's. She was depressed by her inability to extract the truth from Mabel Mainwaring. Even confronted with evidence, Mumsy still refused to have a frank discussion with her daughter.

*She never thought I had any intelligence or talent,* Maxie thought self-pityingly. *That's why she brought me up to be a debutante. She'll never approve of anything I do!*

As she entered the Arms, she could hear Mrs. DeWitt, somewhere, reciting one of Maxie's least favorite poems.

*"Work—work—work*
*In the dull December light!*
*And work—work—work*
*When the weather is warm and bright!"*

In a few hours Maxie would have to go to the Knock Knock and spend her Saturday night serving a crowd of girls bent on fun. Already her new employment was beginning to pall. The novelty was gone, and the usual boredom and impatience had set in.

*What's the matter with me?* Maxie asked herself, dismayed at her own sentiments. *Why can't I be like normal girls, happy with just one job?*

Kathy popped out of her room, when she heard Maxie unlocking her door. This didn't do anything to lift Maxie's spirits.

"Maxie!" She seized the despondent girl and pulled her into the washroom. "We got that bug at the pawnshop up and running, and we struck pay dirt!"

"Oh?" Maxie tried to be interested. But everyone was going to jail anyway, so what did it matter? "Why are you telling me here?" She looked around at the tiled walls and towels hanging on hooks.

Kathy flushed. "I guess I'm getting sentimental," she said with one of her too-intense looks. "Have you run across any mob connections nicknamed 'Little Mackerel'?"

"No." Maxie felt her interest stir in spite of herself. "Who's that?"

"Someone not long for this world, I'm afraid," Kathy told her. "We caught a couple mobsters talking about how the 'Big Tuna' was going to 'hook' the 'Little Mackerel,' who was a 'weak link.' Ring a bell?"

Maxie shook her head. "I'll keep my ear to the ground tonight," she promised.

But in spite of the intriguing information from the would-be agent, Maxie's cloud of confusion and despair followed her to the Knock Knock. She moved in a fog as she went through the routine of getting ready for the busy night. "Maxie, honey, I've told you twice, we're out of stuffed olives." Della's impatient voice cut through Maxie's gloom. "Look alive—it's Saturday night!"

Saturday night, and things would be swinging at the Knock Knock Lounge and across town at the Bay City Women's Club where the DAPs were holding their all-important banquet. But what did any of it mean? Maxie sighed heavily, as she watched the olives glug-glug from the jar to the square container.

The door opened, and a shaft of sunlight shot in like a ray of hope. Maxie looked up and saw, to her astonishment, Pamela standing in the doorway. The Junior Sportswear Buyer was looking around a little anxiously, and Maxie knew, suddenly, that Pamela had come to the Knock Knock to find her. Her heart began to pound with the familiar reunion rhythm. She *had* missed the old grouch—maybe that's all that was the matter with her!

Maxie half lifted her arm to signal Pam, but her ex-girlfriend didn't see her. She was opening the door a little wider, and ushering in a petite brunette. It was Lois Lenz, the abandoned office manager. Yet Lois wasn't looking particularly abandoned, as she smiled up at Pamela.

*She got some sun at Loon Lake,* Maxie thought irrelevantly. With disbelieving eyes, she watched as Lois followed Pam to a table in the back corner. *It doesn't mean anything,* she told herself, as she stood frozen over the olives while Pamela and Lois clasped hands. *They've always been fond of each other, in a friendly way.*

But when Pamela leaned over to lock lips with the supposedly lovelorn Lois, Maxie couldn't deny the truth any longer. A wave of anger engulfed her from head to toe. *Why, that two-faced turncoat! That scheming skirt-chaser!* Maxie wasn't sure whether her unspoken imprecations were aimed at Pamela or Lois or both. *Does Pamela really think she can treat me like an outdated magazine to be replaced by a newer issue?* She scowled at her oblivious ex, squeezing the olive jar in impotent rage. She'd sacrificed everything for that heartless hussy! Family, fortune, the best years of her life had been spent kowtowing to that selfish sportswear buyer!

But no; the churning sea of emotion inside Maxie subsided gradually, and gave way to the calmer waters of melancholy common sense. Pamela had given their affair her all. *If anyone was at fault, it was I,* the ex-deb admitted silently, a salty tear trickling down her cheek. And if Lois found some healing balm for her heartbreak in Pamela's company, who was Maxie to blame her? Hadn't she told both of them it was over, finito? Hadn't Dolly warned her?

Maxie lifted her chin and put on a brave smile. She, too, had loved and lost, at last. This experience would enrich her life, mature her, just as the rest of this summer of trials had. She couldn't help feeling a little forlorn that Pamela had replaced her so fast. And with Lois! A girl who looked so much like her, that when they swapped clothes—

Maxie's jaw dropped. Suddenly she knew how Lon had been eluding her shadowers!

"Maxie!" Della's voice rang out from the other end of the bar. "Stop mooning over the olives and making funny faces and go take the customer's order!"

The two lovebirds at the back table gave guilty starts when they heard Maxie's name. Pamela paled a little when she saw Maxie herself coming toward them.

"What'll it be, girls?" she asked breezily. She was so pleased with herself for figuring out Lon's trick, she forgave her old friends for getting together behind her back.

"You're working here?" Pam said incredulously.

"Scotch on the rocks and a martini," Maxie decided. "My treat. Lois—" The office manager looked up guiltily. "Can I talk to you, alone?"

"Sure, Maxie." Lois got to her feet uneasily, and Pamela stirred. "Should I—"

"No need." Maxie waved her away, and Pamela sank obediently back into her seat. Lois followed the busgirl to the other side of the room.

"We never meant for it to happen," she said as soon as Maxie stopped. "But now that it's happened, it seems like it was meant to be!"

"I'm sure it does," Maxie said kindly. "But I need to ask you a favor. How about swapping outfits with me again? And pretending to be the busgirl for a tiny bit?"

Lois looked down at her clothes. She was wearing her newest dress—a two-toned linen with a tucked white bodice and an apple-green skirt. "Pam and I were going to go to dinner after our drink," she hedged. "Pam made reservations at the Blue Danube."

"You can get dinner later. Don't you think you owe me this *one* favor"—Maxie's eyes bored in on Lois—"after all I've done for you?"

Lois caved. "Of course, Maxie. Right now?" She was ready to disrobe in the middle of the Knock Knock at Maxie's word.

"No—not quite yet—" As if on cue, Lon came in. She was carrying her canvas bag and headed straight for Maxie, instead of ignoring her as usual.

"I need to talk to you." It was Maxie's turn to follow Lon to the tiny office. "I heard about your dockside dip," she told Maxie with her trademark terseness. "You need to leave town. There's a contract out on you."

Maxie's blood ran cold. So *she* was the Little Mackerel. "How do you know?"

Lon gave her a long look. "They wanted me to do the job." After an electric pause, she continued, "I told them no. I'm out."

Maxie was both relieved and utterly frustrated. She was glad Lon didn't want to kill her, but why did the mob girl have to choose this moment to go "straight"? Just when Maxie had figured out how to figure it all out!

"But first," Lon added, "I have one last good-bye." Maxie sagged in relief as Lon bent down to pick up her canvas bag.

"So . . ." Lon looked at Maxie for a long moment, a novel's worth of unspoken words in her sea-blue eyes. "I'll send you a postcard from the Galápagos." And she exited the office.

This was it. Maxie felt it in her bones. Lon was going to lead her to the big boss!

"Now!" she called to Lois, heading for the ladies'.

"Please be careful with my outfit," Lois begged, without much confidence, as Maxie buttoned the bodice. "I just got it cleaned."

"Don't worry," the madcap girl assured her, setting off after Lon. "I've got everything under control!"

# Chapter 34

## Unmasked!

*I*s it because I raised a stink about the trust? Is Mumsy
the Big Tuna? Maxie didn't have time to puzzle out the
answers as she followed Lon on board the bus. Lon
looked over her shoulder after switching buses at Linden
Lane, but she didn't make Maxie, disguised in Lois's two-
toned linen, a paisley scarf over her hair.

At the train station, Lon timed it carefully, darting into
the women's restroom just as a throng of chattering theater-
goers trooped in. Maxie didn't bother to follow. She waited
outside, pretending to pore over the latest issue of *Polish*
(HEMLINES SHIFT FOR FALL) and carefully eyeing each
woman who emerged from the ladies'.

Even knowing what to look for, she almost missed
Lon. The beautiful butch was barely recognizable in the
pink dotted swiss Maxie had last seen in the old armoire
at the Seneca Hotel. Her feet were shod in pumps, there
were rings on her fingers and ears—she was undoubtedly
wearing the engraved gold band, probably picked up at
Pete's pawnshop. She wore a hat that sported a little veil.
She even walked differently, Maxie thought. Kind of minc-
ingly.

Falling in behind her, Maxie marveled at the brilliance

of Lon's disguise. All this time, she'd been hiding in plain sight, fooling Maxie and the Feds, too, with her clever switch from butch to femme.

Confident she'd lost any pursuers, Lon went directly to the line of taxis waiting at the curb and got in one. "Follow that cab," Maxie said, climbing into the one next in line. She was going to net the biggest fish in town, she exulted. And then Lon would be free to swim away to the Galápagos or wherever. . . .

It was like her heart stopped for a second, and Maxie had a queer sensation of being outside her body, hearing in a strange sort of echo chamber, *the Big Tuna's going to hook the Little Mackerel . . . a weak link . . .*"

They'd been talking about Lon!

The insight hit like a steel beam. Of course: Lon's refusal to kill Maxie and her decision to leave the mob made *her* the weak link. And the kind of queenpin who killed cats wasn't going to send her off to the Galápagos with a kiss good-bye—Lon was taking a taxi to her own funeral!

Maxie leaned forward urgently. "You've got to catch that cab! It's a matter of life or death!"

"What do I look like, a race-car driver?" the cabbie hooted. "Anyway, it's stopping."

Lon's cab had come to a halt in front of the Bay City Women's Club. As Maxie watched, Lon slid out and gave her dress a little tug to straighten it. Then she was climbing the steps. The doorman opened the door.

She disappeared inside just as Maxie's cab pulled to the curb. Maxie threw money at the driver, not bothering to write it in her budget book or even note the amount for future reference. She launched herself out of the cab and up the steps, yanking open the door before the doorman could get to it.

She was met by a wall of noise—the well-bred chatter

of hundreds of Daughters of the American Pioneers, blended into a high-pitched, ear-shattering din. Maxie felt rather than heard her pulse pounding in her ears.

There was a banner over the entrance to the dining room, DAUGHTERS OF THE AMERICAN PIONEERS 76TH ANNUAL ELECTION BANQUET, but every member seemed to be in the big hall, catching up with friends or occupied with some last-minute campaigning. Posters propped on easels gave the names of the candidates: Gretta Johannsen, Ingeborg Lund, Hazel Houck, Velma Lindqvist . . . the names blurred before Maxie's eyes as she turned and craned her head, trying to peer past the plump shoulders, the waving, white-gloved hands, the bobbing hats. The smell of perfume and flowers was so thick she felt dizzy.

She worked her way through the crowd toward the dining room. Half-familiar faces loomed at her, and through the roar of noise she heard snatches of greetings: "Maxine, your mother said . . ." ". . . look just lovely," "Sookie told me . . ."

The dining room, when she finally reached it, was almost empty. A few women and the club's maître d' were urging the crush of DAP members in the hall to come inside and sit down.

There was no one in a pink dress with a bolero jacket.

Maxie fought her way back to the hall. A woman clutched at her sleeve, and Maxie shook her off irritably. The woman tugged more persistently. "Maxie, it's me!"

Maxie looked into Kathy's intense green eyes. "Kitty! Kathy! Have you seen Lon? I followed her here, and I've lost her!"

"Lon? No, no one in the least like her has been by." Maxie had to lean over to hear her, although Kathy was almost shouting.

"You wouldn't recognize her—she's wearing a pale pink dress and a hat with a veil!"

The green eyes widened. "A woman answering that description just went into the powder room."

"I've got to warn her!" Maxie leaped at the green-painted powder-room door. Kathy tried to hold her back. "Your mother's in there—don't interrupt my surveillance!" Maxie shrugged free of the grasping girl and pushed open the door.

The maid was handing a towel to a woman at the sink, and two more women wearing DAP pins in their lapels left while Maxie swept the room with a searching glance. "Hurry up, Olive," one of the women called over her shoulder. "They'll be starting soon."

Lon wasn't there. The door to the back room, where long ago Maxie had shared a cigarette with Elaine, was closed. She hurried toward it, Kathy hot on her heels. "Stop!" the aspiring agent ordered. "You're ruining everything!" Maxie ignored her. She pushed at the door. It wouldn't give.

"It's locked! We'll have to break it down!"

"Maxie, are you mad?" Kathy was staring at her.

Maxie tried to explain. "The Big Tuna's inside—Lon's the fish—she'll get hooked or speared or whatever—" It was no use, and there wasn't any time. Even as Kathy opened her mouth, there was a soft "pop" from inside the locked room. Maxie seized the bewildered Bureau girl and ripped open her seersucker suit jacket.

"No, Maxie—not here!" gasped Kathy.

The ex-deb reached under Kathy's unresisting arm and before the lustful agent realized what she was up to, she'd gotten the gun from Kathy's shoulder holster. Taking careful aim, Maxie shot off the lock to the inner room. The maid screamed, as Maxie swung open the shattered door.

Mrs. Mainwaring, one knee braced on the green pouf, grappled with Velma Lindqvist for control of a wicked-looking weapon with a silencer screwed on the end. A rising tide of nausea almost choked Maxie. She'd long suspected her mother, but she hadn't wanted to believe it. But there was Lon, slumped in the corner. The mob girl was clutching her left arm, and blood dripped from her limp fingers onto the green carpet.

"Velma, give me that gun," Mabel Mainwaring panted. "You simply don't shoot people in the Bay City Women's Club!"

Relief flooded Maxie. She sprang at Velma, using the flying leap she'd picked up from Nadia Nemickas earlier that summer. Mumsy wasn't the Queenpin! It had been Velma, all along!

"It was you who killed that cop!" Maxie cried, as she landed on Velma, knocking her flat. "You borrowed a canoe and paddled over to the Schuster pier while I was flirting with Nancy Nyhus!"

She'd knocked the breath out of the faux clubwoman, and it was Lon who croaked an explanation: "He'd seen her with me and then he spotted her at Loon Lake and tried to put the bite on her."

"Shut up, sweetheart," Velma gasped at the bleeding butch. "She can't prove a thing!"

Lon pulled herself up, blue eyes stark in her white face. Maxie saw that the left sleeve of the pink bolero was soaked scarlet with blood. "You were going to shut me up permanently, weren't you? If Maxie's mother hadn't jostled your arm, I'd be fish food!" Her face crumpled. "You never loved me!"

Maxie's heart contracted with sympathy for the betrayed butch. She wondered how the Queenpin could have been so calculating and callous as to dispose of a girl with Lon's fine qualities.

"On your feet, all of you!" Kathy had collected both guns and was pointing them at the group of women.

"Who are *you?*" Velma eyed the green-eyed girl disdainfully as she climbed to her feet. "And what's your price?"

"Kathy O'Connell, Federal Bureau of Investigation, and I can't be bought!" Kathy's voice rang out triumphantly. "I'm taking you and your accomplice in for attempted murder!"

"But I didn't do anything," Maxie's mother protested. "Velma simply asked me to introduce her into Bay City society—"

"And I paid you plenty for the privilege," snarled Velma.

"Certainly, she gave me financial advice—steered me to investments," Mabel faltered. She turned to Maxie and said pleadingly, "She said if I invested the money from the Nyberg Trust in a scheme she had, it would restore the Mainwaring finances!"

"And all you got was bullets at the banquet," Maxie replied. Seeing Mumsy embroiled in her own scandal made Maxie feel sort of sympathetic toward the woman who'd raised her. After all, whatever mistakes Mabel had made, she was still Maxie's mother!

The ex-deb started when she saw Ingeborg Lund's reflection appear in the mirror. It was like dejà vu to have the dowager suddenly come in behind her.

"There you are, Mabel!" said the DAP President in relief. "I've been looking all over for you. It's time for your opening remarks."

"I'm afraid we're holding Mrs. Mainwaring as a material witness, ma'am," Kathy told her politely.

And then the powder room was swarming with police and medics. Lon left first, carried away on a stretcher. Then Mrs. Mainwaring was marched away between two officers.

"I'll have Janet meet you at the station, Mumsy,"

Maxie told her, then added, "Don't say anything to anybody until she arrives!"

The Mainwaring matriarch held her flowered hat in front of her face to protect herself from the curious crowd. Mamie McArdle pushed forward. "Mabel!" she called. "Is it true you own a dockside dive? Has the milk business gone sour?"

Finally it was Velma's turn to go. She looked Maxie up and down before she left, and Maxie felt a faint shock run through her, an echo of that unearthly attraction.

"I'm sorry I couldn't recruit you," Velma told her nemesis with a charming smile. "I would rather have employed you than ordered your elimination."

Maxie watched as the lovely mobster was led away in handcuffs, a queer tinge of regret mixed with her relief. She couldn't help wondering what it would have been like if she'd accepted Velma's offer to join Amalgamated Enterprises and found herself working for the mob. Certainly, it wouldn't have been as boring as she'd believed!

But if she'd been as talented as Velma said, she would have solved the mystery in May. The bankrupt heiress watched Velma's exquisite legs as they slid into a squad car. She would have realized when she admired those legs on the Mainwaring terrace, that she'd already seen them in the Buick next to Lon!

# Chapter 35

# At Home in Bay City

It was Monday night, but Francine's was full of girls. Maxie stopped mid-descent to survey her old haunt. Girls stood three-deep at the bar, and the new bartender was pouring so fast her hands were a blur. Every table was packed. Girls were crowded on the tiny dance floor in the back, gyrating madly to the jukebox.

At the curved corner of the bar sat an older woman, very erect. Her white hair was cut in a 1920s-style shingle, and she held a tiny kitten on her lap.

"Why, that's Francine!" Maxie realized as she compared the woman to the framed photo on the wall. "Francine Flicka!"

"It is," Miss Watkins confirmed from behind Maxie.

Maxie twisted around. "You said once that running a bar for gay girls was just a sideline for her, but you never told me what her true career calling was."

"She's a cat fancier." Miss Watkins urged Maxie forward. "She breeds a superlative sub-species of Siamese. But let's not keep Mrs. Spindle-Janska waiting."

As she made her way between tables, Maxie wondered if the perceptive career counselor sensed how nervous the ex-deb was about this upcoming conference.

She would much rather join the gang at the round table in the center of the bar. Even the sight of Pamela and Lois exchanging enamored looks was preferable to having her career fate finally decided.

And she wished she could sit down in the quiet corner where Kathy was debriefing Lon, and listen in as Lon, looking like herself again in a plaid shirt and pants, laid out the inner workings of the Lindqvist mob. She wondered if the Bureau knew Agent Freitag was still incapacitated, and Kathy was running the case.

Kathy had told Maxie that she thought Lon would be "more comfortable and talkative" in the congenial atmosphere of Francine's. "And how about you?" Maxie had teased. "Will you be more comfortable too?"

As usual, Kathy had flushed. "Maxie, you're incorrigible!"

However, Miss Watkins marched the ex-deb past her friends, to a table in the back, where Mrs. Spindle-Janska was waiting.

The career guru half rose from her seat to take Maxie's hands in both of hers. "Maxie," she said simply.

She was a heavyset woman with short hair, strong features, and deep-set eyes. Later, Maxie couldn't have said what she wore or what color her hair was. A small, strangely carved wooden figure hung from a cord around her neck.

Maxie felt herself relax, as the soothing energy flowed from Mrs. Spindle-Janska to herself. It was even stronger in person than it had been over the phone. Her anxieties seemed to dissolve at Mrs. Spindle-Janska's touch. She felt a little lost when Mrs. Spindle-Janska finally released her hand and they all sat down.

There was a slim folder on the table. Did it contain the answer to her career quandary? The career guru opened it. "Maxie, it's been an honor to analyze your Personality Penchant Assessment, as well as your educational records and the results of the Psychographic Recorder Interview Miss Watkins administered." She paused, and Maxie waited with bated breath. "Our extensive analysis has revealed that you are that unusual creature, a true dilettante."

"A dilettante!" Maxie couldn't help feeling disappointed. "That's what Pamela called me back in May!"

"I'm sure she didn't realize the full meaning of the term," Mrs. Spindle-Janska replied. "Or the range of possibilities the word implies."

"'Subject shows executive ability in fifteen different possible fields,'" Miss Watkins read over her colleague's shoulder. "'Subject will excel as impresario, information broker, and influence peddler.'"

"Really?" Maxie began to feel as if a great weight had been lifted from her shoulders. "But—but my education has been so incomplete and my experience so erratic," she objected, not daring to believe what she heard. "Sure, I know a little about a lot of things, but not a lot about any particular one."

"That's ideal!" chorused the two career counselors. "You have an uncanny ability to make use of others' more in-depth experience and knowledge," Mrs. Spindle-Janska informed her. "Ignorance is no limitation."

"'Delegating is a strength,'" Miss Watkins read. "'Subject will easily subjugate others to her own purposes.'"

Maxie was stunned by this unexpected analysis. "But where should I start? I mean, what about a regular job?"

"It would be folly for you to limit yourself to one job, or even a regular work schedule, at this particular time," Mrs. Spindle-Janska said. "I imagine you have a number of projects fermenting in your fertile brain?" At Maxie's nod, she spread her arms. "Give yourself free rein to bring them to fruition!"

"We understand you have a lawyer on retainer," Miss Watkins added. "That's very wise. She will help you balance your impulsive side, and keep your criminal tendencies in check."

The two older women stood up, and Maxie automatically rose to her feet. Mrs. Spindle-Janska took the dilettante's hand again. "It's been a delight, my dear. Doris will check in with you from time to time, to hear what you've been doing."

"We're coauthoring a paper on your case for the next Career Counselor Conference," Miss Watkins added.

The stunned girl managed to thank the counselors, scarcely aware of what she was saying. She made her way over to the center table and sat in the chair Dolly had saved for her.

"Well? How did it go?" Dolly demanded.

"What did Mrs. Spindle-Janska say?" chimed in Phyllis.

Even Pamela tore herself away from Lois to ask, "Did they find you a new job?" Lois, Janet, and Stella looked at her eagerly.

"I'm an . . . impressario!" Maxie's mind began to move again. "An influence peddler!" An idea bloomed in her head like a flower. "Forget about making Patricia an addict," she told Stella. "I'm publishing your novel as is! It will be the first book from Fifth Floor Editions!"

The aspiring author lit up. "I'm in!" she cried. She turned to Pamela. "You never really worked as a dope fiend," she confided to the mystified girl.

"We'll put out the calendar as well," Maxie told Dolly. "Why give that money away to some middleman?" Now it was Dolly's turn to beam with delight.

"What will you do for funds?" asked Lois with interest. "You'll need to pay for printing, and that's just the beginning."

"I've got the price of the garnet and pearls in my pocket, that's for starters," Maxie told the office manager. She turned to her lawyer. "Janet, what else have I got?"

The young lawyer had been hard at work, untangling the Mainwarings' money mess, and now she pulled out a memorandum of Maxie's remaining assets. "I'm afraid not much," she warned. "The majority of the trust was invested with Amalgamated Enterprises, and of course anything of value that company controlled has been confiscated by the government." She looked down at the list. "The only item that seems to be clear is the title to the Knock Knock Lounge."

"You can sell it," Pamela said instantly. "It'll be good to get rid of that eyesore."

"I'm not so sure," retorted Maxie. Her glance fell on Lon. "It has its regulars, who like it just as much as we like Francine's, and certainly some of us sneak over there from time to time!"

Pamela blushed bright red.

Maxie's mind was racing now, bubbling over with ideas. Hadn't Hal once said he'd do a mob story in *Polish* if there was a society angle? SOCIALITE SAVES BAY CITY BEAUTIFICATION COMMITTEE FROM MOB INFILTRATION! Maxie could already see the headline. She'd sell Hal the story and spin her mother's scandal into something a little face-saving all at once! Stella could write it. She looked over at Lon and Kathy again. She hoped the privacy-nut would cooperate in the creation of *Mob Girl: How I Escaped the Velmqvist Gang*. It would make a saleable second book from Fifth Floor Editions. Stella would ghostwrite that, too. She'd have to give up her job at the photo supply store, Maxie decided. And should she hire another writer?

"Don't forget the public good, in all your entrepreneurial endeavors," Phyllis reminded her gently.

Maxie looked at her frizzy-haired neighbor fondly. Maybe she could salvage something from Sunshine Dairy— surely a few cows remained under Mainwaring control. A dairy farm run by disadvantaged youths—it would be poetic justice.

Stella asked her, sotto voce, "What are you doing later, Maxie? Maybe we can celebrate Fifth Floor Editions, just the two of us."

"I'd like to," Maxie told her, her eyes running over Stella's appealing curves. "But I sort of promised a friend I'd see her off."

Lon was leaving town, disappearing into protective custody until Velma's trial, and Maxie had promised to have a farewell nightcap with her. Would it lead to something more? Maxie hoped so. She looked over at Lon. The beautiful butch's sea-blue eyes met Maxie's in that wordless communication she specialized in. The dilettante tore her gaze away and turned back to Stella. "Rain check?" she asked, pulling out her engagement book. "Are you free tomorrow?"

After all, why limit herself to one girl just yet? Grandma Nyberg hadn't considered her mature enough to manage money before the age of thirty-five. Sure, she was a little in love with Lon, but she and Stella made a terrific team. The world was full of possibilities, and she didn't want to rule out any of them right now. Even the prospect of tempting upright Kathy again held a certain appeal.

The waitress deposited a trayful of drinks on their table. "Compliments of Mrs. Flicka," she said.

"Here's to Maxie," Dolly lifted her glass, "and *all* her endeavors!"

"To Maxie!" the gang cried, lifting their glasses high.

"To Francine's!" Maxie proposed her own toast.

"To the Industrial Workers of the World and Miss Ware!" Phyllis had had a little too much to drink.

"To the fifth floor," said Dolly fervently.

The girls clinked their glasses so hard the liquor slopped over. "To the fifth floor!" The toast reverberated through the room and faded away into the Bay City night.

## Author's Note

I owe several people thanks for their aid as I wrote: Nancy Johnsen and Linda Werner for sharing stories of life in the early sixties, especially the financial details; Peggy for telling me about bartending; Rebecca McBride for answering a photography question; and Jenny Worley for curbing some inappropriate language.

Two dedicated readers, Shari Kizarian and Julie Ann Yuen, gave vital feedback at the last minute. Their comments (sometimes illustrated) were both encouraging and immensely helpful. Thanks to my editor, John Scognamiglio, for his staunch support.

The librarians at the San Francisco Public Library, especially in the San Francisco History Room, were always ready with advice and assistance. Every time I research a book, I'm reminded of how much is *not* on the Internet. I'm grateful for every bit of historical detritus the libraries have saved.